THE DEVIL'S OWN

LL MEYER

This book is a work of fiction. All characters and events depicted are the product of the author's imagination and any resemblance to actual people, living or dead, is purely coincidental.

Cover by: Murphy Rae at Indie Solutions
www.murphyrae.net
Formatting by: Elaine York at Allusion Publishing
www.allusionpublishing.com

Contact the author:
Email: lisalynn_meyer@outlook.com
Instagram: @author_ll_meyer
Facebook: Lisa Lynn Meyer
Goodreads: LL Meyer
Amazon Author Central: LL Meyer

THE DEVIL'S OWN

OTHER BOOKS

The Worlds Collide duets:
Not So Far Away (Scott and Ellie, #1)
The Here and Now (Scott and Ellie, #2)
Fall from Grace (Alejandro and Sophie, #3)
The Devil's Own (Alejandro and Sophie, #4)
TBD (Shane and Desiree, #5)
TBD (Shane and Desiree, #6)

The Penny Books
His Lucky Penny, #1
Pennies for Wishes, #2
Find a Penny, #3
Pennies from Heaven, #4

Written as Lisa Lynn Meyer
A Touch of Silence

For Leila. Her daily encouragement, superior proof-reading skills, and super-star status as an all-round wonderful person have made this duet better in every way possible.

CHAPTER 1

Sophie

I was told to pack for cooler weather. Supposedly, late December is a chilly time of year in Reno. I doubt the cold will bother me though, not with Alejandro to keep me warm.

It's been a week since he came back into my life and despite my best efforts, keeping my feet firmly planted on the ground has proven next to impossible. We've spent every moment together; me, him, and . . .

A paw covers my bare foot. "You can't possibly need to go out again," I say, looking down at Bruce Wayne, whose pitiful expression does its best to convince me otherwise. "We just got back from the dog park." I go back to applying my mascara in the bathroom mirror, trying to keep a smile at bay so I don't stab myself.

Upon arrival at the penthouse on Christmas Eve, I received probably the best present of my life. Alejandro had adopted Bruce Wayne, the dog we found in the wilds of Oregon. Joy, pure and simple, had swept me up. With his wiry gray fur and soulful eyes, Bruce greeted me with a madly wagging tail and as many dog kisses as he could lay on me. His presence had erased any last doubts I'd had about Alejandro. He may be a villain to some, but he's proven to be the hero of my story too many times to count.

Finishing up with my makeup, I consider arranging my hair over my left shoulder to hide some of the jagged scar on my neck. Even after almost eighteen months, the evidence of the gas station hold-up is still the first thing I see when I look in a mirror. At least it doesn't send me into a tailspin of dark thoughts anymore. I'm a survivor, not a victim. I leave my hair loose.

"There. How do I look?" I ask Bruce.

"Good enough to eat."

Startling, I turn. And proceed to drink down the sight of Alejandro leaning against the bathroom doorjamb. After a week of barely bothering with clothes, he's back to his formal self, dressed in one of his trademark bespoke suits that fits him so well, this one the darkest of grays. Absurdly, it's the little V formed by the open collar of his dress shirt that holds my attention. I'd be hard pressed to say if he looks better in or out of his clothes.

"Keep looking at me like that, *mariposa,* and you'll find yourself on your knees."

"You make that sound like a bad thing." Romantic may not be the first adjective I'd use to describe my man, but his calling me *butterfly* makes my heart flutter every time.

"One day that smart mouth of yours is going to get you into more trouble than you can handle."

"I look forward to it," I tell him sweetly and his jaw ticks under his dark beard but it's the love in his eyes that tells me all I need to know.

A knock comes from the bedroom door. "Jefe?" It's Roxanne, his housekeeper. "Skippy's here for Bruce."

That's when I notice the leash in Alejandro's hand.

I crouch down and snuggle into the dog's neck. "Be good for Skippy and Rolando, okay?" While we're flying, he's riding to Reno with the brothers in one of the Tahoes.

"He'll be fine," Alejandro says with a touch of exasperation, clipping the lead to the dog's collar.

I trail behind them into the brightly lit bedroom. Like I have every day of the past week when the blinds are open, I marvel at the breathtaking view of San Francisco. We may only be fifteen floors up, but the position of the building leaves this corner of the penthouse with a clear shot to the east. It's beautiful.

"Sophie."

My head jerks around.

"I have some phone calls to make. Are you good on your own for a while?"

"Oh, yeah, sure." *Is that guilt on his face?* "Don't worry. I still have to finish packing."

Striding forward, he pulls me in for a quick kiss that leaves my knees wobbly. God, the man is intense. The last week has had a fairy tale quality to it that's very reminiscent of our time spent at the cabin, but instead of being squirreled away in the wilderness, it's a penthouse suite. That's about to change, though. This New Year's getaway to Reno is the first time Alejandro and I will be appearing in public together – as a couple. I'm not quite nervous, but I want it to go well.

An hour later, Alejandro reappears as I step into my heels. "Do I look okay?" I ask, studying my black pencil pants and pale pink cap sleeve blouse in the full length mirror. I can't be walking around in jeans and Chucks while he's dressed like a super model.

He comes up behind me and helps me into my wool pea coat. "I think I'd rather keep you here where no man can see you."

I smile. "I'll take that as code for *you look great.*"

Passing me my purse, he gives me a look that registers somewhere between wry amusement and flat disapproval.

Yesterday, I'd had a rather bizarre talk with Niner, Alejandro's best friend and right hand man. He'd essentially laid out the ground rules for being the 'Queen of the Underworld.' And yes, he'd used those exact words, waggling his eyebrows as he said it. He'd quickly turned serious, though.

There were only three rules. Number one, never go anywhere with anyone I don't know. I'd squinted at him, saying it was lucky my mother taught me that one when I was five. He'd laughed in that infectious way of his and told me I'd have to apply it to my adult self in a real way.

Number two, keep my mouth shut around strangers. He explained people may try to get information from me. Since I had no intention of discussing my life with Alejandro with anyone except maybe my sister, Ellie, I had no problem agreeing.

And number three, he said, was the most important. Don't ever try to make Alejandro jealous. He claimed his boss has a possessive streak a mile wide. It reminded me of what Niner had said outside the cabin in Oregon a few months ago about keeping all appendages attached to their rightful owners. I hadn't quite taken him seriously then, but I understand better now after another week spent in Alejandro's presence. The man exudes darkness, and though I feel it more when we're with others, it's always there just under the surface of his tattooed skin, being carefully controlled. I may taunt him in private, but testing his limits in public won't be on the agenda.

Alejandro takes my hand, leading me out to the main room, where the floor-to-ceiling windows let in the bright mid-morning light, making the slate gray tile flooring and slightly paler gray walls appear more inviting than normal. Though I wouldn't go so far as to say he hired an undertaker to decorate, it's close. The man takes minimalism to new heights and there's a serious lack of warm touches around here.

"Rosita Fresita," Niner says happily from where he's sprawled on the couch next to his partner, Ben. I've grown attached to Niner's name for me even if the Spanish version of *Strawberry Shortcake* was probably originally meant as an insult. "You look gorgeous."

I throw a pointed glance at Alejandro, then smile brightly at Niner. "Thank you so much. You look as casual as ever."

"I do, don't I?" he quips, getting to his feet. I've rarely seen Niner in anything but jeans and those T-shirts that he likes to cut the sleeves off of. Today is no exception. "I did wear my best pair of boots though."

We all look down at a new pair of Doc Martens. "A nice touch," I confirm.

"You're not wearing that tonight," Alejandro gripes, heading for the door. Tonight we're going to some kind of fancy New Year's Eve gala.

"Don't worry," Ben says in that soft-spoken way of his that doesn't quite match his appearance. Alejandro has nicknamed him *the Viking* for his fair hair, height, and breadth of his shoulders. "I'll clean him up."

Niner scoffs, but it rings with affection. I met Ben a few nights ago when he and Niner showed up at the door to confirm that Alejandro had, in fact, *manned the fuck up* and 'claimed' me. Turns out there are two penthouse suites in the building and they live across the hall in the other.

In the elevator, Niner rests his head on the outside of Ben's shoulder for a moment and I try not to smile. They've been together for three years and are what I would call adorably in love, though I'm sure Niner would kill me if I said that out loud.

The elevator opens into the cool air of the underground parking garage, where a Tahoe is waiting for us. Alejandro opens the back door for me and I slide in. As Niner and Ben get in the front and we head for the airport, I pull out my phone. There's a short message from Ellie telling me she'll call later to wish me a Happy New Year. I type out an equally short and sweet reply. Alejandro and I decided not to face the music on Christmas Day. We'd showed up to Scott and Ellie's 'separately'. With a house full of people, my big sister had been distracted, but she knew *something* was going on. When I'd announced I had to leave ten minutes after Alejandro did, the weight of her stare had been heavy, but she hadn't asked me directly. I know the disapproving questions are coming though. My sister, Ellie, is not Alejandro's biggest fan. She doesn't believe who he is can be separated from what he does. I disagree.

At the airport, we pull up at a private hanger and I give Alejandro a sardonic look. "You didn't mention a private jet service."

"They don't let me fly commercial."

His use of the word *let* makes me pause. "As in . . ?" I prompt, my hair lifting with the breeze as we get out.

"As in I'm on the no-fly list."

Umm. *What?*

"It's not my fault the FBI doesn't like me."

I squint at him, unsure if he's joking. Then I see the corner of his lip twitch. "Are you in a good mood?" I ask, the question coming out more like an accusation

The quirk of his mouth becomes a full-fledged grin. "Maybe. Maybe not."

"Holy shit!" interrupts our moment. "Are you smiling?" Laney asks, her tone dripping with mock horror as she approaches with JJ.

Alejandro pulls a face. "Yeah, yeah. Just get on the plane." But there's no heat behind his words. He *is* in a good mood.

Following him, I listen to Laney snicker behind us. Laney and I didn't get off to the best start, probably because we're polar opposites. Whereas she couldn't be less interested in the consideration of other people's feelings, I try to get along with everyone. She may come off as standoffish and mean, but I'm hoping deep down she's got a soft spot, because I'm determined to win her over. As Alejandro's executive assistant . . . or maybe she's more like a COO . . . she's an integral part of his life and it would eternally suck to constantly be at odds with her.

Onboard, I can't help but be excited. I've never been on a private plane before. It's small inside, but luxurious, with white leather seats. Alejandro very chivalrously helps me out of my jacket and hangs it on the back of my seat, then does the same with his own. The 9mm sitting in its shoulder holster stares back at me. Another reason to fly privately, I guess; he's always armed.

Niner and Ben sit in the seats facing us and Laney and JJ file towards the back. The pilot appears.

"Jefe, welcome aboard." He's an older man in a pressed uniform.

"Thanks, Derek."

"Drinks are in the fridge and we'll be in the air shortly. Flight time is just over an hour. Skies are clear."

Soon the engines rev higher and we start moving as the loud popping sound of a can being opened rings in the cabin.

"Laney," Alejandro intones. "You drink more than one and you're not driving."

"Sure thing, Dad."

I have no idea what he means by *driving,* but I'm more concerned with the sudden tension radiating from him. It's a sharp one hundred and eighty degree turn from a minute ago. *Because Laney's drinking a beer at ten thirty in the morning? Or because he doesn't like to fly?*

I raise the arm rest and lace our fingers together, laying my head on his shoulder. I'm half-expecting him to snipe at me, but as we take off, his hand tightens on mine. It *is* the flying that's making him nervous. Besides his grip, though, he shows no outward signs. He may be hard on everyone, but he's hardest on himself.

Hoping to distract him, I ask, "So, how come Reno, and not Las Vegas?"

Laney snorts. "Luis would have a coronary if we attempted Vegas." Luis is in charge of security – and he gives me the creeps.

"A coronary would be the least of it," Niner cackles.

"Why's that?" I ask.

Alejandro pulls my hand to his lips for a kiss. "It's not important."

Sitting up, I respond to his condescension with a disapproving look, but it's Laney who calls him out. "You can't possibly expect to hide your entire business from her. How's that going to work?"

He growls something at her in Spanish and she fires back.

"None of us can go to Vegas," Niner says over their bickering, "including you, *Fresita*, because our relationship with Juan Carlos Ortega is not what it could be. You'd probably last less than twenty-four hours before he had you tied up in a basement somewhere."

"For fuck's sake, Niner."

"What? It's true. He can't stand your ass after you –"

"If you finish that sentence, it'll be your last."

Ben reaches over to cover Niner's mouth. "Please don't, babe." Then he turns to Alejandro. "Like me, Sophie doesn't need specific information, but there are certain generalities that shouldn't be kept from her."

I smile weakly at Ben. "Thank you." Alejandro's 'business' is not something he and I have talked about yet. I know it's bad, but I'm hopeful that my sordid list of imagined drugs, guns, prostitution, gambling, loan sharking, etc. isn't quite so long in reality.

When we land, Alejandro holds me back and once everyone has filed off, he says, "I only want to protect you."

"I know. This is new for both of us."

He leans in and brushes his lips to mine. "Are we good, then?"

"Yes, we're good . . . for now."

The amusement on his face at my teasing has my heart lifting. He's irresistible when he's happy.

"Come see my babies," he says.

I blink. "Pardon?"

Pulling me to my feet, he grabs our jackets. "You'll see. Here, you'll need this. It's cold out."

He helps me down the stairs, then hand-in-hand, we start toward a surprisingly large group of people gathered outside of a low building. Only one person notices our approach, everyone else's attention is focused in the other direction.

"Ah, Jefe," the man says, breaking away from the crowd to shake Alejandro's hand. He acknowledges me with a nod. He's not wearing a jacket and his arms are covered in tattoos.

"Jordan. Everything ready?"

"You bet," he says with a wide grin. "Have you made your choice?"

"My girl's going to choose."

A thrill runs through me as the guy turns to eye me with more interest. Alejandro's never called me his girl before. "Choose what?" I ask.

Alejandro leads me through the crowd to stand next to Luis, who I know has been here in Reno for a few days already, preparing for our arrival.

"Jefe," he says in that weird monotone of his.

Then I see what has everyone's interest. It's a line of sports cars, all of them so low to the ground that they weren't visible over the crowd. "Which one should we take?" Alejandro asks, a very sweet note of excitement in his voice.

"You mean, like to buy?" I ask hesitantly.

"No," he says with a soft laugh. "They're all mine. Which one should we drive home?"

He owns them all? There are six of them, but on closer inspection, I see they're not all the same car. I recognize the Lamborghini logo, but that's about it.

He's looking at me expectantly and Niner calls, "Not the red one, *Fresita!*" which sets off a round of good-natured suggestions from the crowd. I feel myself flush slightly as I check out the line of cars again. Some of the colors are completely out of character for Alejandro, and then it clicks. "The black one," I say.

"That's my girl," he says, his voice infused with pleasure, but his face mostly passive in front of all these people.

Jordan leads the way and pulls on the passenger side door first, which opens up instead of out. "Watch your head," Alejandro says.

I squeak with surprise as I get in because the car is so low to the ground. "Good thing I didn't wear a dress."

Alejandro does a decent job of repressing his smirk. "Good thing." He makes sure I'm buckled and then shuts the door, which entombs me in quiet. At least it's quiet until the car beside me rumbles to life. I turn and Niner gives me the devil's sign with such a huge smile that I laugh. Alejandro gets in and Jordan crouches down to explain a few things. Alejandro hits the ignition button and the car's engine roars, sending vibrations through my entire body.

Jordan points to the center console at our elbows, asking Alejandro to pass him a walkie talkie I hadn't noticed. "We'll have eyes on you from the air," he says, turning it on. It crackles a bit and he tests it. It's Niner who responds with, "Let's go!" over the radio. I look over and sure enough he's got one held to his mouth. Then a voice I don't recognize comes on, sounding muffled like it's coming from a helicopter. "You're good to go, Jefe. Take it slow through town, please."

Alejandro takes the radio. "Will do." He puts it back in the console and Jordan pushes the door closed. In the muted quiet, Alejandro's eyes glint with mischief. "You ready?"

Wow, I don't think I've ever seen him so animated and all I can do is beam at him. "Don't kill us, okay?"

"Never." He puts the car in gear and the bystanders back away.

"What kind of car is this?" I ask as we follow the signs to the exit, leading the line of cars.

"A McLaren 720."

"Never heard of it," I say truthfully in an attempt to tease him. We come to the gates of the airport – which I suddenly realize can't be Reno International, but a small, regional one – where more people have gathered. Almost everyone has their cell phones out, taking pictures or video. A little boy waves madly from the sidewalk and I smile at him.

"I thought you said you weren't a celebrity," I joke, remembering that night in the hotel room at my sister's wedding.

He shrugs. "We come every year for New Year's. Word gets around. And you know they're here for the cars, not us."

We pull out onto the road and Alejandro hits the gas a little, pushing me back into my seat. I gasp, then laugh as our eyes meet for a moment of shared joy.

For the first few minutes, we wind our way through an urban area, people gawking from the sidewalks. Then we head North on a two-lane highway. A few miles in and the traffic starts to thin out. In the side view mirror, I can see the other cars following us, Niner's red one right behind us. Another mile or so and Alejandro starts to accelerate almost in anticipation of something. The radio crackles, but before I hear a single word, Niner tries to pass us.

"All clear," comes from the radio and Alejandro hits the gas, swearing under his breath. The car jumps forward and I inhale sharply, surprised by the force with which I'm pressed back into my seat.

Once Niner backs off, Alejandro risks taking his eyes off the road for a second. "You okay?" His voice shimmers with boyish delight as he continues to accelerate, moving away from the edge of the highway to straddle the center yellow line.

Exhilarated, I laugh, the scenery flying by now as the car hugs the road around a bend. Apparently, I trust him with my life because I'm not scared at all despite the way the speedometer keeps rising. Everything about Alejandro screams control, even over the laws of physics.

It's all rural land out here with only a few scattered houses set against the dry, rolling hills. Every few miles there are people out with cellphones at the ends of their driveways or parked at junctions in the road to watch the cars go by. Only once are we warned from above to reduce speed and move back into our proper lane.

I love every second of it and I'm almost disappointed when, fifteen minutes later, we slow down. My senses must be warped because it feels like we're crawling even though the speedometer still reads 45mph. Then we come to an almost complete stop before we turn off onto a paved lane. Following it at a snail's pace, we finally come to a simple metal gate that connects to a barbed wire fence. The set up wouldn't be out of place on a cattle ranch . . . if a cattle ranch had a checkpoint with surveillance cameras and men armed with assault rifles.

I lift my brows at Alejandro as the gate is opened for us. "Just the way it has to be," he says as he eases the car over some speed bumps.

Winding further into the hills, we come to the walls of an estate . . . no, a compound. They have to be twelve feet high. Though they're painted an innocuous cream color, I catch the glint of the sun off the broken glass that's affixed to the top. I guess it's more aesthetically pleasing than razor wire. I reach for the St. Christopher medal Alejandro gave me all those months ago and start running it along the chain, officially nervous.

We're waved through another manned gate, this one an arch in the wall, and enter a huge courtyard. "Oh, wow," I breathe, the pendant forgotten. Set back from the walls is a stunning cream-colored Spanish style mansion with a red tile roof. "Finally," I say as we follow a long circle drive which flanks the central desert rock garden.

"Huh?"

"I *knew* you had a lair somewhere."

"A what?" he says on a choked laugh.

"A lair. The Garden was so disappointing." And it's true. His offices in downtown San Francisco are utterly normal.

"Is that right?" he says, laughing outright now. I love that he's so much freer with his emotions when it's only us.

As we approach the house, people file out of the big double doors, drawn by the rumble of the cars. He pulls up at the front steps, cutting the engine. The sudden quiet is almost deafening and makes the way my entire body tingles from the vibrations much more noticeable.

"Sophie."

I swing my head around and find myself pinned by the intensity of his gaze.

"Before we go in . . ."

"Yeah?"

"I need you to know that every single person in that house owes you respect." He must see my confusion, or maybe it's skepticism, because he goes on. "This isn't the outside, okay? Anyone disrespecting *you*, is disrespecting *me*, and that can have serious consequences."

I'm not sure I like what he's saying, but Alejandro knows best how to navigate this world, so I take his words at face value and nod.

"If anything happens when I'm not with you, you have to tell me. Is that understood?"

Narrowing my eyes, I decide not to take him to task for patronizing me twice in one day since this is clearly important to him. "Yes, it's understood."

His lip tugs up at the corner, loosening some of the unease that's been coiling itself around my spine. "Now," he says, glancing at the people who've begun to surround the car. "Give me a kiss so everyone knows that you're mine."

Smiling, I lean in to brush my lips to his. He surprises me, though, by pulling me closer and slipping his tongue into my mouth, sending electricity surging through me. When I've been thoroughly kissed, he pulls away, looking pleased with himself. "Let's do this, then."

In a mild haze, I watch his features harden as he unbuckles his seat belt and reaches for his door handle. "Oh, and Sophie?"

"Hmmm?"

"Don't touch that door."

He gets out, leaving me wondering why not as I watch him come around the front of the car, acknowledging people but not stopping to talk like they so clearly want. Every single one of them seems to be vying for his attention with looks that border on . . . reverence . . . or maybe it's fear.

CHAPTER 2

Alejandro

I don't regret it.

The last week with Sophie has righted so much of what's been wrong with my life over the past months. But of course I've second guessed myself a time or two, and now, as I get out of the car, is no exception.

I've brought my mariposa into the heart of the viper pit. This place, this time of year, is crawling with men and women who don't see the world like she does. Bent moral compasses and ruthless brutality are the norm. And it's all held in check by a sense of loyalty to me. Whether that loyalty is inspired by fear, necessity, or genuine feeling is irrelevant – and it all has to extend to Sophie.

I need to set the tone, to impress upon every single one of these motherfuckers that she's mine and completely off limits. I do *not* want a repeat of something like that memes disaster. Of course, I can't go overboard either. Too much interest will hint at what she really means to me, which could be equally disastrous.

Mostly ignoring the clamor as I go around the car, I open her door and offer her my hand. Her delight at the gesture is obvious but I remain neutral.

16

As I get her on her feet, Niner shows up. "How was that, *Fresita?*" he asks, pumped up by the rush of the drive.

"It was awesome!" she gushes.

More of the cars rumble up to the house, parking haphazardly near the entrance. Luis gets out of his and stomps over to Laney's car and yanks on the door handle as soon as it comes to a stop. My brows go up as we all watch him pace in a tight circle, waiting for Laney to get out of the car. He has her by the throat almost immediately, jerking her toward him to hiss something in her ear.

Niner starts laughing. "Holy sh_t. He's going to fuck her right on the hood of that car."

I can only see Laney in profile, but the curve of her lips says it all.

Sophie stiffens though, asking quietly, "Shouldn't you do something?"

"You mean like get the popcorn?" Niner says.

Ignoring him, I put my hand to Sophie's back and manoeuver her toward the doors. "Don't worry about Laney," I tell her. "She can handle herself." I hope. Maybe I'll have a word with them later. The last thing we need around here is telenovela-level drama.

Inside the cavernous entryway, Rocio is waiting for us. *"Buenas tardes, Jefe."*

"Rocio." My estate manager is one of the most no-nonsense people I've ever met, which is why I like her. Her gray streaked hair is pulled back into its usual severe bun at the nape of her neck and she's dressed more conservatively than a nun in her calf-length, long-sleeved black dress. "This is Sophie," I tell her in English. "She's to be extended every courtesy you would me."

Affronted, she clips out, "Of course. It's nice to meet you, Sophie."

We turn and find Sophie gaping. At first I think she's checking out the enormous Christmas tree that sits in the middle of the foyer, but then I realize it's the giant *Santa Muerte* mural on the wall that's got her attention. Even if I don't subscribe to such cultish bullshit, I have to admit the image is pretty bad-ass. Standing two stories tall, she's perched on a pile of skulls in all her black and white glory, her robes swirling around her, her skeletal hands clasped in prayer. The only color is the halo of blood red roses surrounding her hooded skull and the matching red of the sash around her waist.

Maybe I should have warned Sophie.

Slipping my arm around her waist, I say gently, "Soph, this is Rocio. She's in charge around here."

"Uh, hi," she says, tearing her eyes away, sticking her hand out. "Nice to meet you."

"You —"

Rocio is cut off by Niner shoving his way in. "Rocio! Tell me how much you missed me."

"Not much, actually," Rocio says dryly, but she accepts his kiss to her cheek with a ghost of smile playing at her mouth. As soon as he pulls away, she's all business again. "Your room is prepared, Jefe, and the *perro*," she says, her lip curling, "has arrived and is out back."

I smirk at her disdain for Bruce Wayne. "He'll grow on you, just wait."

"I doubt that. Dogs are not to my liking."

Sophie perks up at the word *dog*. "Come on. Let's go find the little punk." I know she's worried about him.

The house is busy. In the main hall, people murmur greetings as we pass by. I acknowledge them but don't stop. Niner follows in our wake, being more social, making jokes, and keeping his finger on the pulse of the organization. It's a system that we've perfected over the years. I'm the one everyone fears, he's the one everyone loves.

"It's huge," Sophie says as we enter the kitchen, where at least ten people are working.

"It is," I agree, leading her to the French doors that lead out to the pool area. I catch sight of our mutt playing in the distance. He's running circles around one of the guard dogs under the watch of two men and what looks like a kid.

I whistle and the dogs lift their heads. Seeing us, Bruce comes running at full tilt. When the German Shephard gives chase, he snarls at him, making him back off.

"Good boy," I say as I bend over to pet him. He wastes about two point four seconds on me before he heads into Sophie's waiting arms, a trembling mess of adoration.

I still cringe at all the baby talk Sophie uses around him, but I've gotten used to it . . . mostly. The boy comes jogging up. "Hi, Jefe," he says, out of breath. He must be Brandon's kid, though he's grown a lot since I saw him last. "Is your dog's name really Bruce Wayne?"

"It is."

"Is it because he's gray?"

I incline my head. "That, and because he's got the bat signal stamped on his ass." The distinctive black patch on his hind quarters is the best thing about the mongrel. Then I notice Sophie's reproving look. *What?* I ask her silently and she moves her eyes meaningfully to the kid. Shit, I guess I'm supposed to watch my language.

"Hi, I'm Sophie. What's your name?"

"Justin."

"Is it you, Justin, who's been taking care of our dog this morning?"

He can't be more than six or seven, but his chest puffs out with pride. "Yeah."

"Well, you've done a great job," she says, straightening, the dog continuing to dance at her feet. "Thank you."

Justin preens under Sophie's praise as Brandon comes up, putting a hand on his son's shoulder. "Jefe," he greets. "How was the trip?"

I shrug. "Fine. This is Sophie." He merits an introduction because he's my representative here in Northern Nevada and he lives at the compound. Every major region under my jurisdiction, from Washington State and Oregon to Salt Lake City and over to Denver, has local guys who keep an eye on things. I don't run actual chapters of *Los Santos del Diablo*. Those had all died out before my time. Instead, existing groups pay 'taxes' in exchange for access to my product, as well as certain rights, privileges, and protections. The practice has made me a very rich man. But unfortunately, this is our yearly 'sit down' and I have meetings out of my ass to look forward to.

Sophie picks up on my restlessness. "Well it was nice meeting you guys," she says, seamlessly extracting us from the conversation. Bruce follows us back into the house.

"You all right?" she asks, taking my hand and giving it a squeeze.

"Yeah. Let me show you our room." We backtrack to the foyer and then take the stairs up to the second floor. "There are two wings," I tell her as we head to the left. "And I'd prefer that you stayed on this side of the house."

"Oh, yeah? Why's that?"

This woman. Always questioning me. "I guess you won't accept a 'because I said so'."

"That would be a good guess."

I grunt with disapproval, but I answer her. "Because the other side is full of riff-raff."

Coming to a stop, she forces me to do the same with our hands still entwined. There's mischief written all over her. "You mean as opposed to the riff-raff on this side of the house."

I can't stop a smile from forming. "You're cruising for a spanking."

"And now you're just buttering me up," she sasses, planting a fleeting kiss on my lips before she starts walking again.

My laughter rings in the hallway. She's going to do a serious number on my hard-earned reputation if I'm not careful.

Admittedly, my room here at the compound is excessive and Sophie busts my balls about it. "Are you sure your ego fits in here?"

"You know, I'm appreciating the dog's inability to talk more and more."

"Please," she says, checking out the enormous bed. "You totally love me." She pauses, inspecting the wrought iron headboard more closely. "Roses and skulls? I'm sensing a pattern here."

I snake my arm around her from behind, pulling her flush to my body. "Face it. I'm not a classy guy."

"Actually, I've got you all figured out." She snuggles back into me, tilting her neck to give me access. "I know all of this is mostly for show."

"True," I say into the soft skin under her ear. "I'd be just as happy with you bouncing on my dick in a shack somewhere."

"And you say you're not classy." She gasps at the end of that sentence as I slip my hand down the front of her pants and into her panties.

"You dirty girl," I accuse, finding her wet. "Was it the car that turned you on?"

"More like you driving the car." She groans as I circle her clit.

"Careful," I whisper, nibbling at her earlobe. "Or my ego really won't fit in here."

She starts rolling her hips between my groin and my fingers, and now I'm the one groaning.

Bruce Wayne gives a low growl and we freeze. Over my shoulder, I meet Skippy's eyes. "Sorry, Jefe," he says, standing there in the doorway, more interested than apologetic. "Laney sent me to find you. Meeting in five minutes." The little shit is lucky he makes a quick exit. I've mostly gotten used to Skippy being my principal driver, but every once in a while I get vibes from him I don't like. But I guess everyone who works for me is *off* in some way or another.

"I can't believe we forgot to shut the door," Sophie whispers.

My phone starts buzzing against my ribs in my suit jacket's inside pocket. Heaving a sigh, I pull my hand from her pants.

"It's fine," she claims as she turns. "You go do whatever it is you have to, and I'll go check out the rest of the riff-raff."

I take hold of her jaw. "Don't test me."

Her expression softens. "I was kidding."

Searching her face, I decide she's telling the truth and I kiss her. "Good. Find Ben and stick with him. And keep the dog with you. Seems he's more than just decorative."

"I will." When I make no move to leave, she lifts her hand to stroke her nails through my beard. "I'll be fine, Alejandro."

Some kind of resigned, growly noise slips from my throat. Too bad I can't keep her chained to my side 24/7. "Okay. I, uh, I love you."

She immediately lights up. "I love you, too." Sometimes the trust and adoration that radiates from her makes me nervous as fuck. Planting one last kiss on her lips, I leave her there and head down to the conference room.

Outside the door, I see Rolando frisking the brothers from Eugene-Springfield in Oregon and curse under my breath. These two douches test my patience on a good day. We went with them despite their name being The Loud Boyz – yes, with a Z – because they've got the client base to go with their big mouths. I almost wish they'd mess up somehow so we can get rid of them. It's been two years, though, and so far, no such luck.

I go in and JJ's set up at a desk in the corner, his laptop open. He's a smart guy and I like having his take on more than the cyber security stuff, which is why he's here. I take a seat at the head of the small conference table, Luis on my left, Laney on my right, Niner next to her with his feet up on the table, throwing a ball up in the air, already bored.

The morning drags by because with outsiders in the room, we can't joke around like we usually do. It's all one hundred percent professional. We listen to grievances and praise alike as we go over each group's numbers which are based on Laney's many indexes. We work through lunch, and by three o'clock I've had enough. The problem with running a well-oiled machine is that it doesn't squeak. Luis doesn't even have to threaten anyone.

I dismiss the last group and Niner groans. "Remember when Sal Benson came at you with a knife a few years ago?"

I snort because he sounds wistful. "Those were the days?"

"Yeah," he moans. "This shit is so boring. Whatever happened to the hunger for power? Or internal strife? Nobody's even tried to collect that crazy bounty on your head yet."

Pushing tiredly to my feet, I lean over and kiss the top of Laney's head. Without her organizational skills and reports, we'd still be dealing with the Sal Bensons of the world.

Niner throws that stupid ball against the wall and catches it as it bounces back, saying, "At least we've still got your Christmas present in the basement for entertainment."

There is that.

The junkie who held a knife to Sophie's throat all those months ago has been cooling his heels downstairs for the last week. "How's that coming?" I ask Luis, whose usually stoic features fill with distaste.

"Still detoxing. A couple more days should do it."

I nod and head for the door.

"Jefe, hang on," Laney calls. "Let me walk with you."

She catches up in the hall, scrambling to maintain pace with my longer strides. "Haven't we spent enough time together?" I gripe.

"I figured you're heading in Miss Spun Sugar's direction and so am I."

I stop, then get momentarily distracted by her T-shirt, which reads *Two words, one finger*. How did I not notice it earlier? "Laney, I get one whiff of you undermining her and we'll have a problem."

"Relax. No one's being undermined. I just assume she's checking out the dresses with the rest of the women."

Right. The dresses. Another one of Laney's ideas that's gone over so well. Every year for the New Year's bash, she gets a truck load of designer dresses delivered for the men's significant others to choose from. She claims it's so popular that the women put pressure on the men year round to stay in the good graces of the organization.

We make our way to the great room at the back of the house where a good thirty women are picking over racks of dresses and shoes. I spot Sophie somewhere near the middle, an obvious furrow between her brows.

My arrival causes a stir as I make my way into the fray, but I barely notice anyone else with my girl in my sights. "Hey," she says, pushing up on her toes to kiss me.

Cautious with so many ears listening to us, I keep it simple. "Find anything?"

She chews at the corner of her lip. "Not yet." She leans in closer and whispers, "So, is this the kind of stuff I'm expected to wear?"

Expected? Unsure of what she's trying to say, I cast my eyes over the dresses but don't see anything of note. She reaches for a dress at random and holds it up. It's made of a shimmery aqua-marine blue fabric, but there's not much of it and what there is, looks like someone took a pair of scissors to it. She'd be all T and A in that thing. "You are *not* wearing that."

"Thank you," she mouths, looking comically relieved.

"Laney!"

Sophie jumps at the volume of my voice, so I pull her close and rub soothing circles on her hip.

"Oooh," Laney enthuses, coming down the row. "I love the blue." She takes the hanger from Sophie's hand and holds it up higher. "This would be amazing on you."

"The color *is* nice," Sophie says with a weak smile, clearly hedging, not wanting to offend Laney.

"My girl is not going anywhere with her ass cheeks hanging out," I declare, earning me a glower from Laney.

"Don't be such a Neanderthal. There's nothing wrong with this dress." She holds it up again. "Though you are a little taller than average," she muses. "It might be a little short on you."

"Is there anything a little classier?" I deadpan.

"Sorry, they were all out of Amish chic."

I set my jaw, about to throw something back at her, when Sophie interrupts. "I was thinking maybe this one." She quickly goes back down the line of dresses and pulls out a dark gray one. "Do you hate it?" she asks me, considering the dress.

It's still short, but it would at least cover the important parts. It certainly doesn't have cut outs. "Better," I grumble.

"I'll try it on then."

"Jefe!" We turn and Rolando is at the door. "Luis needs you."

I blow out a breath, supposing if I don't go, Luis will maim someone for the hell of it. "You okay here?" I ask Sophie. "Where's the dog?"

"I'm fine and Ben took him outside so I could find something to wear."

"Have you eaten?"

She nods and Laney gags. I swing a glare in her direction, but Sophie puts a hand on my arm to tell me she can take care of herself.

"Hopefully this won't take long," I tell her, then lean in and whisper in her ear, "Be good," before I kiss the scar on her throat, making her shiver.

CHAPTER 3

Sophie

I watch him go, enjoying the view of his broad shoulders from the back in that suit he's wearing.

"So is it true?"

I turn to Laney. "What?"

"That your vagina is made of spun sugar?"

I'll give it to her, she holds a straight face for longer than I do. I fold about five seconds into our stare down, laughter bursting from my chest.

"Yes," I tell her, sarcasm dripping, and she finally cracks a smile. "But the real question is how you know that."

"Oh, I have my sources."

"I bet you do." We turn back to the dresses. "So," I say, not wanting to waste the opportunity to get to know her better. "I hear you're the one who organizes all this." I give the room a vague wave.

"Yeah," she says like I'm the most boring person on the planet.

"You're not a fan of small talk, I take it. Fine, what I really want to know is what's going on with you and Luis. He didn't hurt you earlier, did he?"

"Hurt me?" She pauses in her perusal of a hot pink, booty-shorts jump suit. "How El Jefe ended up with someone as sweet and innocent as you is a complete mystery to me, but I suppose you're all right."

"Gee, thanks. So he didn't hurt you," I insist.

"No, Sophie. He didn't hurt me."

"You two are together then?"

"Oh, that'll be the day," she jeers. "I'm more of a play the field kind of woman and Luis is . . . well, Luis. Let's just say he wouldn't approve of this," she shakes the pink jump suit at me, "any more than El Jefe would."

I nod, understanding completely. "You don't like controlling and bossy."

She raises an eyebrow and I feel my cheeks heat, because I guess I've just admitted that I do. "Okay," she says. "Maybe it's not such a mystery after all." Thankfully, she turns back to the racks and changes the subject. "I've got you down for the full spa treatment, starting in," she reaches into the back pocket of her jeans for her cell phone to check the time, "about an hour. Hair, nails, makeup, massage."

"Oh, okay. Thanks. I'm going to pass on the massage though."

After the violence of the gas station attack, I'm still not comfortable with a stranger's hands on me. I may never be.

"Okay, then. Let's go try these on."

· · · · ·

In the end, the charcoal gray dress turns out to be the one. Twirling in front of the mirror in Alejandro's enormous walk-in closet, I'm satisfied with my reflection. The snug, sleeveless bodice fits me perfectly, the beading sparkling in the light. While the V neckline might be a tad deep, my boobs are mostly covered and I love the matching V in the back. Plus, the short A-line skirt floats nicely around my upper thighs and combined with the tall Louboutin classic black heels, my legs look amazing. I just wish I were feeling a little less off-kilter.

I hear the door to the bedroom open and Bruce Wayne jumps up from where he's curled in a ball on the carpet. "Hey, buddy," I hear Alejandro say, then louder, "Soph?"

"In here." Off-kilter becomes downright edgy. What if he doesn't like the dress? And what if he doesn't want me wearing my hair half-up, half-down? It does nothing to conceal my scar.

He comes in, pulling off his shoulder holster, all business. "That took for*ever*," he grouches, putting the gun down on the center island dresser and starting in on the buttons of his dress shirt.

"Is everything okay?"

He sighs. "Yeah, just let me jump in the sho–" He finally spies me and pauses, his eyes raking all the way down and then back up again.

I briefly touch the St. Christopher medal. "How do I look?"

"Turn," he orders.

"Not a single visible ass cheek," I joke, trying to convey a confidence I'm not quite feeling. When I'm facing him again, he studies me, almost as if he's taking stock of my anxiety levels. "So?" I prompt, nerves singing. "Do I pass muster?"

With a jerk of his head, he calls me to him, but I shake my head. His brows lift in that imperious way of his that says *are you defying me?*

"It took all afternoon to get these kinds of results. You'll muss me up."

His fingers start working the buttons of his shirt again and I watch as he peels it off. "I'll do more than muss you up if you don't get your ass over here."

"Oh, yeah? Like what?" I relax by a degree, officially distracted by the sight of his chest and the tattooed skin covering his defined arms. This is our familiar rhythm when we're alone, playful and full of innuendo. "Maybe you'll tell me how pretty I look in my new dress?"

"There's that. Or I could bend you over this thing," he says, gesturing casually at the island dresser, "and spank you before I sink myself deep."

A wash of desire heats my skin. I love the way he talks to me, dirty and demanding yet never harsh. I fiddle with the hem of my dress, watching him undo his pants as he toes off his shoes. "That would definitely muss me up." It only comes out as a whisper because the intensity radiating from him says he's serious. Come hell or high water, he'll be inside me within the next few minutes. Another wave of heat washes over me.

Removing his pants and boxer briefs, he straightens and my gaze zeroes in on that incredible V in his abdomen and the quickly swelling member between his thighs. "Nah," he says, calling my attention up again. "When I'm done with you, you'll look as put together as you do now . . . unless . . ."

"What?"

"Well, that lipstick you're wearing would look incredible smeared all over my cock." He palms himself, giving a languid stroke. My stomach swoops and I shift nervously in my heels as, slowly, he covers the distance between us. "Don't you think? You on your knees, lips stretched around me as I push into your throat, tears streaming from those big, innocent eyes. Now that *would* muss you up."

My clit pulses as I tentatively take the hand he's holding out to me. Like we're out for a casual stroll, he leads me back to where he was, still stroking himself. Standing there, face to face, he examines me, his fingers grazing over a loose curl at my temple. The inspection has my core tightening. "If your makeup runs, every man tonight will know you have a belly *full* of my come. I like that idea."

I whimper and he smirks before he leans in to whisper, "Turn around." I do as I'm told and he continues at my ear from behind. "You're lucky we don't have time for me to do a thorough job of *mussing you up*."

There's something heady about not being able to see him, about not having any inkling of what he'll do next. The feel of his fingers between my shoulder blades makes me jump slightly. "Hush," he admonishes softly, the sound of the dress's zipper coming down echoing around me. "Arms up."

He pulls the dress over my head and throws it aside, leaving me standing there in nothing but a black thong and the Louboutins. He groans. "Put your hands flat on the island." When I comply, he makes me spread my fingers. "Wider." Running his fingertips along the sensitive inner skin, he taunts me. "Are these black nails for me? Did you think they'd turn me on?"

I consider trying his patience by insisting they're not black, but the same charcoal as the dress, but I decide to hold my tongue and not press my luck.

"Well, you were right. They make me hard." He punctuates the statement by brushing himself against my thigh. "Spread your legs."

With every gruff, unapologetic command, my body twists itself further into knots. It doesn't matter how benign the order is and he knows it. He loves to play with me, to wind me up, but I think I love it more.

"Are you wet?" he asks, now running a single finger down my spine. Jerkily, I nod my head. "You are?" The finger curls into the back of my thong and pulls. He keeps increasing the pressure on my clit until my knees are weak and I can't stop myself from panting softly. "I asked a question, *mi amor*. Are you wet?"

"Yes," I hiss as he drags my underwear from side to side, again and again, sending bolts of pleasure radiating out from my clit.

"Let's hope so, because I'm about to bury myself in this tight cunt." He starts to pull my thong down my thighs and I make to close my legs to let it fall. "No." The single syllable has my pussy clenching on air. "Don't move." He gets my underwear halfway down my thighs and leaves them there, digging into my flesh, then he leans in and whispers, "Bend yourself over. Let me see what's mine."

He's not satisfied when I go down on my elbows. "All the way," he croons and I lay my breasts against the cold dresser top, then my cheek. "Keep your chin up," he says disapprovingly. "We don't want to ruin the makeup."

A sound I'd have to classify as a mewl slips from my lips, making him chuckle as he presses himself over me, his hard body molding itself to mine. "Such a good, dirty girl, doing everything you're told."

I groan outright now. The feel of his weight, his words in my ear; it's all too much. "God, I wish I had time to torture you properly." Planting a hand next to me, he pushes himself up.

"Reach back and spread yourself for me."

I do as he bids without complaint, so deep in the fantasy now that I can't imagine refusing him anything.

"More," he demands. "Up and out. That's it." He's quiet for long moments and my face starts to get hot at the thought of him seeing me like this. I finally squirm only to feel him pushing in at my entrance. I gasp loudly. He stalls out. "Chin up," he insists harshly and my pussy spasms so hard that I see stars.

As soon as I comply, he shoves himself deep, all the way deep, his pelvis pressing into the fingers he hasn't allowed me to move from my ass cheeks. Then, his fingers dig into my waist. "Come if you can," he grits out. "This is gonna be hard and fast."

He's not lying. He comes at me in long, powerful thrusts that set off every nerve ending in my body, keeping me hovering on the edge of bliss until I'm panting and whining with need. His threat of *come if you can* hovers in the back of my mind, taunting me, igniting sparks of deliciously screwed-up yearning. When his strokes slow down into a more languid rhythm, anticipation surges inside of me. Because what if he really does leave me hanging? He must feel the slight, tell-tale clenching of my pussy because he shoves one last time and then stalls out, balls deep inside of me.

He comes down on one elbow, hovering over me again. "You're not going to come, then?" he admonishes and we both groan as my inner muscles clasp at him. I'm so close. "I should leave you like this, needy and wanting all night." Except, contrary to his words, a hand snakes between the edge of the island and my hip. The first jolt from the pressure to my clit is dizzying, but he's being too gentle . . . and he knows it.

"Please," I beg in a hoarse whisper.

He licks a line up my spine between my shoulder blades, tasting my skin. "Please, what?" he asks just as softly.

I open my mouth to plead some more, but without warning, he increases the pressure of the circles he's rubbing, and that incredible feeling of inevitability laps at me, then swells, then obliterates everything in an explosion of ecstasy.

His last thrusts set off sweet aftershocks as he shudders over me. Trying to collect myself, I listen to our panting breaths until he carries my boneless body to an armchair in the corner, murmuring sweet nothings to me and covering me with a throw blanket.

"I'll be right back," he says, kissing my forehead.

I watch him leave and then Bruce places a tentative paw on the chair to sniff at me. "It's all good," I reassure him, sneaking an arm out from under the blanket to scratch behind his ear, which he takes as an invitation to join me on the chair.

Alejandro, in all his naked glory, comes back with a wash cloth. "What the hell, dog? That's my girl." But he doesn't force him to get down, only lifts the blanket and cleans me up. "You feeling better?" he asks.

I nod. "Thank you. It's been a stressful day."

"I know," he says, giving me another kiss. "And it's not over yet. I'm going to get in the shower, then we'll go." He looks to Bruce. "Take care of her."

Bruce and I sit there in peace for a few minutes before I re-engage my brain and go in search of a new pair of underwear and my dress. I'm checking my makeup when Alejandro reappears, wearing only a towel.

"So, the plan tonight is simple," he says, pulling on a pair of boxer briefs on and picking a dark suit from the rack behind him. "First, there'll be dinner in a big ballroom."

Nodding, I walk over so he can zip up my dress, knowing he's letting me know what to expect to head off any unnecessary anxiety on my part.

He goes to work on the buttons of his dress shirt, then gets his pants on. "After, we'll watch the fights."

Right, the MMA stuff. The thought of witnessing that kind of violence turns my stomach, but I don't complain. He's already warned me that he, Niner, and Laney sponsor a bunch of fighters.

"Then at midnight, we'll be in the night club."

"Sounds good." Going back to the mirror, I smooth down my dress and check for anything amiss. I spin to check out the back and see him pulling on a suit vest, something he never wears.

"Grab me a tie out of the cabinet, will you?" He jerks his chin across the space. *A vest and a tie?* I think I'm liking this formal version of Alejandro.

Opening the cabinet door, I'm greeted by an almost solid wall of dark colors and a rush of love for him settles over me. Understated and minimalist is so him. I snag the one that most closely matches the gray of my dress, and on a whim, also grab the only red one that would go so well with the soles of my shoes.

Biting back a smile, I present the choices and am rewarded with a sarcastic eyebrow lift that says *nice try* as he plucks the gray one from my hand.

When he finishes with the tie, he hands me a pair of cuff links and holds out his arm. "You've done well so far."

Irritation scratches at my placid mood as I get the first one attached. "I'm not a child," I huff as he holds out his other sleeve and I get it done as well.

"No, but maybe you need another lesson, this time in manners. I'm sure eating you out for an hour will work wonders on that attitude."

My glare dissolves into several blinks of lust-induced embarrassment. *Who says things like that?* He sits down on the bench to pull on his socks and shoes and pretends like he's said nothing at all.

Shaking my head, I go back to my reflection until he comes up behind me. "You look incredible."

"Thank you," I say, melting with the compliment. "So do you."

He glances at his watch. "Where's your coat?"

I go for my new St. Laurent angora coat and he helps me into it. When we leave Bruce Wayne behind the bedroom door, he's clearly devastated. "He'll be okay, right?"

Alejandro snorts. "I'm sure he's already mounting a revenge-assault on the trash can in the bathroom."

I wrinkle my nose. "He is obsessed, isn't he?"

He begins to outpace me. "Only because he knows it pisses me off."

When he starts down the main stairs without me, I stop at the landing and cross my arms over my chest. With visions of breaking my ankle in these shoes, I survey the empty foyer before I say, "Who's the one lacking in manners now?" He pauses halfway down and turns to me.

With a surprisingly rueful look, he heads back up and offers me his arm. "Maybe I'm a little out of practice with this dating thing."

"Maybe?"

He retorts with a low, "Don't push your luck," making me smile.

The main doors are wide open and I can hear voices and the loud rumble of at least one sports car. As we exit onto the steps, a cold wind swirls around my legs and I shiver.

"About time," Niner calls from down on the driveway where he and Ben are standing next to the red Lamborghini. When Alejandro ignores him, he yells, "Looking good, *Fresita!*"

"Thank you," I call back as Alejandro opens the back door of an idling Tahoe for me.

I slide across the seat and find Luis's stony gaze on me in the rear-view mirror. "Oh, hey," I say lamely, feeling strangely deflated all of a sudden. The way Luis seems to look through a person instead of at them is hair-raising.

"Took your sweet time, didn't you?"

Shit. I didn't even notice Laney in the passenger seat.

"Not like they're going to start without us," Alejandro mutters, pulling the door shut.

The Lamborghini roars past us and heads for the gate. "That idiot is going to get himself killed one of these days," Laney says.

Luis scoffs. "You're one to talk after what you pulled today?"

In response, Laney licks her lips suggestively and Luis's eyes go from there down to her lap . . . where I assume she does . . . something. Something that would surely require bleaching my mind.

Alejandro chuckles. "Whatever that thought was, mariposa, it's exactly right."

I motion with my finger between the two seats in silent question.

"I certainly hope not," he retorts.

As I get myself buckled, I ask him, "You didn't want to drive your car?"

He grunts. "Of course I did. But my head of security is a pearl-clutching, alarmist pussy who wouldn't let me."

Luis flips Alejandro off, and for a moment, I smile. But then Alejandro's words sink in. "Why? Were you threatened?"

He gives a dismissive wave. "When am I not? But now I have you."

Laney makes a retching noise from the front seat while I try to figure out his meaning. "You have me now so . . ?"

"So, it's one thing to risk my life, but another to risk yours."

"Oh." I'm not sure if I'm scared or flattered or horrified . . . or just plain-old madly in love.

CHAPTER 4

Aléjandro

The ride to the casino is mostly quiet, which suits me fine. It's been a long day with the flight, all the meetings, and then JJ's report on some private chat room threats against me. Luis wanted to cancel my attending tonight's event, but I vetoed that immediately and Laney agreed. If I give the impression I'm running scared, I'll have half the underworld gunning for me. I may as well dig my own grave and hop in.

But that doesn't mean I can't take precautions, especially with Sophie by my side. *Who cares if I don't get to drive my McLaren?* Okay, fine, I'm pissed about that, but in the grand scheme of things, it's a minor inconvenience in exchange for the armor and bullet proof glass of the Tahoe.

We pull into the casino's underground parking garage without incident where a woman with a clipboard is waiting. Niner is already here – chatting her up because he can't not – with Ben standing sentinel at his side.

"Wait here," Luis mutters, getting out. Laney, of course, doesn't give two shits what he says and gets out along with him.

"Oh my god," Sophie whispers, sounding appalled. "Laney told me earlier they weren't, but they're definitely doing it."

"Probably," I say as we watch Luis pat the woman with the clipboard down for weapons.

"She's got guts, that's for sure. Luis scares me to death."

I take in the beautiful planes of her face in the low light. "Good. He's not someone you should ever be friendly with."

Luis pulls open my door and I help Sophie out, admiring her legs in that dress and those heels as she steps down. Damn. She's stunning. I suppose it's a good thing I'm not armed tonight. Shooting my allies for leering at my girl wouldn't be good for business.

The woman from the casino introduces herself as Ursa Bolana, Director of Public Relations, and I almost smirk at how obviously ill at ease she is in our presence. By the time the casino's main investors found out who I was, it was too late to return my twelve percent stake in the project. Roberta, my accountant, is a former forensic investigator for the IRS, and she knows her stuff. My corporate investment firm passed due diligence with flying colors.

We follow her inside to a swanky VIP coat check area where Laney strips off her trench coat to great effect, revealing the blue dress with the cut-outs from earlier. Niner whistles low as he hands over his leather jacket and Luis looks ready to do murder.

"Oh, wow," Sophie says, shrugging out of her own coat which I pass to the woman behind the desk. "You look amazing."

Laney smiles like the Cheshire Cat. Even I have to admit she's making a statement wearing heels that lace all the way up her thighs and disappear under the dress.

"Good luck tonight, buddy," Niner says, slapping Luis on the back.

"Uh," Ms. Bolana stammers, her eyes flicking between Niner and Luis because they're openly armed. My hard look warns her to drop it, so she plasters on a fake smile and says, "This way, please."

We take the elevator up to the main level and when the doors slide open, we're greeted by the musical sounds of the slot machines. Since it's New Year's Eve, the casino floor is crowded and people openly gawk at us as we make our way across the room. I glance at Sophie to gauge her reaction to the crowd, and I'm pleased to see that my earlier attempts to knock back her anxiety weren't in vain. Not that making my woman come would ever be in vain.

"Can we play roulette later?" she asks happily.

"We can do anything you want." I'm not sure if she catches the suggestion in the comment because her sweet, naïve expression only gets brighter. Fuck, I love her.

As we approach the ballroom, there are still people waiting to get in. Respectful murmurs of *Jefe* and louder exclamations directed at Niner ring out. Not one man or woman looks in Luis' direction as he leads us forward. His nasty reputation is legendary.

Nearing the front of the line, the metal detector looming, Ms. Bolana wavers with uncertainty.

"That will be all, thank you," Laney tells her. The woman is comically relieved to be rid of us.

Rolando, who's keeping watch over the men as they search bags and frisk those who don't clear the metal detector, gives me a nod. Most of us, including Laney, set off the loud protest of the machine as we walk through. It might seem unfair to some, but my men will be the only ones armed tonight.

Sophie's steps falter slightly when she notices a big plastic tote bin half-full of confiscated weapons; guns, knives, brass knuckles, lighters, and what I think are a couple of garrotes. *And is that a pair of handcuffs?* Whatever that's about, I don't want to know.

I pull Sophie closer as we walk and whisper, "Welcome to my world."

Her wide eyes meet mine. "Who brings handcuffs to a dinner gala?"

"Kinky bastards?" Clearly that hadn't occurred to her and I can't resist needling her a little more. "Maybe I'll go back for them later."

Swatting at me, she giggles. "Very funny."

I almost break character and smile back.

At our table, JJ and Tony, along with his date who can't be much more than legal age, are seated, as well as Roberta and her newest boy toy. Introductions are made and as I sit, I notice the other tables are round, whereas ours is rectangular. I'll give Laney credit where credit is due; she's making a statement, one that includes Sophie since the table is wide enough for her to sit at the head beside me . . . like she's my queen. I meet Laney's gaze and she winks playfully. I'll have to increase her bonus.

Dinner is fine. I get some champagne into Sophie and she completely loosens up. With Niner on her left and Laney on my right, she spends a lot of time laughing at the insults they throw at one another. And as she relaxes, so do I.

As I nurse my second drink of the evening, I watch her and wonder what I'd do if she ever tried to walk away from me. Let's hope I never have to find out. Having to pin my mariposa to a board wouldn't be pleasant for either of us.

Only three men have the balls to approach me during dinner, hoping for an introduction to Sophie, I'm sure. One of the fuckers even tries to kiss her cheek, but as she shrinks away from him into me, Niner saves his life with an amused, "Not sure that's the way to play this Montora."

The cretin appears indignant until he sees my icy stare. With a possessive arm around Sophie, I take the opportunity to get the word out. "Any man stupid enough to touch her will find himself in a shallow grave." I'm forced to give him the watered-down version because Sophie would probably freak out if I said *castrated and left to bleed out in a shallow grave*.

He slinks away and I incline my head at Niner in thanks.

"Was that really necessary?" Sophie asks in a low voice, sounding distressed.

"Would you rather spend the night letting skeevy assholes kiss your cheek?"

"Oh." She considers. "Well, when you put it that way."

"The sooner you realize I know what's best for you, the better." That lights a spark in her, and as her face twists, I almost laugh.

"That's a horribly misogynistic thing to say."

"And yet, it's true." Her eyes narrow further and I feel my dick start to grow heavy.

"We're going to talk about this later."

"I look forward to it," I say, throwing her words from earlier back at her.

She makes a noise of disgust, but there's no real acrimony behind it. "Why is it so hard to be mad at you?" she grouses.

I hook a hand behind her neck and pull her close. "I'll let my cock explain it to you later." Her lips part slightly and I barely restrain a groan.

When dinner is over, we make our way as a group to the locker rooms adjacent to the casino's small arena. Finding

MMA fighters and building them up to greatness is something Niner, Laney, and I do together. And I've got high hopes for Fernando Silva. Laney's brother in Peru discovered him in the *barrios* of Lima and thought he had potential. He was right. We brought him here to the U.S. and he's been steadily moving up as a welterweight. We hope to get him a fight in the UFC if he wins this one tonight.

The kid's English is terrible, so everything is in Spanish and half the room is bored senseless, including Sophie. When her phone rings, she pulls it out of her little purse and shows me that her sister is calling. She gestures to the back of room and I nod.

Unfortunately, Monika takes the opportunity to move in. She runs PR/social media for all of our fighters and I put up with her because she's good at her job.

"Jefe," she purrs, using her claw-like nails to caress her ample cleavage as if to draw attention to her tits. Like I could miss them; they're practically spilling out of her dress. "Our boy's about to hit the big time."

Her come-ons have always been obvious. I'm not sure why she keeps trying when I've never once given her the impression I'm interested. Tawdry simpering has never been my thing.

I stick with business. "How's his follower engagement shaping up? You're making sure to get his input when responding to comments?"

She's insulted by the question for a moment before her features even out. "Of course. You don't pay me for my looks . . . although . . ."

And I've had enough. "Listen, Monika—"

She titters. "Oh, Jefe, you're so serious." Then she has the gall to run her fingers along the lapel of my suit jacket.

"Is there a reason you're touching him?" Sophie demands.

Monika's hand falls away as I turn, but Sophie's not looking to me for an explanation. She's homed in on Monika, who's not conveying a single iota of repentance. "Oh, honey, relax."

I open my mouth to put Monika in her place, but Sophie holds up an index finger tipped with a dark, polished nail to stop me. With fascination, I watch my girl's gentle manner transform into incredulity, which she punctuates with a condescending lift of her brows.

"So, what . . ." Sophie starts. "He's going to fuck you in the bathroom while I'm on the phone? Surely you can scrape together a bit more self-respect than that."

Outrage ripples across the woman's features and suddenly I'm worried about the possibility of a catfight.

Sophie must see her intention too, because she says, "I wouldn't if I were you. I don't fight fair."

The distinctive snick of a switchblade echoes in the room. "Hey, *Fresita*, maybe cut her up a bit," Niner suggests, holding it out to her.

My girl reaches for the knife, still not taking her eyes off of her prey. *The hell?* Now my dick is showing some serious interest. Indecision wars within me. *How far do I let this go?*

Before things can escalate though, Monika backs down. "There's no need to go all psycho," she says, trying to sound exasperated, but she's clearly shaken by the knife's appearance. "I was just saying hello."

"Fair enough, *honey*," Sophie says with mocking sweetness. "Next time keep your hands to yourself."

As Monika steals away, I wrap an arm around Sophie's waist and get a frosty glare for my trouble. Pulling her closer,

I let her feel how hard her little display has made me. "That explanation you have coming from my dick? You're going to feel it for days."

"I better. You owe me."

I laugh. "How do you figure that?"

"She was touching you," she practically hisses, putting that sexy index finger in my face again. I take hold of it and bring it to my lips.

"What in the ever loving . . ?" Laney trails off and I look up to expressions running the gamut from disbelief to astonishment.

"Did you just laugh?" JJ asks.

"Oh, fuck off," I tell them. "I laugh."

"He does," Niner confirms. "I heard him once the summer after sophomore year."

I scoff, but Sophie giggles, softly at first, then the sound morphs into outright joy and my annoyance sloughs away. *"Vámonos,"* I grumble. "Fernando, *buena suerte.*"

After that, I feel oddly upbeat and I walk out onto our mezzanine box seats with my girl proudly displayed on my arm. For once, I let myself bask in just how good my life can be.

The arena only holds a couple thousand people, but it's packed and the first fight is already in progress. Fernando is the headliner so he's up last, the fourth match of the night. I get Sophie settled on my left, making sure she's got another glass of champagne. As the next round starts, I find myself leaning forward on the rail with Niner beside me and we get absorbed in the all-out brawl in the octagon.

When a round ends, I notice Sophie on her phone. "Are you bored?" I ask her.

"A little, but I don't mind. I just don't like the . . . uh, carnage."

I guess I didn't think of that.

In between fights, I have to make nice with some guys from an outfit in Minneapolis. It's only a preliminary meet and greet, but doing business with them would be a big step for us. We're slowly pushing our influence east, much to Laney's satisfaction. I, however, am more cautious. New territory means new problems. How big can we get before we're stretched too thin and things start to collapse?

Returning to my seat, I see that Tony's girl is now sitting on Sophie's other side. Thankful she s got someone to talk to, I give my attention to the second fight. Halfway through, I see the girls giggling at something on Sophie's phone. Then they get up and look over the rail. Sophie then answers a call. With all the noise I can't hear what she's saying. *Who, exactly, is she talking to?*

Sophie sits down again and gives me a rueful look as she holds out her phone to me. On the screen, it says: *Jorge Alberto*. My back immediately goes up and she must notice because she rolls her eyes. "Just talk to him."

I take the phone. "Who the fuck is this?"

"Tío! Sophie says you're not going to let her go."

It clicks then. Jorgie, my nephew. I suppose he's harmless enough, but my sister, Nora, is always on my case about keeping her son away from *Los Santos* and Jorgie is always throwing himself in. I didn't know he'd be here tonight.

"Go where?" I growl.

"Over to the club. Let me take her dancing. She's bored out of her mind."

My knee-jerk reaction is to say *over my dead body*. But a glance at Sophie tells me she's hopeful. *Shit*. I lean over the rail and meet Jorgie's eyes. His friend Mike is beside him. "Let me arrange security first. You can meet her at the stairs."

He flashes me a thumbs up.

Handing Sophie back her phone, I call Tony over from where he's standing with his date. "Jenny already asked me," he says and it takes me second to figure out Jenny is his girl's name. "I'll make sure they don't get into trouble."

Tony being with Sophie eases my mind a bit, even if I'm cognizant that *I* should be the one to take her. Though I'm sure I'll be as bored there as she is here. Sighing, I sit next to Sophie. "You don't leave Tony's sightline for any reason."

She nods, her smile wide and grateful and if I were a different man I'd feel guilty for ruling her movements. But she and I seem to have found an understanding. I keep her safe, she lets me. I dominate, she submits. And we both like it that way.

"Take three other guys," I tell Tony and Sophie makes a choking sound. I hold up a hand to stop her from protesting. "Or you can stay."

"But isn't that too much trouble?" she asks.

My sweet girl, always considering others before herself. "They *work* for me."

She nods reluctantly.

Before they go, I put my mouth to her ear. "No man touches you. Is that understood?"

"Not a problem. I only want you."

I watch them go, the girls arm-in-arm, their heads together. And I hope this isn't a huge mistake.

• • • • •

It takes Fernando until the fourth round to finally get his opponent to tap out, and by that time, I'm anxious as fuck. I've already had four reports that everything is fine, but I won't feel better until I see Sophie for myself.

Leaving Laney and Niner to congratulate Fernando, I take Luis and Rolando and cross the casino to the night club. It's almost 11:30 and the line to get in is long. I guess not everyone knows who I am, because there's some bitching when we walk right in. The pounding music invades my senses, some kind of techno shit that brings on a wave of nostalgia for the raves I used to love as a teenager.

As we're shown to the VIP section upstairs, I keep an eye out for my girl, but I don't see her in the throngs of people. Near our table, Tony and Jeremy are standing at the rail, watching the dancefloor below. Stripping off my suit jacket and tie, I undo the top buttons of my shirt and join them.

"Where is she?" I ask, almost having to yell over the music as I remove my cufflinks and start rolling up my sleeves.

Tony points and I spot her right away. She's with Jenny, Jorgie and Mike, and two of my junior guys who are trying to maintain a bit of room around them. She's beautiful and carefree with her arms up and her hips swaying, lost in the music. I almost smile until that no-good nephew of mine moves in on her. And she lets him.

Tony grabs my arm as I turn for the stairs. "Jefe, it's innocent," he informs me. "They've all had a lot to drink, but it's just PG-13 stuff." I hesitate, watching Jorgie turn to Jenny and do the same. I still don't like it.

Waving Luis off from following me, I head downstairs and push my way through the crowded dancefloor. When she sees me coming, she dances right up on me and claims my mouth, her arms snaking around my neck. Jesus. She's temptation incarnate, tasting of alcohol and pent-up desire, pressing her breasts into my chest. My hands cup her ass and we start to move, the beat throbbing around us. Our tongues tangle, fanning the flames of desire. She slides a leg between my thighs and we groan into each other's mouths. It goes on and on right there on the dancefloor, rubbing, groping, making out like fucking teenagers. There's not a single other place I'd rather be . . . except inside of her. Yes, that's what I want. To slide into that tight heat, to make her come, to spill myself deep inside of her.

I pull her in tighter against my raging hard on, letting her ride my thigh. She breaks the kiss with a gasp and her lust-drenched, drunken gaze hits me like a semi-truck. "Want you," she pants. Our hips rolls together and her cry gets lost in the pounding music. Her neck bared, I lick over her scar and then bite down.

"Jefe," I hear. It's too close and my eyes snap open. It's Luis and he's pissed. He jerks his head back the way I came, but Sophie chooses that moment to bite me back, right under my ear and my eyes sink shut again.

"Now, Jefe. There're cameras."

My synapses take their sweet time connecting the dots. "Shit," I finally moan, placing my mouth at Sophie's ear. "We gotta go."

I start her moving, my arms still around her. Following Luis under the stairs instead of returning to the VIP section, we come out in a hallway where he opens a door marked private. "Get it out of your system," he snaps, ushering us in and then closing the door behind us.

"Finally," Sophie says, sounding like she's been waiting a lifetime as she palms my dick through the fabric of my pants.

I crash my mouth back onto hers and she fumbles with my zipper. Getting me free, her hot hand strokes me a few times and I almost forget what I'm doing it feels so good. As always, though, the need for control takes over and I push her back against the door. Reaching up under her dress, I give her thong an experimental tug. The soaked material yields, so I yank and come away with the only barrier between me and that sweet pussy of hers. Taking hold of the back of her thigh, I pull it up high on my hip and dip down to get myself into position.

"Do it," she pants and I don't argue. The angle is shit, but I barely notice because she's like molten lava, tight and soft and all mine. With her back to the door, I lift her other thigh, taking her weight as she wraps her arms and legs around me. "Yes," she hisses, impaling herself deeper.

Planting my palms on the door I want to warn her I need to *fuck*, but words fail me as her nails dig into my scalp. We quickly find a hard rhythm and the burn in my muscles only compounds the bliss of it all.

Her pussy contracts and I grunt, stalling out. "Make yourself come," I demand. "Put your fingers on your clit and make yourself come."

I'm half expecting her to defy me, to push my buttons a bit, but apparently drunk-Sophie is much more compliant than her sober counterpart. She goes right to work, rubbing her clit in small circles in the sliver of space between our bodies. And damn, it doesn't take long. Speared on my cock, clinging to my body, she comes apart in spectacular fashion. I see, hear, and feel every nuance of her orgasm; every wail, every clench, every shudder. And two more thrusts is all it takes for me to join her.

CHAPTER 5

Sophie

I'm in heaven. Even when he sets me down on my feet and my legs are like rubber, I'm in heaven. And I'm drunk . . . god, it feels so good to let go.

A loud thump at my back makes me jump. "Jefe, let's go! It's almost midnight."

I giggle, watching Alejandro tuck himself back in his pants. "You think he knows?"

"That I fucked you against the door? Definitely. I bet half the club heard you over the music."

I smirk proudly as he straightens the bodice of my dress for me.

"You good to go back out there?"

"Yeah, just let me clean up." I scan the room for some tissues or something.

"I don't think so. When New Year's hits, I want my come sliding down your thighs."

I choke on a laugh. "You're such a barbarian." Spotting a box, I totter to the desk in an imitation of a newborn foal.

"Are you disobeying me, woman?"

"Sorry, but some things are only sexy in theory."

Dimly, I'm aware of how tawdry I must look, tossing a third wad of tissues into the trash can, but when I meet Alejandro's eyes, I get nothing but satisfaction from him. That pleases my champagne-soaked brain to no end.

"*Now* can we go get a drink?" he asks, bending over to grab my panties from the floor, stuffing them into his pocket.

"Yes, dear."

On the other side of the door, I give Luis a sly grin and I'm not even disappointed when he shows no reaction. "They want you and Fernando to do the countdown," Luis says as we make our way back, the music getting louder.

"Fine, whatever," Alejandro says. "Just find me a drink, would you? My mariposa is miles ahead."

It's obvious by the clamor our re-appearance causes that practically everybody in this place knows what we did. The old me would have been mortified, but this me, the one who's extremely tipsy and under Alejandro's protection? She wants to announce, *'That's right, bitches. The hottest man on the planet just made me come.'*

Alejandro barks out a laugh.

"Did I say that out loud?"

"I didn't hear a thing," he says, drawing me closer.

There are a lot more people in the club than there were earlier and Alejandro's men have to make a path through the crowd. We end up near the bar where there's a dais set up with a rail around it. Good thing or I'd probably fall right off. Niner, Ben, and Laney are already there, along with the fighter from earlier who's pretty beaten up. Glasses of champagne are being handed out and I notice a big countdown clock on the wall. It's 11:57.

Alejandro leans into my ear as he puts a glass in my hand. "Fernando wants you to hit the plunger on the confetti canon. Are you okay with that? It's going to be loud."

Sober, I'd balk. Drunk, I'm game. "As long as you're with me." I slide a foot out of my high heel so I'll fit under his arm properly.

The music is turned way down and a man who I assume is the manager or the owner of the club says a few words, welcoming everyone and thanking Alejandro, Laney and Fernando. Then the countdown to New Year's is on, everyone yelling out the last thirty seconds. Five, four, three, two, one, and I hit the plunger. BOOM! I jump, yes, but I'm happy as Alejandro holds me steady in his arms.

He stays with me through all the congratulations, not letting me go for a second and only allowing Niner and Ben to hug me. And when we get a slice of a moment for ourselves, he says, *"Feliz año, mariposa."*

"Happy New Year, my devil."

I have the greatest night. I drink more delicious champagne, I sit on Alejandro's lap, I dance with Jenny and Jorgie, and even Niner. After a fight breaks out on the dancefloor, Alejandro makes me stay upstairs in the VIP section with him, but it doesn't put a damper on the fun at all.

If this is what my new life with Alejandro is going to be like, I'm all in.

It's past four in the morning when we finally go upstairs to our suite in the casino, where I promptly pass out.

· · · · ·

Of course the piper has to be paid in the morning. I don't think I've ever felt quite so much like death warmed over . . . at least not since my undergrad days. And Alejandro is just as worse for wear. He's beyond cranky, and worse, being hung over doesn't dull his need to always be in motion. It's barely nine o'clock when he informs me we'll be leaving in thirty minutes. If only looks could kill, I'd still be in bed and not struggling to pull a pair of yoga pants onto shower-moist skin while a marching band wreaks havoc in my skull.

I hear the outer door to the suite open, then close, and I brace myself for whatever callous comment is going to come out of his mouth.

"I brought you some coffee."

My body slumps with relief as I take the Starbucks cup with a slightly shaky hand and offer him a weak smile, a *thank you* on the tip of my tongue.

"Is your shit together?"

And there it is. "Yes, *darling*," I whisper, "my *shit* is together."

He grabs my bag off the bed and heads for the bedroom door. Once I've got my socks and sneakers on, I pull a hoodie over my head and follow. He's looking out at the view in jeans and a black Henley. Too bad I don't have it in me to admire the picture my man makes wearing aviators.

As soon as he sees me, he moves with the grace of a panther and ushers me out the door. There are men I've never seen before at either end of the hall, and one who's holding the elevator for us. Alejandro doesn't acknowledge them, so neither do I. As the elevator starts its descent, my stomach wobbles and all I can think of is why I'm not still under a blanket, dead to the world. We come out into the cold, underground parking garage and get straight into a Tahoe. Rolando is driving, Luis beside him. "Morning," I mutter, trying for polite, but they pretend I don't exist. Fine with me. Placing my coffee in the cup holder between the front seats, I reach for my seat belt, but Alejandro takes hold of my thigh and pulls me to the middle seat. My mood buoys a bit, but as the muted light of the parking garage is exchanged for the stark brightness of the desert sun, I groan, shielding my eyes.

"Here," he says so softly I almost don't hear him. He eases his sunglasses over my eyes and then pulls my head to his shoulder. Well, shit. He may be a grumpy ass, but his need to take care of me is . . . what? Heart-melting? Swoon-worthy?

I sigh and snuggle against him.

Arriving back at the compound, I realize I'd forgotten all about Bruce Wayne. Some mother I am. He's fine though; Rocio, the estate manager, let him out this morning and fed him. Right now, he's playing in the back with Justin.

Alejandro takes me up to our room and puts me to bed. "You're not staying?" I ask, disappointed.

He shakes his head. "I feel like road kill. I need to eat something. Get some sleep."

"Kay."

I don't know how many hours later, he joins me for a bit, but when I finally wake up, feeling more human, he's gone again. After a coat of mascara and a high pony tail, I deem myself presentable and I make my way downstairs. The halls are deserted, but as I get closer to the back of the house, I hear voices.

Entering the kitchen, I see the large dining table at the far end is busy with people. A quick scan tells me that Alejandro isn't among them, but almost right away, I hear, "She's alive!" from Niner. "Come sit, *Fresita*. I've been saving a spot for you."

"Oh, please," Laney says to Niner as I approach. "You're such a brown-nosing opportunist. You were fawning over Rocio not two minutes ago in that very spot."

"You're just bitter because you've got some competition for the title of baddest-ass bitch now that *Rosita Fresita* is here."

"True," Laney concedes.

"True?" I sputter, taking the seat.

"Oh, yeah," Laney says, directing a smile my way for the first time ever. "That was some crazy shit last night." She holds her fist out across the table and I stare at it stupidly for a second before I bump it.

"Miss?" comes from beside me. A woman sets a cup of coffee down for me and asks, "What would you like to eat?"

"Oh, um. Just some plain toast, please. I'm still not feeling very well." Heat licks its way across my cheekbones for unexplained reasons. I don't even know this woman.

Ben laughs low. "Oh, I bet you aren't."

Laney snorts. "That was quite the display you put on last night."

My expression must convey my confused dismay, because JJ starts laughing. "You don't remember?"

"Oh my god, remember what?"

"Making out with el Jefe on the dance floor."

I relax. "Oh, that." I wave a dismissive hand, then stir some cream into my coffee. "That was his fault." My mind provides me with the incredible replay of him pushing through the crowd in that suit vest, his collar open and his sleeves rolled up, showing his tattoos . . . yeah, not something I'll ever forget.

Again, Laney holds out her fist to me, and I again, I bump it, this time with a bit more confidence. "Personally," Laney says, "I'm not into all that broody testosterone, but if you're willing to put up with it, you have all my respect."

Niner bursts out laughing. "The fuck are you talking about? You don't like broody testosterone, my ass."

Tony, chuckling as well, says, "Just tell us, Lanes."

"Tell you what, you fuckers?" she gripes.

"Have you guys done it yet?" JJ teases as I check the table for Luis. He's not here though.

Laney gives him the most scathing look I've ever seen. "What is this, high school?"

"If it was," Niner says. "You'd be the scary goth chick who has secret voodoo dolls in her basement."

I try to smother my reaction, but Laney hears me and points an accusing finger in my direction. "What are you laughing about? Miss cheerleading prom queen."

"I'll have you know I went to an all-girls school. We didn't have cheerleaders or prom queens."

"Oh, ho. Now we're talking," JJ says, waggling his brows at me playfully.

Tony then says, "Tell me there were sleepovers with spin the bottle and pillow fights."

I can't help it. I laugh. "What a bunch of pervs."

"Well, that's nothing we didn't already know," Ben says.

A French door opens and Bruce Wayne rushes in, his nails scrabbling against the tile in his desperate attempt to reach me. I push my chair back to lean down and give him some love, but not before I get a glimpse of Alejandro in a bathing suit, shirtless and glorious in the afternoon sun. He hasn't been swimming though.

"Ah, yes, the prom king and the mascot," Niner jokes, and they go off on a tangent about what our high school should be called. Feet clad in mint green flip flops appear in my field of vision.

"My turn, you little bastard," Alejandro says, using his foot to move the dog aside, then pulls me up out of my seat and takes my place so I can sit on his lap.

I shiver at his skin's temperature. "Why are you so cold?" I ask, rubbing at his arms.

Nuzzling into my neck, he murmurs, "I was going to go for a swim but the delinquent, here, was threatening to jump in the pool, so I took him for a walk instead."

"You're actually a big softie, aren't you?"

He scoffs as my toast is put down in front of us. In low Spanish, the woman asks Alejandro what I assume is if he wants anything. His answer is echoed by Niner. "You want some eggs?" Alejandro asks me.

"Oh, no thank you," I say, directing my words to the woman.

The teasing conversation starts up again, this time including Alejandro in the high school debate. I'm pleased that he joins in with them, not just shutting them down . . . or out, like he usually does. These people are his family, and maybe mine now, too.

• • • • •

After our early dinner, Alejandro wants to go for a drive in his McLaren. He keeps it mellow and a Tahoe follows us as we wend our way along the two-lane desert highway. The vibration of this ridiculous car is soothing to my still slightly nauseous body and the sky is pretty as the sun sets. I'm loath to break the pleasant quiet of the moment, but I don't know when I'll find him in such a laid back mood again.

"So, my sister called last night."

Not taking his eyes from the road, he gives me a non-committal hum of agreement.

"She, uh, kind of guessed that I was with you and I didn't deny it."

That gets me an amused glance. "I didn't realize I was your dirty little secret."

"You're hardly a secret – at least not anymore."

"Well, don't keep me in suspense. What did she have to say?"

"She wants me to bring you to the house."

"For my reckoning?" he jokes.

"You don't have to worry. I'd never let her say or do anything insulting or offensive."

That gets me a rare, wide smile with a flash of teeth from behind his beard. "You going to protect me?"

"Of course," I say, sounding offended. Then to keep it light, I add, "Though she does have a few inches on me, and don't tell anyone, but she's freakishly strong."

He laughs. "When do we have to go?"

"I was thinking for Daniela's birthday?" We can't miss his goddaughter's party even if we wanted to postpone the coming *reckoning*.

"In February?" He visibly relaxes and I realize he's not quite as blasé about this as he wants me to believe. "Works for me."

"Thanks, prom king."

"I told you. I'm the bad boy," he deadpans. "I'd never go to a *prom*."

Sometimes life is so close to perfect it's scary.

On our return, Alejandro's good mood continues and after stopping by our room for a blanket, he leads me to the back of the house and up some stairs. Since it's only a two story house, he's either taking me up to the attic or . . . "Oh, wow," I say as we come out onto a large roof-top terrace with Bruce Wayne at our heels.

Tilting my head back, I take in the night sky. There's not as many stars as there were at the cabin that night in Oregon, but it's pretty nonetheless. My attention is brought back to earth, though, when I hear voices. Involuntarily, I move closer to Alejandro who's eyeing a partially hidden seating area on the far side of the patio. It seems Bruce Wayne has found some new admirers.

"Come on," he says, tugging me with him.

There are two couples lying on lounge chairs around a gas fire pit.

I'm about to suggest we come back later, when Alejandro's voice pierces the chilly desert air. "Clear out," he orders and I think I might gasp softly at his rudeness. My eyes cut to his, but he's erected his business persona, the one that's harder than granite and leaves zero room for disobedience. He must sense my mouth opening to protest because he squeezes my hand in warning.

"Sure thing, Jefe."

The four of them gather their stuff and are gone within a minute, the door closing softly behind them.

"Was that really necessary?" I ask him. "Surely they've got as much right to be here as we do."

He doesn't answer, only chooses a two person chaise in front of the fire and pulls me down alongside him. Once we're settled under the blanket, though, with the remnants of my hangover still nagging at me, I don't let it go like I should. "Are you going to tell me what that was about?"

"Just drop it."

Lifting my head, I glare at him. "We could have come back later."

"And have it get around that I'm being polite to lackeys?" *Polite* comes out like it's the worst insult imaginable and *lackeys* turns my stomach . . . until he adds more. "I'd be dead in a month, and you with me."

"What?" I whisper in horror.

He mutters something darkly under his breath that I can't make out, then says, "I shouldn't have said that. But come on, Sophie, this isn't some kind of PC democracy."

Not wanting to see his stupidly handsome face anymore, I lay my head back on his shoulder.

"Anyway," he goes on gruffly. "I'm responsible for everything and everyone under this roof. It all rests on *my* shoulders, so if I want to sit on my goddamn patio, I will."

What a broody ass. Though I suppose he has a point even if his words don't erase the bad taste in my mouth. Everyone is here by choice, aren't they? If they jump when he snaps his fingers, it's not my concern. But not treating people with decency? That seriously goes against my grain.

Bruce distracts us both from our thoughts as he slowly lifts a paw onto the end of the lounger and then slinks up next to our legs as nonchalantly as possible. "Such a rotten pain in the ass," Alejandro complains.

"Kind of like his daddy?"

He huffs, then tightens his arms around me. "Exactly."

At least he hasn't lost his sense of humor.

With the flames of the fire pit holding back the darkness, the tension slowly begins to evaporate and is replaced by the bone-deep contentment that was with us earlier. I guess I knew this thing between us wasn't going to be easy. How we treat people is just one of a million ways we're different, and we're each going to have to learn how to adjust.

I run my hand up under his hoodie and soak up the warmth of his skin. There's a chill in the air, though I don't think the tremor that runs through his big body is from the cold. My fingertips find the scar on his right side near his waist and trace the two inch vertical line.

Without thinking, I ask, "Why won't you tell me what happened here?" At the cabin, I never got the chance to ask about it, and this past week, he's changed the subject twice.

"You don't want to know."

That gives me pause. "Of course I do. I want to know everything about you."

"No you don't," he says, once again bordering on condescending.

I try not to take offense. It's just the way he is. "You know what happened to me," I coax. "It's only fair I know what happened to you."

"Drop it, Sophia."

Drop it twice in one night? Maybe I *am* offended. "I assume you didn't have your appendix removed," I say dryly.

He can't quite stifle a laugh. We both know the position is all wrong. "No, all my internal organs are present and accounted for."

"Then tell me."

"Fine," he says, exasperated. "But don't say I didn't warn you." He exhales, long and loud as if resigning himself to something. "If you must know, I got shanked."

The moment stretches out while my brain tries to process the word. "Shanked?" I finally choke out. But *shanked* implies . . . "In prison?"

CHAPTER 6

Aléjandro

I'd laugh at the way the word *prison* comes out of her mouth all strangled and pitchy, but I kind of hate the idea of her thinking less of me. Not that I was ever a saint in her eyes, but any illusions she's been holding on to throughout our tempestuous relationship are about to be yanked away. But at this point, we may as well get it over with. I was always going to have to tell her.

"Yeah," I say flippantly. "In prison. I did seven months while awaiting trial."

"Seven months . . ." she repeats, aghast, "Awaiting trial?" A few beats pass. "You couldn't make bail?"

My surprise at the direction of her thoughts quickly fades. *Does she think they would hold me on some kind of minor charge?* The last of my good humor slips away at having to disabuse her of the notion.

"Bail was denied. Mostly because the charges were serious." Wincing, I admit, "Felony murder."

I feel her bristle against me. "But you're here . . . obviously."

"Obviously," I retort. "The charges were dropped due to lack of evidence." A sudden burst of anger has me adding, "Since I didn't do it."

She nuzzles into my neck, placing little kisses up to my ear. "I'm sorry that happened to you."

She's sorry? Just because I didn't do *that* job, doesn't mean my hands are clean by any stretch of the imagination. She can't be that naïve.

"It must have been traumatizing," she goes on gently. "How long ago did this happen?"

Her tone is soothing, filing down a few of my rough edges, and my greedy soul laps up her compassion as she continues to stroke over the scar on my side. "I . . . I was twenty-three."

"So a *long* time ago." We both chuckle and then she says, "That's about how old I was when I returned from Haiti. Big experiences leave big impressions, don't they?" My girl talks about her trip to the island as a volunteer often.

"Yeah," I sigh. "They do." This woman is too perceptive by half. "I felt like a totally different person when I got out. I couldn't sit still anymore. I always had to be doing something. I still do."

She hums in agreement.

"Sometimes," I go on, "the anxiety builds up to the point that I feel like I'm going to come out of my skin."

"Is that why you go down to the gym at weird hours?"

"What?" I say sardonically. "You mean not everyone goes at two o'clock in the morning?" This past week between Christmas and New Year's saw me at the gym in my building less than usual because she was with me, but I'd still needed the release a few times. "Exercise helps dial it back a bit."

She nods against my chest. "I wish I had something like that. My instincts seem to kick in out of the blue and I never know when to trust them."

The attack at the gas station really messed with her self-confidence, I know. "You should always trust them, but the trick is to not let them cripple you. After I got out, I was paranoid too. Eventually, though, it turns into common sense. The last seventeen years of my life have been lived with an eye to not going back inside."

Feeling so much more at ease than a few minutes ago, I slouch further down in the chaise and watch the flames dance, enjoying the feel of her body next to mine. If incarceration gave me anything, it's a true appreciation of moments like this.

"Did it ever make you think about leaving it all behind?"

"Hmm?" I murmur. "You mean doing time?"

"Yeah, you say when you got out you didn't want to go back . . ."

My guard down, I answer truthfully. "Of course I thought about it. But by then, I had responsibilities."

"Really? Like what?"

Oh shit. I realize my mistake then. But maybe I should cop to everything now. She'll find out eventually and she deserves to hear it from me. Sighing heavily, I admit, "I had big responsibilities that couldn't be met by starting over somewhere new." I hesitate. "Or I don't know, maybe I could have. But at that age, my pride was almost as big as my ego."

I get no response, probably because I'm feeding her cryptic bullshit. Her silence provokes a bit of a pang in my chest. What if she's so put off by what I have to tell her that she tries to leave? *I'd like to see her try,* my brain supplies stubbornly, but then my more practical side feels a rush of fear. It pushes me to plow forward. "Child support," I say, blood rushing in my ears, though not so loudly that I miss her quick inhale. "I had child support payments to make and I couldn't do that by working at *McDonald's.*"

Long seconds pass before she whispers, "You have a child?"

"Yeah," I grit out as if the admission hurts. "I have two."

"Two?"

She sounds breathless . . . with surprise? Or is it horror? Well, if it isn't horror yet, it might soon be.

"Alejandro?"

She sits up and by the light of the fire, her shock is laid bare. My girl has always been so easy to read.

"I've never heard any mention of you having kids."

"It's not common knowledge," I admit.

"What? What does that mean?"

"It means they don't live in California." My mind sorts through all the possibilities, searching for the least damaging way to tell this story. "My, uh, ex-wife made the decision to leave while I was locked up."

"Excuse me?"

God. Am I really trying to make myself out to be the victim? "Don't be outraged on my behalf, mariposa. She did what was necessary. Believe me, it took guts to strike out on her own with a toddler and a baby on the way." I rub a hand over my face and swallow another sigh. "I was never a good husband or a good father. I was young and stupid and full of anger. For her, my getting collared for murder was just the icing on a very messed-up cake. She wanted out for the sake of her boys, and I . . . I couldn't argue with that."

Anguish sparks, hot and unexpected, in my chest. I've never told this to anyone. There are people, like Niner and Laney, who *know*, but I've never explained it before. *How did I not know it would hurt so much to talk about them?*

I press my forehead to her shoulder, trying to regroup, trying to contain it all before I completely unravel. Her fingers slide into my hair and the soothing graze of her nails against my scalp is enough to hold the unheard of emotion at bay.

"Tell me about them?" she asks, her tone nothing but sweetness again. *She's really not going to condemn me?* When I don't immediately respond, she qualifies it with, "Well, tell me as much as you're comfortable sharing."

"What do you want to know?" I ask huskily, lifting my head.

"I'm not even sure. You've thrown me for a loop here, my devil. Maybe start at the beginning. How did you come to be married with children at such a young age?"

I rest the back of my head on the chair. "Fuck if I know. Charlene and I were mostly monogamous and when she told me she was pregnant, I married her. It was just the done thing."

"You didn't ask for a paternity test?"

I laugh, short and sharp. "When I say *mostly monogamous*, I meant me. Honestly, I don't know what she saw in me."

She gives a hum of contemplation. "And what did you see in her?"

"That's easy. Besides being the prettiest thing I'd ever laid eyes on, she was stable. And to a guy who'd lost his family and was knee-deep in violence and mayhem, she represented . . . home, I guess. Everything I'd had growing up."

Her nails continue their calming motion in my hair as she asks, "How did you meet her?"

"Uh, by accident one night. Some guys were hassling her and her friend outside a restaurant. Things grew from there. I was cagey about who I was and what I did in the beginning, but eventually she figured it out."

Again, she's quiet and I can only imagine what's going through her mind.

"The pregnancy wasn't an accident," she says, making my breath catch.

"Probably not," I concede. "We didn't really talk much. But I think she thought a baby would be enough to change my self-destructive patterns."

"She loved you," she says simply, like it explains everything.

"Well, it's a good thing she loved her boys more."

"Why do you keep referring to *her* boys – wait, they're both boys?" A wide, beautiful smile spreads across her face.

"Yeah, they're both boys. And they're *hers* because they don't know who I am."

"What?! Why not?" she asks too loudly and Bruce Wayne lifts his head to study us.

"Because I live a very dangerous life." I'm braced for the onslaught of her condemnation because it has to be coming now. What kind of a man chooses *anything* over his own children?

"Oh, Alejandro," she whispers, leaning in to kiss the side of my mouth. "I can't even imagine what that's cost you."

I blink, taken aback.

"Do you really not know anything about them at all?" she asks gently.

"No. I mean, yes." I can't think straight around my surprise. "I mean, Charlene sends me their school pictures every year and tells me a bit about them." Emotion starts to rise again. I really thought I'd made peace with this eons ago. "Um, Samson is the oldest. He turned seventeen a few months ago."

"Seventeen?!"

"I know. He's halfway through his senior year."

"Does he look like you?"

I consider. "Not as much as his younger brother, Tyler. But they both have my dark hair and eyes." I can't help the note of pride in my tone, though being a sperm donor isn't at all the same as being a father.

"Do they like school? Or sports? Or what?"

"I . . . I don't know if they *like* school, but Samson is a really good student. Tyler not so much, but they go to the best school money can buy. At least I've done that for them."

She keeps her own counsel, but the approval shining in her eyes keeps me talking.

"They played baseball when they were younger," I say hesitantly. "Their stepfather . . . well, he's really their actual father, he used to coach their Little League Teams."

"Your ex-wife is married again?"

"Yeah, Doug. He's an insurance adjuster. A good guy." I cringe, surprised by how hard that is to say. "Charlene likes to say he's everything that I wasn't; dependable, respectable, decent. He's the man my father wanted me to be." My next words come out bitter. "He ended up with my life."

"I don't know," she muses. "I can't really see you in insurance."

I snort, loving that she always knows how to make me feel better. "Well, I would have gone in a slightly different direction of course."

She giggles and the sound of it fills me with well-being, at least until she sobers and asks her next question. "So you've never met them?"

I shake my head. "Not as their father, no. I saw them briefly before Javier was killed. Charlene introduced me as a friend from work, but that was almost ten years ago."

"Have you ever thought about . . . making contact with them?"

Shaking my head, I give her the same answer I always give myself. "That would be selfish. They don't need me messing up their lives."

Sophie tsks. "That's not what I asked."

"What? If I've thought about it? Of course I have. Almost every day. But I made my choices long ago and I have to live with them."

She must agree because she leans into me again and places her head on my shoulder, pulling the blanket back over us. We sit together for long moments, listening to the sounds of the night. With her nose pressed to my neck, the hollow feeling inside of me begins to fade away.

CHAPTER 7

Sophie

The next morning, I wake up alone, but his side of the bed isn't cold yet, so he hasn't been gone long. I lie there, staring at the ceiling, letting myself reabsorb everything he confessed to last night. *Holy shit.* The man certainly knows how to take a girl by surprise. I guess the part about being in prison wasn't too shocking, but the kids? And then the ache in his voice when he talked about them? That about did me in. This life Alejandro has built for himself has definitely come with a very hefty price tag. First losing his family, and then his wife and kids. In that light, his decision to let me go last September makes a lot more sense. Once Alejandro chooses a course of action, he sees it through to the end. I have to wonder if I'm the only exception he's ever made.

Suddenly the need to lay eyes on him and make sure he's okay pushes me from the bed. Maybe if I hurry, we can have breakfast together. I get in the shower and then throw on some jeans and a T-shirt.

The house is decidedly empty. I'm assuming Alejandro's invitation to all and sundry was revoked once New Year's came and went. Either that, or Luis told them all to get out . . . with only his glare.

Alejandro isn't in the kitchen, but I do find Laney sitting at the table with a cup of coffee and her phone. "Hey," I say, taking my own coffee to join her.

Her head jerks up. "Shit, you scared me."

I'm about to apologize when her brow furrows and she says, "Why aren't you downstairs?"

"Pardon?"

"Downstairs," she says like I'm being deliberately obtuse.

I frown. "I just got up. Is something going on?"

Outrage blooms on her face. "That *rat* bastard."

"What? Who?"

"*Pinche Jefe*. This should be *your* show, *your* closure."

I look down at my coffee. "I think I'm missing some caffeine, because I don't have a clue what you're talking about."

"Come on." She gets to her feet. "He's not getting away with this."

I follow her, trying to keep up with her brisk pace. "What's this about, Laney?"

"You'll see."

She leads me through the house, over to the other wing, the one Alejandro told me to stay away from. "Listen, um, I don't think this is a good idea. He's going to be angry with me for snooping around."

Laney stops abruptly and I almost collide with her. "Let me give you a piece of advice, Ms. Spun-Sugar Prom Queen. If you don't make your stand early on, he will crush you."

My head jerks back with alarm. *What on earth is she talking about?*

"Maybe not intentionally," she goes on. "But what does it matter if it's intentional if you've already been trampled."

"Trampled?" I echo. "That's all very dramatic, Laney, but I still don't know what's going on."

Turning on her heel, she keeps walking. "There's something you need to be a part of and I'm not letting him shut you out."

"Shut me out of what?" I say, irritated now.

She has the nerve to ignore my question and I almost turn back. The thought of Alejandro's piercing disapproval being directed my way for directly disobeying him is not a pleasant one. Something keeps my feet moving though.

Laney enters a room at the end of a long hall and the guy I met on the first day, Brandon, is sitting behind a desk, working on something. When he sees us, he gets to his feet. "Laney?" he asks cautiously.

"Open the door," she orders, and I look around in confusion. The only door is the one we came through.

"I, uh, don't think –"

"I'm not asking, Brandon. Open the door."

"He said no interruptions."

"Well," she says in a saccharine sweet voice. "If anyone has the authority to override that, it's me. Don't make me ask again."

Clearly ill at ease, Brandon comes out from behind the desk and leaves the room. "What's going on?" I whisper as a heavy *click* fills the air, making me jump slightly. I don't like that I'm getting jittery. Alejandro telling me not to ignore my instincts last night comes to me, but I'm not sure if this is just paranoia or what?

Laney walks to the book case and yanks on the edge. Like something out of an Agatha Christie mystery, it swings forward to reveal a set of concrete stairs, descending into a brightly lit passageway.

"What the hell?" I almost hiss, my pulse fluttering. "I am *not* going down there."

Laney shrugs. "Suit yourself. But what he's doing down there is for you . . . supposedly." She gives the last word such an acidic bite that I edge away from her. "Just don't come crying to me when he's completely run roughshod over your life."

With that, she leaves. *Leaves!* And for good measure, she shuts the door behind her. I hear her saying something to Brandon out in the hall, but he doesn't come back . . . to save me from myself. My gaze swings back to the stairs.

Okay, I'm not stupid. I can guess why there's a secret basement in this house. What I can't guess at is what Alejandro is doing for *me* down there. Inching closer, I stare directly down the steps, listening hard, but all I get is the soft buzzing of fluorescent lights.

CHAPTER 8

Aléjandro

He's pacing his cell, and every few minutes, I hear his hoarse, muffled yells coming from down the hall.

The first thing I did this morning was check in with Luis and I was rewarded with what's on the monitor in front of me. After nearly ten days, it seems Sophie's attacker is enough of himself that I'll finally be able to have a chat with him. Which is convenient really, because we're going home tomorrow.

"Does he know why he's here?" I ask Luis, who's sitting at the control room desk.

He shakes his head and Niner laughs. "What a mind fuck."

Oh, he's fucked all right. There's already a vat of acid with Paul William Gallagher's name on it out back. It's just a question of how long it's going to take him to reach his final destination. Unfortunately, despite my blood warming at the thought of getting this done, something about the situation feels off.

Like he's reading my mind, Niner pipes up with, "Shouldn't *Rosita Fresita* be here for this? She's the one this asshole owes."

I fail to suppress a pained sound and I get dual looks of *what the fuck?* Then Niner groans. "You didn't tell her."

The need to defend my decision gets the better of me. "She wouldn't . . ." I want to say *approve*, but I don't want anyone knowing how soft she really is, so I go with, "understand." But I think that's worse.

"I know you think you're protecting her," Niner starts. "But you're not doing her any favors by taking this from her. She deserves to know."

My uneasiness grows, probably because he's right. "Telling her leaves us exposed," I hedge.

"Then we wait until we're sure she won't run to the cops."

"Fuck that," Luis gripes. "She'd never make it to the cops."

Is he threatening her?

Niner distracts me before I can fully digest Luis's meaning. "Anyway, you're more afraid she's going to judge you than go to the cops."

"Enough with the touchy-feely bullshit," Luis says, pulling a Taser out of a drawer and smacking it down on the desk. "He needs to be restrained. You want to do the honors?"

"You should at least give her the choice," Niner nags, ignoring Luis. "If she finds out later, she's going to be pissed."

"How's she going to find out?" I demand.

His expression says he thinks I'm more than a few beers short of a six-pack and I grit my teeth.

"You are *not* telling her, do you hear me?"

"I didn't say I would, but it's my job to point out potential cluster-fucks."

"This is my personal life and *none* of your business."

"Reconsider," he insists mulishly.

"No."

"Give it a rest," Luis says with disgust, getting to his feet. "She's just a fucking whore."

With his earlier threat still fresh, rage ignites and without a second thought, I draw my gun. My thumb almost gets the safety off before he disarms me and I'm staring down the barrel of my own weapon.

The next thing I hear is Niner disengaging his own safety, pointing his 9mm at Luis's head. For a very long moment, everyone remains frozen.

"What *the hell* is going on?" sounds from the doorway.

My eyes bore into Luis's, daring him to do it. "Make your decision now," I tell him coldly. "If you can't accept her, then pull the trigger." The flicker of surprise on his face tells me he really did believe Sophie was *just a whore.*

"What?!" Sophie squawks with panic. "No!" She's moving then. Despite the firearms, despite the tension, she slides herself into the space between me and the gun. "Put it down," she orders Luis.

I'd be proud of the steel in her voice if she wasn't risking her life. My hands grip her upper arms to push her aside, but Luis relents, slowly turning the gun around and offering it back to me, butt first.

Once it's in my hand, Niner puts his arm down. *"Puta madre, cabrónes,"* he says, obviously shaken up by the unexpected turn of events. As usual with Niner, that lasts until his next breath when he starts with the jokes. "Fuck, that was like a real Mexican standoff."

"You think this is funny?" Sophie squawks, crossing her arms over her chest, probably to hide how much they're trembling.

"Get. Out," I growl and Sophie whirls on me, outrage flaring in her features. "Not you," I tell her. "Them."

Luis makes to grab the Taser on his way out, but I stop him. "Leave it. Just go upstairs."

He offers me a very disgruntled look, but Niner is all smiles as they leave. "Someone's in trouble," he sing-songs, prompting Sophie to flip him off. Jesus Christ. It's like a circus around here. "I'd keep that Taser away from her, Jefe," is his parting shot.

Sophie is pale and drawn, but it does nothing to disguise her anger. Well, it's nothing compared to mine. "Sit down before you fall down," I command.

"Don't talk to me like that," she says, her tone still surprisingly even. She does as she's told, though, sinking onto the chair.

"What the fuck were you thinking?"

"He wasn't going to shoot me," she claims.

She is so wrong. "No, he wasn't going to shoot *me*. You, he couldn't care less about."

Whatever color that was left in her complexion drains away, leaving the scar on her throat a bright-scarlet half noose. I can't seem to muster any sympathy, though, with so much rage and fear and adrenaline running through my veins. "Don't *ever* do that again." Her mutinous glare doesn't change. "Do you hear me? Ever."

She pushes to her feet on unsteady legs. "You're a *jack*ass," she says, heading for the door.

Circling her around the waist I pull her to me, her back to my chest.

She paws at my arm. "Let me go."

Despite her protests, I turn her in my arms and hold her close, forcing my brain away from images of her dead on the floor with a bullet hole in her forehead. "Promise me," I demand, shoving my nose to her neck to reassure myself she's here and alive and breathing. "I don't ever want to live without you. Do you hear me?" If I'm embarrassed by all the emotion that's bleeding into the room, I don't care. "I won't lose you."

"But it's okay for me to see *you* with a gun to your head?" she asks, her ire giving way to distress as she slowly returns my embrace.

The enormity of what she did washes over me. "Dammit, mariposa. My life is not worth yours."

"Says who? You think I want to live without you any more than you want to live without me?"

How does she not see the absurdity of that statement? "How did you get down here?"

"Laney –"

"For fuck's sake." I pull back to get a look at her, wanting to gauge how much she knows. All I see is worry and stress.

"Please tell me what's going on," she whispers, her trusting blue eyes pleading with me. "I don't like not knowing."

I can't hold back a grimace; a lot of Sophie's anxiety stems from uncertainty and now that Laney has opened this can of worms, I'm not sure it can be re-sealed. Swallowing hard, I reconcile myself to the inevitable and jerk my chin at the monitors behind her. She turns and studies the screens. Of the four, there's only one that shows anything of interest.

"Who is that?" she rasps, sounding fearful.

There's no chance this isn't going to affect how she sees me. I used up every spare ounce of luck last night by confessing to fatherhood. "Paul Gallagher."

She stiffens, but keeps quiet, continuing to stare at the screen. My insides begin to writhe with foreboding. She's not like me. Her moral compass isn't twisted all to hell and I *know* this is beyond the pale.

"What are you going to do to him?" she finally asks.

Caution wars with my need to be honest with her. Telling her the truth wouldn't be wise. What if she *did* go to the cops? Sophie knowing I've done some bad shit in my time in the abstract, can't compare to telling her I'm going to slit this fucker's throat from ear to ear without an ounce of pity.

Before I can finish working it all out, she comes out with, "Can you send him to rehab?"

I snort derisively. "He's already been – twice."

She looks over her shoulder at me, clearly surprised.

"In fact," I go on. "He was released from a court mandated program twenty-two days before he found you at that gas station." She lurches herself out of my hold, turning troubled eyes on me. I'm not sure if my goal is to press my own advantage or to present her with the stark reality, but I keep talking. "You know how we got him? He showed up in Salt Lake City at his mother's place. Picked him up outside a pawn shop where he was unloading everything he took while she was at work."

"He's sick," she whispers, excusing him. "He needs help."

"Tell that to the woman he carjacked with her kid in the backseat a month after he ran from the gas station where he attacked *you*." I don't even have to lie. It's all true. But I hold back on telling her I think the guy is a waste of skin since I doubt it would help my cause. She doesn't share my contempt for humanity.

"Can I talk to him?"

I swear my eyebrows hit my hairline. Don't know why, though. Under it all, my girl has an iron spine. "You sure?"

She pulls her lips between her teeth, then nods.

Getting out my phone, I text Luis. When he reappears in the doorway, Sophie is sitting on my lap in the chair.

Not sparing us a glance, he grabs the Taser off the desk and disappears. To her credit, Sophie watches the guy get stunned on the monitor without flinching. And neither does she balk as he's handcuffed to a metal chair.

"You want me to do this?" Luis asks from the door, hands on his hips.

"No, but I do want your word where she's concerned," I tell him, tilting my head to indicate Sophie.

His lips tighten at the corners, but he gives a cursory nod. He turns to go, but I stop him with an, "And . . . I ever hear another insult out of your mouth, we'll have a real problem, Luis." I'm only letting this one go because I messed up so badly in front of my men months ago when Sophie and I came back from Oregon. I sowed the seeds of *she's just a whore*, and now I have to pull the growth out by the roots. But there's a very fine limit to my patience.

Of course, Luis could end me and Sophie, and I'd never see it coming. He's a trained killer, something I was reminded of ten minutes ago when he disarmed me like it was child's play. But doing away with me – or Sophie – would rock a boat that he'd prefer to keep on an even keel. He likes to kill people and working for me gives him a long list of 'deserving' victims. Men like Paul Gallagher. Our co-dependent relationship isn't something he wants to see the end of.

"*Vale,*" he says simply, telling me in Spanish that he agrees to my terms.

When he's gone, I twist the chair so we're facing the monitors again. Dickface seems to be getting back to lucid. "You sure about this?"

"Yeah, but you'll be there, right?"

"Please. Stop insulting me, woman." I set her on her feet and then take her hand.

The door to his cell is open and we can hear the metal cuffs clanking against the chair as he struggles to free himself, muttering panicked curses. When we come into his line of sight, he freezes, then starts bitching. "What's going on, man? Why am I here?" He looks like shit after ten days of detoxing

When we don't say anything, he tests his bonds again. "Fuck!" he yells with frustration. "Is this about that cunt in Vegas last month? Because she had it coming."

Sophie's grip on my hand tightens and I have to quash the urge to grin. What a dumb-ass. I watch his eyes catch on Sophie and then he plays even further into my hands. "What happened to you?" he spits. "Your boyfriend here try to slit your throat?"

I hear her soft intake of breath, but she quickly composes herself. "Do you know who I am?" she asks, her voice wavering slightly.

He gives her a brief once-over. "Sorry, don't know any dumb bitches with permanent neckties."

Every ounce of the disbelief and horror she's feeling plays out on her face. "I . . . I've seen enough."

Are you sure? sits on the tip of my tongue, but I swallow it back. Pressing her would only further bruise her psyche.

I walk her back upstairs, telling Luis, who's sitting with Niner and Brandon, not to have *too much* fun with the guy. In Spanish, of course. Sophie's had enough for one day.

"Should we get some breakfast?" I ask gently, feeling her out.

"Nah, I think I'm going to lie down for a while."

So that's what we do. On the bed, with Bruce Wayne beside us, I keep her close, my front to her back, my palm molded to her ribs how she likes it. We don't sleep and neither do we talk. I just let her work it all out for herself in the quiet while she strokes the dog's ears. After about an hour, I start to get antsy and when her empty stomach grumbles, I ask her again about breakfast. This time she agrees and I text Rocio to have it ready.

Before we get up though, Sophie whispers, "I always imagined if I came face-to-face with him that he'd be sorry . . . or something. But he doesn't even remember me. How can something so monumental to me be nothing to him?"

"Oh, *mi amor,*" I say, stroking her cheek. "I wish I knew what to tell you."

She gives me a small smile. "I wish you did too."

Honestly, I'm waiting for the part where she insists we turn him over to the cops so justice can be served. But when she speaks again, it's nothing of the sort.

"You'll make sure he *never* hurts anyone again?"

Adrenaline surges through me, followed closely by approval and pride. My girl has a bit of dark streak in her after all. To combat a lip curl of satisfaction, I kiss her. A sweet peck at first, but her lips quickly coax mine into more. One thing leads to another, and soon, we're naked and I'm determined to erase this morning's events from her memory.

I take my time, working her body until she's a panting mess while in the back of my mind, I worry that my life – our life – will eventually become too much for her. My only comfort is that today is a one off. Vengeance won't ever be something she has to contend with again. I hope.

Lifting my head from between her thighs, I soak up her glazed expression. She lets out a low, gasping, "Holy shit." Trying to catch her breath, she crooks her finger at me, but I shake my head.

"Tonight," I tell her, knowing I'll need her later. "Right now, Rocio is expecting us downstairs for breakfast."

The incredulity on her face is hilarious.

"Come on." I swat at her bare hip with a laugh. "Up. I haven't had a single drop of caffeine yet today." Holding out her panties to her, I'm relieved when she takes them from me, coming across much more like her usual self. The shadows that were hanging over her a few minutes ago are not quite as dark as they were.

Downstairs, I notice Laney has made herself scarce. Smart woman. She and I are going to have a serious talk.

We eat outside by the pool in the sunshine, and Brandon's son, Justin, shows up. The kid can't get enough of Bruce Wayne and he chatters away about wanting a dog of his own. Normally I'd tell him to get lost – well, I suppose the kid would normally never try to approach me – but Sophie seems willing to humor him, so I follow her lead. He even convinces her to go swimming with him after he explains that the pool is heated. When he hesitantly asks if I want to come too, I feel the weight of Sophie's stare, silently asking me to agree.

"Sure, buddy," I tell him. After the morning Sophie's had, I'd do anything for her. "Just make sure you ask your mom first, all right?"

And I don't regret my decision. Brandon, his wife, Tony and JJ join us and we have a great afternoon fooling around in the pool, especially when Bruce Wayne jumps in, much to everyone's amusement. It makes me a tiny bit heartsick to think that my boys, now fifteen and seventeen, are already well past this stage and that I'll never experience it, but it's fleeting. I'm happy now, in this moment.

I keep a close eye on Sophie all day, watching for any signs of distress. I'm not so naïve as to believe she'll be able to brush off a man's impending death, but she seems fine. So after dinner, when JJ comes to me, wanting a private word, I don't feel guilty for leaving her with a glass of wine in her hand, chatting with Brandon's wife.

I follow JJ all the way back to the office. "You do know we're on vacation, right?" I ask. I've had a couple of rum and cokes so I'm feeling loose and I almost don't notice how much the man's mood has changed since dinner.

"Yeah, well, I'm thinking you need to see this sooner rather than later, Jefe." He takes a seat behind the desk and turns his laptop to face me. It's some kind of list of names, along with what I assume are timestamps.

"What's this?"

"The names that the casino's facial recognition software generated from New Year's Eve."

I gesture for him to get on with it. "And?"

"And a very . . . concerning name came up. Center of the screen."

At first I don't see anything of note and I'm about to snap at him when a name finally jumps out at me. "Holy shit," I whisper. I read it twice, three times. "Is this right?"

"As far as I can tell, it is. Though he did his best to avoid looking directly at the cameras."

I slump back in the chair, my mind racing. My lawyer. My missing and presumed-dead lawyer, Harvey Sharkane. "Have you seen the footage?" I demand. "Is there any indication where he's been for . . . what? Almost eight months?"

JJ shakes his head. "Nah, nothing like that. I can show you who he met up with though." He makes a few clicks and turns the laptop back to me.

My gut clenches. I'm not sure if I want to laugh or rage. The only ones wearing straight-rimmed ball caps at my New

Year's Eve bash were the Loud Boys. "They still in town?" I ask.

"No, they left this morning."

I gesture at the screen. "How long did they meet for?"

"Three minutes, fourteen seconds."

Frowning, I consider that. "Let me see it."

There's no audio, but their body language says it all. Paxton and Hayden Erdmann are clearly not interested in what Harvey has to say. *What is going on?* "And there's nothing else?" I ask. "He didn't talk to anyone besides these two?"

"Not that I know of, but I'll try to tweak the parameters of the search to get some more hits. The chances aren't great, though. It's like looking for a needle in a haystack."

The urge to bitch him out and tell him to do more than *try* almost gets the better of me. But JJ isn't an amateur. If it can be done, he'll do it. "Have you told anyone else about this?"

He gives me a withering look and I feel some of the pressure in my skull ease. "I'm not stupid, Jefe."

"No, you're not. Make sure this stays between us for now, all right?"

"You got it."

I push to my feet, thinking maybe things will make more sense after I take care of that pending business in the basement.

CHAPTER 9

Sophie

The trip back to San Francisco the next morning is a much more subdued affair than the one into Reno. There are no fast cars or lines of people. Alejandro's not even wearing a suit for the flight home. JJ and Laney are working on laptops, Ben and Niner are talking quietly behind us, and as if going back to real life has flipped a switch, Alejandro is in a black mood, sitting next to me, stabbing out a message on his phone. As for myself, considering how sore I am physically, and how much I have on my plate mentally, I'm feeling surprisingly grounded.

Alejandro had disappeared for a few hours after dinner last night. Ostensibly it was for a meeting with JJ, but I knew better. When he found me later in our room, an air of lingering violence had clung to him along with the smell of cigarette smoke and the taste of rum on his tongue. His clenched fists and glittering eyes told me to surrender without a fight, and it's not a night I'll ever forget. He'd been rough, demanding, and unapologetic, making me come over and over as he lost himself in my body.

So far, the emotional repercussions of what I'm sure Alejandro has done haven't surfaced yet. I worry that I should be sickened, or at least appalled. But I can barely rally an ounce of pity for Paul Gallagher. All I *feel* is more tightly connected to Alejandro than ever before.

He pulls me from my thoughts by lifting the armrest between us and pulling me close. "You okay?" he rumbles next to my ear. I realize I was running my St. Christopher medallion along its chain, a sure sign that I'm nervous. I drop it and nod against his shoulder, soaking up the reassurance of his presence. "Good, when we land I've got a surprise for you."

I smile. "Oh, yeah?"

"Yeah." He leaves it at that, just kissing the top of my head before he goes back to his phone.

I do my best to keep my eyes away from the screen of his phone, but I notice he's messaging Tony, who he's sent somewhere in Oregon for a 'sit down' with the Erdmann brothers, whoever they are.

Though Alejandro's business is mostly a mystery to me – thank goodness – I've put together over the last couple of weeks that Tony is some kind of fixer within the organization, a kind of communications director; he feels people out, talks to them, negotiates with them. And everything he does is with the weight of El Jefe behind him, just like Niner, Luis, and Laney. I've never witnessed anyone question them. To do so would mean contradicting Alejandro himself and nobody would dare.

I've also put together that *El Jefe* is an image that's been cultivated to great effect and is actually a reflection of all five of them put together. Of course Alejandro bears the heaviest burden, but I'm grateful he has people to help carry the load.

There are two Tahoes waiting for us on the tarmac when we land. Niner gets behind the wheel of one with Ben beside him, and Alejandro and I slide in the back. "You ready for this, *Fresita?*" he asks, shooting me a grin in the rear view mirror.

I perk up. "Ready for what?"

"Just drive," Alejandro grouses. "It's a surprise."

"Oh, come on. I deserve a hint at least."

Alejandro lifts a wry brow. "What you deserve will be a smack on the ass if you're not careful."

I give him a smile and Niner gags. "That was way too much information."

"Please," I tell him. "With how much bull you spout, you must love it when Ben spanks you."

Ben laughs, Alejandro shudders, and Niner gives me a smirk. "Wouldn't you like to know, you little wench?"

"Wench? That's a new one. I like it."

He starts the engine, shaking his head. "Then I obviously need to step up my game."

We head north and Niner and I trade insults in the light Sunday traffic. We end up in Sea Cliff, a very upscale area of San Francisco, though the house we pull up to seems modest compared to its neighbors. I can't see beyond the trees that are thick on both sides of a high wall, but if I'm not mistaken, the house overlooks the ocean.

"Have you got another lair to show me?" I tease as we get out.

"A lair for Bruce Wayne maybe."

With that vague remark, he leads me to a solid black metal gate that Niner has opened. And from there, I'm a bit stunned.

The world on the other side of the wall is so unexpected. There's space for a single vehicle outside the main doors, but the drive that runs along the front of the house and exits further down the block barely registers because the house is so beautiful. It's reminiscent of the house in Reno with its white Mediterranean façade and red tile roof.

We go inside and Alejandro appears pleased by my reaction as the understated grandeur continues. The foyer is bright and airy, but instead of a staircase that goes up, it goes down. We descend into a living area with the most incredible view I've ever seen and I realize the house is much bigger than I thought. It's built into the hill and I can even see the far end of the Golden Gate Bridge. "This house is yours?" I ask, having a hard time not gaping.

"Yeah, I bought it." Standing there all casual-like in boots, jeans, and a black T-shirt, hands in his pockets, he's gorgeous and . . . expectant. "You like it?"

"Well, yeah." I turn back to the windows, soaking up the view of the dark water, the hills on the other side of the strait, and the unusually blue sky for a January day. "What's not to like?"

I wander to the adjacent kitchen, running my fingers over the stone countertops. It's all so perfect.

"Come on," he says. "Let's check out the bedroom."

There are three bedrooms on this level, but there's no doubt which is the master. It's enormous and boasts the same view as the living room. There's even a private balcony.

"So," he starts, following me as I check out the walk-in closet, "we won't be able to move in for a couple of months while they do the security upgrades, but –"

"What?" My steps stall out and our gazes collide. "We?"

"Well, yeah."

"You think I'm moving in with you?"

His expression darkens. "I don't think, I know."

What? Crossing my arms over my chest, I search him for some sign this is a joke. Because he can't really be serious. "I'm sorry, when was this decided?"

"Come on. Of course you're moving in."

"Funny, I don't remember that particular conversation. Perhaps you'd care to refresh my memory."

He must not appreciate my sarcasm because he fires back with his own. "The *conversation* would've been irrelevant, Sophia." Then he has the audacity to turn his back on me and walk out, and I swear I saw the beginnings of an eye roll.

"Uh, excuse me," I say, following him. "You may think it's irrelevant, but I don't."

He ignores me, heading for the balcony and disbelief slithers through my belly. "As I was saying, it'll take a while for the upgrades, but once –"

"You better be messing with me right now."

My biting tone must hit a nerve because his hand freezes on the balcony door handle. "Don't," he says, the word laced with warning. He turns to give me a hard look. "I don't do this."

"This?" I say incredulously. "You mean have a conversation?"

"I mean have a conversation that's –"

"Do *not* say irrelevant." I can only stare at him, desperately hoping he's about to say *got you!* "Alejandro," I whisper, my heart suddenly thumping uncomfortably hard in my chest. "I won't do this with you if you . . ." I take a second to regroup and start again. "If you want to make your pitch to convince me to live with you, that's fine. I'll listen. But I won't be ordered around like one of your men."

He huffs with irritation. "You already admitted you liked the house. I don't see the problem."

"Let's reverse it then. What would you say if I told you to pack your stuff because we're moving to Amelia's apartment?"

"I'd say the same thing I'm going to say now. Don't waste my time with your bullshit."

He can be so cruel sometimes, and right now I'm unsure if I should slap him or simply retreat. The latter wins out because I'm not interested in hurting him either physically or emotionally.

"Sophia," he calls, the aggravation in his voice following me down the hall. Back in the kitchen and living area, Niner comes bounding up the steps from the lower level.

"You gotta see the downstairs, *Fresita*. It's awesome."

"Well, it'll have to be awesome without me," I say, starting up the stairs to get back to street level.

"Hang on," he says, getting in front of me. "What's going on?"

"Nothing." I try to go around him, but he moves with me. "Please move."

"What'd he do?"

"He's just being his usual, full-of-joy self. Now let me by."

"No can do, prom queen." Taking my hand, he starts back down the stairs.

I pull back. "Would you let go of me?"

"How about this?" he says, making it sound like he's going to negotiate, but no, he ducks his shoulder into my hips and hoist me up in a fireman's carry.

"Niner!" I screech as he heads down the next flight of stairs to the lowest level of the house. I'm too scared he's going to fall and kill me to struggle. "Put me down," I grit out when we get to the bottom.

"Oh, babe," I hear from Ben. "What are you doing?"

"I'm showing Sophie everything this house has to offer."

"But the lady asked you to put her down."

"Oh, fine," Niner says, sounding put out as he sets me carefully on my sneakers.

Once the head rush passes, I give him a good whack to the arm. "Don't be a bully. I get enough of that from him," I say angrily, jerking my hand at the ceiling. And damn it, I can feel tears welling now.

Niner's eyes widen, conveying something along the lines of *now what do I do?* I might find it funny if I didn't feel like my legs had been cut out from under me. I get that Alejandro is not the most easy-going or even reasonable man alive, but blatant indifference to me and my feelings?

You knew, whispers through my mind, taunting me.

I guess I did know how over-bearing and stubborn he can be. But that doesn't mean I have to go along with his controlling behavior.

"Hey, uh, *Fresita,*" Niner says. "Come see the yard with me." It's not quite a question, but at least it's not a command. I've had enough of those for today.

He leads me out the sliding patio door to a deck, which leads to a small grassy area. The yard has been fenced in with glass panels that don't obstruct the view. Standing with our elbows on the railing, we don't say anything right away, just admire the scenery while the breeze lifts my hair.

"He bought the house for you, you know?" he finally says.

I let loose a strangled guffaw. "Even I know you can't close on a house in a week, let alone the week between Christmas and New Year's."

"True. But this has been in the works for a couple of months. He was always going back for you. It just took him a little longer to come to terms with it than I thought it would."

"Exactly what every girl wants to hear," I say, not sparing an ounce of disgust. "That the man she loves has finally *reconciled* himself to a life with her.'

"Eh, but this was never going to be a fairy tale. And if it makes you feel better, it's no picnic for him either. Him being clueless is as hard on him as it is on you."

"Oh, I doubt that," I say, but the words are accompanied by an unexpected titter at the idea of Alejandro being clueless.

"I'm serious," Niner says with his own chuckle. "He's used to knowing what needs to be done and doing it. Simple. No fuss. That he can't pin you down or bend you to his will is frustrating for him. Just give him time to adjust."

I swing my head around to glare at him. "And how long is this clueless period of adjustment going to last? Or will it go on until he succeeds in bending me to his will?"

His smirk is maddening. "Listen. He's already made a million tiny concessions –"

I scoff, but he keeps talking.

"– that you may not recognize. And he's *never* done that before."

"So, you're saying . . . what?"

"I'm saying, show up for every round you go with him. If it's vital, fight hard. If it's not, give him the benefit of the doubt. He's trying."

We hear the door open, but neither of us turn around. Niner leans closer and nudges my shoulder with his own. "I'm rooting for you," he says in a low voice before leaving me to the tender mercies of a man who doesn't seem to have any.

Alejandro comes up next to me, but I keep my gaze fixed out over the water, steeling myself for whatever razor-sharp comment he's about to direct my way next. For some reason,

I'm not expecting him to touch me, so when his hand settles on my back, I flinch.

"Hey," he admonishes softly, slipping the hand around my waist. "You don't ever have to be afraid of me."

Without thought, I lean into him. Then once I'm surrounded by his warmth, I don't want to give it up. *God, I'm so weak.* He's quiet for a moment, probably trying to come up with a way to make nice with me without having to admit to any wrongdoing.

"I should have asked first," he finally says.

I blink. Damn, he's good at this. It's not quite an apology and not quite an admission of guilt. "Yes, you should have."

More quiet.

"I just need to keep you safe and I can't do that if you're living in some random apartment."

Displeasure re-ignites, but I manage to keep my mouth shut.

"Mariposa . . ." It's the closest I've ever heard him come to using a cajoling tone.

If I look at him, I'm going to fold. "Yeah?"

"Are you going to make me say it?"

I'm not sure what he thinks I want him to say. "Yes."

"Fine," he grumbles. "Will you move in with me? At the penthouse for now and then here at the house?"

I smile weakly against his shoulder. Good grief. It sounds like this is actually paining him. "Yes, Alejandro, I'll move in with you."

He takes hold of my shoulders and pushes me back, glowering, probably because I gave in so quickly. "Were you fucking with me?" he accuses.

"What? No!" I knock his hands away. "Why are you such an ass? I just needed you to *ask*."

"And I just need you safe!"

"That may be, but you can't *dictate* my life."

"What the hell?" His face pinches like he smells something foul. "I'm not dictating anything."

"Aren't you? *Telling* me what I'm going to do is not okay. I don't work for you."

His lips press into a thin line.

"And I'm not Bruce. You can't order me to do things."

"He doesn't listen to me either."

"I'm not being unreasonable. You can't expect me to be some kind of doll that you pose to your liking." I watch him consider my words. "Okay?" I prod

"Fine. Except if we're in the bedroom, and then I'll *pose* you any way I want." He doesn't wait for my agreement, just pulls me close again, muttering, "At least you're not making my life difficult on *that* subject."

"I never try to make your life difficult."

"It just comes naturally, then?"

I stop him from trailing kisses along my neck since I won't be able to think straight once he gets started. "Come on," I say a bit wearily. "Let's see the rest of this beautiful house and then I have a ton of laundry to do before tomorrow."

"Why? What's tomorrow?"

Is he serious? "You know I have to work." I had the week between Christmas and New Year's off, but I'll be glad to get back to some semblance of a routine.

"Work," he repeats in an oddly flat voice that raises the hair at the back of my neck.

"Yes, *work*. I told you. Mondays, Wednesdays, and Fridays."

"You want to go back to that crappy job? Why?"

I feel my jaw slacken, but I don't have the wherewithal to stop it. "Tell me you're kidding," I whisper. "Tell me you're not belittling me after what we just talked about."

"Stop with the dramatics. It was a simple question."

"It was loaded and you know it."

"You don't need to work, Sophia."

"I *like* working. That job got me out from under my mother's thumb and I'm *not* going to exchange one thumb for another."

His dark eyes flash in the sunlight; I've clearly offended him, but I don't care. "I didn't mean it like that," he growls. "I'm . . . surprised, that's all."

"Well, I'm not quitting my job. What are you expecting me to do all day? Clean your house? Bake you pies?"

"I have a housekeeper and I wouldn't object to pie."

"Do not joke," I say, finally giving in to the need to reach for the medallion around my neck. "This isn't funny."

CHAPTER 10

Alejandro

Well, fuck me.

Sometimes I'm baffled by what comes out of my mouth when I'm with her. And today, I've turned what should have been a nice surprise into a shit show from the Stone Age. I didn't even mean what I said to be sexist. I *do* need her safe and I *don't* understand why she'd want to waste her time working for little more than minimum wage.

But none of that is important now because once again I've pushed her too far, too fast. After the upheaval of the last few days, I suppose I'm lucky she's not rocking herself in a corner. I wish I could slit Paul Gallagher's throat all over again because blaming myself doesn't appeal to me in the least.

"Look at me," I say, keeping it gentle.

She takes her sweet time, but eventually her big blue eyes lift to mine. The hurt radiating from them almost has me cringing.

"Come here."

I hate the way she hesitates, but I hate the way the mutiny in her demeanor fades even more. The last thing I want to do is snuff out her fire.

When she edges closer, I fold her into my arms and hold on tight. "I don't mean to be an insensitive asshole. I guess I got too far ahead in the narrative and I didn't make sure we were on the same page." I nuzzle at her hair. "I assumed you'd want to live with me. I assumed you'd be happy to leave your job."

"Well, you know what they say about assuming things, right?"

"Yeah, yeah. And for the record, I don't want a doll . . . or anything like it. I want *you*. Okay? I love *you*. Even if you're a constant pain in my ass, I want you calling me out. You know how my ego gets otherwise."

She sniffles a bit. "You and your ego are completely insufferable sometimes."

"But you love me anyways?" I ask, sounding hopeful.

"I do. I love you so much."

"That's good, because there's one more assumption we need to talk about."

"God, there's more?"

"Yeah, and it's a big one that you're probably not going to like."

She rests her forehead on my collar bone. "Just tell me."

"You need security. You'll have men with you at all times." I don't sugar coat it because this isn't optional. It's fact. And I'm ready to shut down every single objection she's got.

She sighs and I feel her nod against my chest. "I figured."

What? "You figured?"

"Well, yeah. It was pretty obvious. I'm just having a hard time picturing it. Can I still drive my car?"

Jesus, I was expecting Armageddon. "No, mariposa, you can't drive your car." I hesitate for a second, then say, "I'm sorry."

Lifting her head, she graces me with a watery grin. "Pardon? I didn't quite catch that. Was that the S word?"

"Don't be a smartass. And why are you being so understanding about armed men following you around, but you have me by the balls about the house?"

She snorts. "I don't really have to explain that, do I?"

• • • • •

Despite having important shit that needs my attention, I rearrange my day for her. Not that I want a medal or anything, but I make the trip down to East Palo Alto with her. We pick up all her stuff from where she's been staying, including her car which I have driven back to the penthouse. Then we go for lunch with Niner and Ben at fucking IHOP because my girl wants pancakes.

Don't ever let it be said that I didn't make every effort to *be* with this woman.

Anyway, though I refuse to admit it out loud, I have a pretty good day hanging out with my girl, and my best friend and his partner. It's so . . . normal

But real life calls when we get back to the penthouse later that evening. "I need to work," I tell her.

"Okay," she says, still crouched down, greeting a very excited Bruce Wayne.

"We're going to work here, in the penthouse."

"Okay," she says again, but this time it sounds more like *so, go ahead.* She looks so much better than she did earlier.

Laney takes that moment to saunter in without knocking, using her laptop as a tray to carry all her crap. She's followed closely by Luis.

Sophie gets to her feet, her brows lifting in question. "They all live in the building," I explain, then I give it to her straight. "The thing is, I need you to make yourself scarce."

"Can't have me overhearing your evil plots to take over the world?"

I snort out a laugh.

"Don't you have an office building for this sort of thing?"

I shake my head to clear it. "Yeah, I didn't quite think it through, did I? I just didn't want to leave you by yourself."

Her smile is unexpected. "That's actually sweet and not a problem because I have laundry to do, and unpacking." She turns to go, but I grab hold of her arm and pull her back.

"You're not pissed? Because I would be. This is your home now."

She comes right up to me. "See this is why I love you. When you want to be, you're the sweetest man."

The skepticism I'm feeling must be obvious on my face because she laughs.

"Alejandro?"

"Yeah?"

"I'll be sure to keep my AirPods in." And with that, she pecks my lips and disappears down the hall, rolling her hips as she walks, Bruce Wayne following her like a besotted fool.

I can relate.

I turn and Laney, who's got herself set up at the dining room table, says to Luis, "If I ever get that lovesick, you'll do me a solid and take me out, right?"

From the furthest spot away from her at the table, Luis just glares.

"Actually," I tell her. "Sophie and I aren't the ones making everyone nauseous."

"Right." She draws the word out to form at least ten syllables. "Do you want to tell him or should I?" she asks Luis.

"She's right, Jefe. You and her are the stuff of nightmares."

Sitting in the chair next to Laney, I flip him off to the sound of her cackling as Niner comes in wearing only a wife beater and basketball shorts. *"Güey, where are your shoes?"*

"Fuck that," he says, heading to the fridge for a beer. "If I gotta work from home, I'm doing it in comfort. Zoom me the fuck up."

Laney rolls her eyes. "We're all here, you moron. Zoom is for virtual meetings."

"Huh." He plops down across from me, cracking the beer open. "That's disappointing. I'll have to leave that one on the bucket list."

My laugh starts low in my chest and slowly gains momentum. I love these idiots. They're my family . . . and they're all staring at me like I've grown a dick on my forehead.

"Are you high?" Niner asks. "Because that's twice in two days. And let me tell you, this shitty, non-Zoom meeting better be important. I had to leave my man stretched out on our bed."

Laney sighs dreamily. "Damn, I so need a good dicking."

"Well, don't look at me," Niner says. Then we all swing our gazes pointedly to Luis, who's got his phone out. Cool as can be, he turns up the volume on some game he's playing, pretending we're not here.

Laney opens her laptop, shaking her head. "Where's JJ, anyway? And what's with all the secrecy."

Like he's been summoned, JJ comes rushing in. "Sorry I'm late, but I got some more hits from the footage." He sits next to me, ablaze with triumph.

"What's going on?" Laney asks

JJ looks to me for permission and I nod. "Harvey showed up in Reno for New Year's Eve."

Dead silence.

Niner recovers first. "I'm sorry, what?"

"Yeah, crazy, right?" JJ says, then fills them in. When he's done, we watch the footage from the casino and sure enough, the Loud Boyz weren't the only ones Harvey approached.

"What. In the. Ever. Loving. Fuck?" Niner says at the end.

Laney is as dumbfounded as the rest of us. "How is he not dead like the others?" Last spring, three of my men disappeared around the same time as my lawyer and all three turned up dead.

"He was in on it," JJ throws out.

I shake my head. "Does Harvey really have the balls?"

"He might," Niner says. "Depending on what he had to gain."

"What if," Luis says, thinking out loud, "our guys were taken to *hide* his disappearance?"

Well, shit. That hadn't occurred to me. Rubbing at my beard, my mind starts making new connections. "As in he can't be a suspect if he's a victim."

Luis nods.

"But you do remember that our guys were *beheaded*, right?" Laney says. "There's no way Harvey did that on his own."

"And it was the cartel that put up the money for the hit," Niner adds.

"But can you really see Harvey Sharkane sitting down with Enrique or Miguel Sandoval," I say skeptically, "and convincing them that he's going to take me down? Because I can't. He's too . . ."

"Mickey Mouse?" JJ provides.

"Exactly."

"So there's a middle man somewhere," Laney says.

"More likely, there *was* a middleman," I muse. "After two failed attempts on my life, no one was willing to try again."

"Maybe," JJ says, "but what's he doing talking to our allies? Looking for support?"

Niner's face screws up. "Support for what? We still don't know what he wants. Or even what his motive is."

"Well, what are our options?" Laney asks. "There's money, love, power, betrayal . . ."

"Maybe it's money," I say. "Harvey was always trying to get me to cut him in on the bigger projects – the casino, this building, that strip mall we did last year."

"But is that really motive enough to turn everything upside down?" Niner asks. "The man basically faked his own death."

"How about . . ." Luis starts. "How about the Sandoval Cartel is blackmailing him."

"Better," I concede. "There's a bit of logic there."

Laney drums her electric blue nails on the table for a moment. "But what about those pics that were sent? Especially that one of you and Sophie, Jefe, right before the first attempt. That was definitely personal."

I swallow in an attempt to loosen up the anxiety that's starting to ball up in my throat. "True."

"So, maybe love," Niner says. "What's the word on that woman? Leilani?"

JJ frowns. "Harvey's mistress? There's no word. She's gone without a trace."

Everyone's quiet for a moment, but then Laney, sounding doubtful, says, "I don't see what she has to do with us."

"This is not adding up," I bitch. "We're obviously missing a piece somewhere."

"And Harvey's the one who has it," Laney says. "Seems like all we have to do is find him. Has Tony called in?"

"Not yet. The meeting with the Loud Boyz is tomorrow morning. But at this point I don't think they'll have much to say."

"Harvey may have given them a way to contact him."

"Or not," I snap, hating how tight my throat is getting. Fucking anxiety.

Laney opens her laptop. "Let me put out some feelers. Now that we know who we're looking for, he may turn up."

JJ nods. "I've started digging too."

To the sound of JJ and Laney clacking away on their keyboards, I say, "Let's go down to the gym."

Luis nods, but Niner scowls. "Not happening. I'm going home."

I wasn't actually talking to Niner and we all know it. Him I trust in the apartment with Sophie, Luis not a chance. "Fine. But we meet back here in ninety minutes."

Pushing to my feet, I go in search of my girl. The familiar view of the San Francisco night sky that's framed by the big window at the end of the hall settles my nerves a bit, as does Bruce Wayne's appearance. "Hey, buddy. ¿Dónde está tu mamá? Hmm?"

He leads me to *where she is* in the laundry room, talking to someone on the phone. I lean on the door frame and watch Sophie move her clothes from the washer to the dryer and listen to her make noises of agreement in a mostly one-sided conversation. When she catches sight of me, her smile is wide. Gotta say, it makes me feel pretty good.

"Hey, Bea," she says, pulling her phone from her back pocket. "I'll have to call you back in a minute . . . okay, yeah. Bye." She removes an AirPod from her ear and her smile only increases if possible. "Hey, everything okay?"

"Yeah," I tell her truthfully, because no matter the bullshit going on, having her here in my space is soothing. "Who's Bea?"

"A sorority sister," she says, sounding so happy that I stifle my laugh. *A sorority sister?* Jesus, she and I could not be from more different worlds. "Actually," she goes on, more hesitantly now. "She was with me at the gas station when, uh," she waves her hand at her neck, "this happened."

Sophie's mentioned before that her friends haven't really been in touch with her since the attack. Assholes. "And you're glad she called?"

"Yeah. She wanted to make sure I'm going to the sorority luncheon they're having for alumni next month."

"Oh, yeah? Are you thinking of going?" My brain is already flipping through security scenarios and rejecting them all.

"I think so. Alexis is going too. It'll be nice to reconnect with them."

After our meltdown this morning, I'm not going to get away with telling her she can't go. And ruining her happiness isn't actually on my to-do list, so I roll with it. "You'll let me know when you firm up your plans?"

"Sure." She saunters forward. "You all done for the night?" Her voice is low and seductive.

"No," I say with a bit of petulance. "I'm going down to the gym to straighten out my head. Are you okay with them working out there while I'm gone?"

"I don't mind at all. I've still got a ton of clothes to put away."

"All right." After a quick parting kiss, I move into the bedroom and . . . *puta madre.* Her shit is everywhere; spread out on the bed, hanging over the armchair, laying in open suitcases. Okay, so her clothes and shoes aren't quite as soothing as the woman herself. Whatever. I change into a tank and a pair of basketball shorts, liking that the closet is more organized than the rest of the room. But then in the en suite, my eyelid almost starts twitching. Makeup, shampoo, perfume, lotion, and I don't know what else covers the entire countertop. And this bathroom is not small. I grit my teeth.

I slip out while she's still in the laundry room, chatting away to her friend again.

I hit the treadmill first. The gym is busy for a Sunday night, but I ignore the attempts to greet me, which are annoyingly frequent. Everyone who works for me, once they pass a two-year probationary period, has the chance to buy a unit in the building. Roberta runs the mortgage fund for me. Sounds like a bit of scam, having money I pay out come back to me in the form of a mortgage payment, but it's extremely popular, even with the stipulation that units can't be sold without my approval. Most of the people who work for me are never going to qualify for a traditional loan and the loyalty it breeds is well worth the hassle of things like noise complaints, which Laney handles anyway.

I've done 1.1 miles when Luis gets on the treadmill next to mine. I've done three when I feel the anxiety begin to loosen its grip on me. At four, I quit and move to the weights, letting the burn in my muscles further set me free. I'm spotting Luis while he does his dumbbell bench presses when Jeremy and Aaron approach.

"Jefe, you wanted to see us?" Jeremy asks. He's a big-ass dude, an ex-Marine and Niner recommended him.

"Yeah. I need to know if you're going to accept the job."

"Of cour –"

"And before you agree, you need to be aware that if anything happens to her, I'll kill you both myself."

Aaron, who hasn't been around as long, looks a bit worried, but Jeremy has no qualms. "Jefe, it's a step up for me and if you'll have me, I'd like to take the offer."

"All right." I like his answer. I turn to Aaron. He's younger, but he's also a veteran and knows what he's doing. I'm hoping he'll agree because I want at least one of Sophie's detail to speak Spanish. Swallowing hard, he says, "Yeah, me too."

"Good. You start tomorrow morning. JJ will get you security clearance for the penthouse level and you'll be outside my door at 6:45 a.m."

"Yes, sir."

They turn to go but I call them back. "Just remember that you work for *me*, not her."

I get nods of agreement.

CHAPTER 11

Yesterday's showdown with Alejandro and then the quality time we spent together afterward proved to be very cathartic. I'm feeling incredibly upbeat this morning despite having to drag myself out of bed practically at the crack of dawn.

Alejandro is less thrilled.

"You don't have to take me," I tell him as he steps from the shower. I almost miss the glare he sends my way with all the wet, inked skin stretched over muscle in front of me. He came back from the gym last night comparatively relaxed, and after meeting with the others for a few minutes, he'd thrown them out and demanded my 'attention'. It had been divine.

I go back to applying my makeup while stealing glances of him toweling off in the mirror. I could get used to mornings like this.

Without a word, he leaves the bathroom and Bruce Wayne lets loose a discontented sigh from next to my feet. He was hoping for a morning greeting from his master. I grin to myself. Alejandro is the furthest thing from a morning person. Until he's had some coffee, he's basically a beast who will bite the head off of anyone who gets too close.

Finishing up, I go in search of my pink Chucks that match the little dogs on the scrub top I'm wearing for work today. Scavenging the sneakers from the enormous pile near the closet door is not an easy feat. I grimace. There's still a lot of organizing to do. Alejandro hasn't said anything yet, but I know his need for order is needling him.

"Let's go!" comes from the down the hall. "Or we won't have time to stop for coffee."

I grab my hoodie, my phone, and my purse. "Ready," I call, coming out into the bright light of the main room. The view of San Francisco is gorgeous. "You're sure Roxanne will take Bruce for his walk when she gets here?"

Alejandro grunts a, "Yeah," at me, giving me a once-over from head to foot. "They let you wear that to work?"

I nod. "Lucky me, right?" Jeans and sneakers, and my hair in a high pony tail is a world away from what I used to wear when I worked at the lab in LA. Like I told him yesterday, I like my job.

I crouch down and practically hug the dog. "I'll be back in a few hours. Be good, okay?"

"That dog was born bad," Alejandro grumbles as he pulls open the door.

"You two have so much in common," I say sweetly. I don't get the chance to laugh at my own joke though, because there are two men standing outside in the hall, which immediately makes me tense.

"This is Jeremy," Alejandro says gruffly, gesturing at the first guy. He's extremely tall and broad. I remember him from New Year's but I've never been introduced. "He's in charge of your detail."

"My detail?" I say dubiously, earning myself the second glower of the morning as I get to my feet.

"And this is Aaron." The other guy isn't as tall or as confident, but he gives me a small nod.

"Hi, I'm Sophie," I say, a little off-kilter at not having any warning but doing my best to go with it.

"They'll address you as Ms. Summers."

I start to laugh but it chokes off when I get hit with glower number three. Okay, then. Not the right moment to object. I would never directly challenge him in front of his men anyway.

Since my one true love is in such a foul mood, the elevator trip down to the parking garage is tense. There are two Tahoes waiting for us and I smile when I see Skippy and Niner, but I can only wave because Jeremy holds open the door of the second vehicle for us.

First thing, we hit the Starbucks drive-thru and slowly, the caffeine begins to work its magic on Alejandro. Near the end of our half hour commute, I speak up. "So, you guys?"

Jeremy's attention snaps to the rear view mirror and Aaron turns in the passenger seat.

"I'd really prefer that you call me Sophie, okay?" Alejandro tries to stare a hole into the side of my head, but I ignore him.

"Uh, well, um," Jeremy waffles and I take pity on him.

"I know this puts you in tough spot with Alejandro," I say, almost laughing at the way the man's eyes bug out at my use of his boss's given name. I'm convinced I'm the only person on the planet who uses it. "But Ms. Summers is my mother's name and I'm not going to answer to it."

"Sophia."

I finally turn to Alejandro. "And it would attract unwanted attention if we're out in public. Better to keep it informal, don't you think?"

He's wavering, but I don't dare let any kind of triumph show on my face. "Fine," he mutters. "But they gotta respect you."

"That won't be a problem, will it, guys?"

"No, ma'am," comes in unison from the front.

At the *ma'ams*, Alejandro smirks as if he's getting his way after all.

We pull into the small strip mall that houses the veterinary clinic. "Do they have to stay here all day?" I ask. "Or will they just come to pick me up?"

"All day," Alejandro intones.

"Okay," I say, feeling guilt creep up on me until my next sentence. "So, I have to take the dogs for walks in the park out behind the building and I'd appreciate it if one of you could come with me." Alejandro's eyes immediately sharpen on me. "Is that okay?" I ask, a bit confused by his reaction. If these guys aren't here to watch out for me, what are they here for?

"One of them will be with you *every* time you leave the building."

"Oh, okay, then. Isn't that what I said?"

He crooks his finger at me, his expression inscrutable. I lean in and he whispers, "Don't be a smart ass." Opening his door, he graces me with a grin as he gets out. I follow him and suddenly everyone's getting out.

"Send her a message so she has your numbers," Alejandro orders, then he puts his hand to the small of my back and ushers me toward the front door.

"Are you really walking me all the way?" I ask.

"Yes."

I can see two of my co-workers in the window, craning their necks for a better view of the shiny Tahoes and all the men milling around. The receptionist, Darlene, has gone all googly-eyed at the sight of Alejandro in his suit. I can't blame the woman, but I'm not sure how I'm going to answer all the probing questions that are about to come my way.

At the door, Alejandro plants a kiss on my lips. "I'll see you later tonight at home."

"Yes, dear," I say, making his mouth quirk. He may be infuriating a lot of the time, but the playful moments make up for it tenfold.

Our goodbye sets the happy tone for my workday. My co-workers gush with me over my new boyfriend and I don't even have to lie to them. How did you meet? *He's my brother-in-law's uncle.* What does he do? *He's a businessman.* Who were all those men? *He travels with security sometimes.* He's hot as sin. *He is.*

Even Doctor Badawi gets in on the action by stopping by the front desk in between appointments. "So, a new boyfriend?" she says. "I hear he's a keeper."

I smile up at her. "Fingers crossed." I'm so grateful to the doctor for giving me a chance with this job. She's an acquaintance of my father's, but she wasn't under any obligation to hire me. With a Master's in biochemistry, I'm seriously over-qualified in an irrelevant way to be an office assistant, but thankfully the last two and a half months have worked out for both of us.

I mostly succeed at not worrying about Jeremy and Aaron having to wait around for me. They're being paid, I tell myself, and this wasn't my idea. We have a quick lunch together at a nearby restaurant where I start getting to know them. Turns out Jeremy is a mama's boy who's a serial one-and-done type of guy, and Aaron is married with a two-year old daughter.

They're both veterans and honestly, their presence makes me feel better, though probably because of my own issues with personal safety and not the dangers posed by Alejandro's work. But whatever. I'll take my victories where I can get them.

On the way home, we stop for pie.

• • • • •

The only hiccup in my pie surprise is the lack of the intended recipient. When I get back to the penthouse, I chat with Roxanne, Alejandro's housekeeper for a while. She's an older woman, one who adores him because she claims that he saved her from a life of prostitution years ago. I try to keep my eyebrows from lifting, but I'm not at all sure I succeed.

"He picked an innocent one in you," she says. "It makes sense, though. What with all the trash he wades through in a day, I don't blame him for wanting something good in his life."

My thoughts ping pong all over the place, uncertain if I should be offended or flattered. Perhaps it's for the best that she doesn't give me a chance to make the call before she's asking if I'd like some help organizing the closet. "I'd say yes, if I were you," she warns. "El Jefe doesn't like clutter."

"You don't mind?"

"That's what he pays me for."

In the end, I'm glad for Roxanne's company as well as her organizational skills. After she leaves at six o'clock, though, the apartment gets a bit lonely. By eight o'clock, I still haven't heard from Alejandro and the way I keep checking my phone begins to grate on me. I debate calling him to find out what time he'll be here, but that strikes me as very . . . domestic and my instincts caution me Alejandro wouldn't be pleased. But hunger and impatience begin to claw at my level of caring. I don't see why he can't simply let me know what's going on. Finally, at close to nine o'clock, I've had enough. I get Bruce Wayne's leash, thinking I'll take him out for a quick walk and find some dinner at the same time. We make it to the lobby before we're stopped by the doormen, who wouldn't be out of place at a nightclub.

They know who I am. "I'm sorry Ms. Summers," one of them says. "But I have strict instructions not to let you go out without an escort."

I give him a look my mother would be proud of, one that conveys exactly what I think about said instructions. He's unmoved. Sighing, I lead Bruce over to a sitting area and call Jeremy. It goes to voicemail. I call Aaron. He answers and I very awkwardly ask if he can take me. He apologizes profusely for being at Costco with his wife. Ugh, how embarrassing for both of us. My thumb hovers over the call button beside Alejandro's name, but I'm swamped with doubt. Plus, I think I might snap at him if I hear his voice right now.

I'll fix this myself. "Excuse me," I call to the one who appears to be in charge. "Can you find someone to take me, please?"

It's like I've asked him to strip naked and sing the national anthem. "I'm sorry," he stutters. "But I don't know who's authorized to –"

"Fine. Do you have Niner's number?" Him I could talk to without snapping.

More horror. "No, ma'am."

I bite the inside of my lip, running through the people I could call. Laney would laugh at me. JJ? JJ would have no idea what to tell me. "Whose number *do* you have?"

Blank faces.

"Well, who do you report to?"

"Uh, Mr. Arraya."

"Skippy?" I ask, sounding completely incredulous.

"No, Rolando."

Right, they're brothers and that makes a whole lot more sense. But Rolando likes me about as much as Luis does. Great, those are my choices, Rolando or Alejandro. Or I can starve. *Melodrama, anyone?* Just then, my phone starts buzzing in my hand. Jeremy.

"Hello?"

"Hey, you called? Sorry, I'm at the gym."

Right, because everyone's free to do whatever they want except me. I can barely pry my jaw apart to speak. "I'd like to take my dog for a walk and find some dinner. Do you know who can take me?"

"When do you want to go?" he asks.

"Fifteen minutes ago." God, now I'm being an asshole.

"Okay, I'll be up in ten-fifteen minutes."

"I'm in the lobby."

"Ah," he pauses, "I'll make it five."

Remorse finally catches up with me. "Thanks," I say weakly as I end the call.

Patting the couch beside me, I get Bruce Wayne to jump up and then I bury my nose in his neck. He whines impatiently. "I know."

It takes Jeremy a bit more than five minutes and when the elevator door opens, his hair is still dripping wet from the shower and he's struggling into his shoulder holster, carrying his hoodie.

I stand and Bruce Wayne wiggles excitedly around his feet. "I'm so sorry," I tell him. "I should have called first, but I didn't want to be a pest."

"You're never a pest." He hands me his hoodie so he can untwist his holster. "So where are we going?" His grin eases my guilt.

"To find something to eat. And Bruce needs to go out." I bite off the *Is that okay?* that's trying to sneak out of my mouth. I feel like I'm five years old.

He pauses his adjusting of the holster. "It's almost nine. You haven't eaten yet?"

"Oh, well. I wasn't expecting them to take so long." I feel myself start to blush. "I guess I didn't plan things properly."

"Yeah, they said they'd be late." He reaches to take his sweater back and I try to hide my dismay. *He knew they'd be late?* I want to ask how he came by this information, but I don't think Alejandro would appreciate me implying . . . *what?* . . . to his men.

"You ready?"

"Yeah."

Getting *out* of the building is like getting *into* Fort Knox. I've always entered through the parking garage with Alejandro, so I'm surprised that going through the heavy revolving door only leads to another smaller lobby where there are more 'doormen' along with a woman who sits behind a desk.

"Bruce," she practically squeals when she sees him. Scurrying over, she bends down to receive his dog kisses. "Oh, that's a good boy."

She looks up at Jeremy, smirking. "You're on dog duty now? Bit of a demotion, isn't it?"

He snorts. "Not likely. I've been upgraded to Princess Patr–"

The horror on the big guy's face overrides my own mortification. Laughing, I ask, "Is that what it's called? Princess Patrol?"

"Oh," the woman from the desk says. "Are you her?"

"Yeah, I'm her. I'm Sophie."

She smiles. "Savanah. You've sure got the rumor mill spinning."

"And it's all good, right?" I say dryly.

Her giggle is genuine and I warm to her.

"Okay, we'll see you later," Jeremy says, ushering me through the actual doors.

Out in the cool night air, we head down the sidewalk and Jeremy tries to apologize. I wave him off as Bruce checks out a parking meter. "It's fine. Things will die down soon, I'm sure. It's going to take a period of adjustment for everyone."

"Okay, well, what are you in the mood for?"

Oh, right. Dinner. I don't tell him my appetite has mostly disappeared. "Uh, something cheap. Is there a Subway close by?" I'm still learning how to manage my money. It's been a steep learning curve since my dad cut off my allowance in September. And *someone* spent fifty bucks on two gourmet pies this afternoon without thinking. *Princess Patrol* is more apt than I like to admit.

"Yeah, there's one a couple blocks over."

On the way, I'm cheered up by Bruce Wayne who's incredibly happy to be in the outdoors, proudly strutting along the sidewalk, tongue hanging out. Jeremy waits outside with him while I go in for my sandwich.

When I come back, he's on the phone. "Yes, sir," he says. Pause. "No, sir. Yeah, of course." Pause. "Okay."

Even though it's none of my business, he looks a bit spooked, so I ask if he's all right.

"Yeah, I guess I'm not used to getting calls from the boss yet."

My head snaps up. "That was Alejandro?"

"Yeah," he says sheepishly.

I fish my cell phone out of the back pocket of my jeans. There's nothing; no missed calls, no texts, no notifications at all. On the walk back, I keep my phone in my hand, waiting for something. Anything at all. It doesn't come.

CHAPTER 12

Alejandro

All damned day.

All damned day, I think about her, worry about her, daydream about her. I can barely keep my mind on my business – where it belongs – especially after an almost two-week absence over Christmas and New Year's. 'El Jefe' needs to be seen and heard regularly. Over the years, I've learned that wolves get bold if they're not kept in check on a regular basis. One whiff of weakness and they'll lunge for the throat. And with Harvey running around, I can't be taking any chances.

So I go through the motions: meet with my local guys, collect taxes, give out a few bonuses, listen to grievances, and mete out some justice (well, not me personally, but I watch with detachment while Luis and Rolando do their thing). It's all . . . usual. And boring as fuck. Why can't I be at home, in my bed, inside my girl's tight, hot pussy?

Okay, so maybe *daydream* isn't accurate.

It's a lot closer to *fantasize*. All. Day. Which only makes the boredom more acute. The urge to call her, to text her, to interact with her in some way almost overwhelms me a few times, but I don't give in to it. The last thing I need is for it to get out that I'm pussy-whipped. Because I'm not.

Of course, I track her ass. Work – some bakery – home. I try to tamp down on the self-righteous satisfaction at knowing exactly where she is in real time, but it's a lost cause. I revel in it. At least I do until Rolando informs me she tried to leave the building on her own. That pisses me right off. By the time I find out about it, though, and call Jeremy to find out what's going on, everything is resolved. He's with her now at Subway of all places. *What does she need with Subway at nine o'clock at night?* I down the rest of my drink and order another from Khalen's latest woman. That this sit-down will take another hour or so is probably for the best. I should cool off before I go home.

But an hour turns into two, and then we decide to hit up Khalen's new strip joint. Luis couldn't be happier, but Niner curls his lip. But for obvious reasons, Niner's never been a fan of tits and ass. He leaves, and five minutes into the experience, I wish I had too. But business is business.

The time is pushing two in the morning when I finally open the door to the penthouse, exhausted and disturbingly sober. There are no lights on, but by the glow of the city below, I pet an excited Bruce Wayne. "Hey, buddy. How'd it go today? Did Sophie keep you out of the trash?" To my annoyance, my stomach twists as I say her name, but that doesn't stop my dick from swelling. It's going to be heaven getting between her thighs.

I head down the hall and frown when I see the blinds in our bedroom haven't been shut. She knows I don't like to sleep with them open. The windows on two sides of the room make me feel like a bug under a microscope. The thought falls away when I realize she's not in the bed. I check the bathroom. It's dark. *What the . . ?* I pull out my phone and check the tracking app. She's here somewhere. Or at least her phone is.

Worry begins to churn inside of me. "Where is she?" I ask Bruce, but then notice he's not with me. I check the laundry room, the spare bedrooms, the main bathroom. Nothing. Kitchen/dining/living. Empty. I follow the hall down the other side of the apartment, worried she's in my office. But no. Then, the other bathroom. Empty. That only leaves the last spare bedroom. Bruce meets me at the door, wagging his tail, then goes back to settle next to Sophie . . . who's sitting on the floor, back to the wall, leaning her head against the floor-to-ceiling window.

Relief and irritation collide. I hit the light switch. "Soph?"

She lifts her arm, covering her face. "Turn that off."

I do as she asks. "What's going on?" She doesn't answer. She doesn't even look at me. I take a few steps into the room, a hint of uncertainty picking at my nerves as I sink down onto the foot of the bed.

"Soph?"

She lifts her head to spear me with glittering anger and hurt. Even in the low light, it's obvious she's not happy.

"What is this?" I half demand, gesturing at her on the floor, in the dark.

"I guess it's our goodbye," she says hoarsely.

My head jerks back in surprise. "What?"

She looks out over the city again.

"I asked you a question." I have zero patience for drama. "What is this?"

"I don't think our ideas of what a relationship is are compatible," she says to the window.

"Compatible?" I echo with contempt and her head swings in my direction. "The hell are you talking about?"

"Don't worry. I've already ordered you a blow-up doll to replace me." The cruelty in her tone catches me off guard. It's so unlike her. "I hear they make them pretty life-like, and you won't have to interact with her at all if you don't want to."

Is that what this is about? Self-righteousness fuels my terse response. "I was working."

The air between us doesn't crackle like it usually does, probably because her face is unnervingly blank. She finally breaks the silence with, "Okay."

"Okay?"

She shrugs before turning back to the window. "Yeah, okay."

When she doesn't move or say anything more, my temper flares. "So let's go to bed."

That gets me a scathing look. "Tempting. But I'll pass."

I groan loudly. "Can we stop with the games?"

"Games, Alejandro, would imply I have a man on the board which I clearly do not."

"Would you just tell me what's going on," I grind out.

"What's going on is I spent all night wondering if I'm being unreasonable for wanting to be treated like I matter." She pulls a face. "Which sounds just as pathetic out loud as it does in my head. I've decided, however, that I'm not interested in wondering about your take on esoteric questions that have obvious answers."

My patience runs out. "English!"

"Fine! In plain words, when you said yesterday to make myself scarce, I didn't know you meant permanently."

"I said I was working!" I don't even realize I'm on my feet until I'm looming over her.

Bruce Wayne growls, but she doesn't shrink away. "And I said *okay*. You're obviously a very busy man. Too busy to call . . ."

I turn away from her in disgust.

". . . too busy to text." She pauses for effect. "But, that's not quite true, is it? It's just *me* you're too busy for. I can't believe you'd even want a woman who'd let herself be humiliated like that."

"Humiliated?" I start pacing, genuinely baffled now. This is not the homecoming I was envisioning. "You're delusional. How did I humiliate you?"

She gives me that creepy smile she reserves for when I'm saying something she finds particularly repugnant. It's only the second time I've seen it, the first being when I left her on that balcony all those months ago. My level of uncertainty climbs.

"You made me look like a fool in front of Jeremy. Do you know how shitty it is trying to fish for information without asking, without giving away that *El Jefe* hasn't bothered with me all day?"

"You could have called," I say, but the indignation that's been burning in me all day and night isn't quite as hot anymore.

"You think I didn't spend the first half of the night debating *that* question with myself?" She laughs grimly. "Don't do it," she mimics. "He'll think you're nagging. He's probably busy. He'll call you when he's free. He'll –"

"Okay, I get it. You didn't call."

She swallows, then goes on in a quieter voice. "Niner said you were trying for my sake, but –"

"Niner?" I scoff.

She ignores me. "But from where I'm standing, you expect me to fall into line for nothing in return."

I stop in front of her, my hands on my hips, and hang my head. "I'm not sure what you want me to say here, Sophie." The situation is getting away from me.

Her withering laugh chills my insides. "Like I said, we're not compatible."

I rub at the back of my neck, trying to quash the sense of doom that's creeping up my spine. *All this because I didn't call her?* I have a choice to make here. Standing my ground leaves my pride intact, something that's infinitely preferable to retreating. I don't retreat, ever. It's for cowards and weaklings, and I'm neither. Except I don't want *us* to die on this hill, and my instincts are telling me that's exactly what's going to happen if I don't cede some ground.

I strip off my suit jacket and throw it on the bed. It's followed by my holster and then I toe off my shoes. Sophie watches warily as I join her on the floor, Bruce between us. "My brain did as many laps around the crazy track as yours did," I admit. "It pissed me off."

At that, she blows out a heavy breath and goes back to the view, but I put a finger under her chin and pull her back around. "I don't know how to do this." A flicker of contempt appears on her face, but I push on with the truth. "You're a distraction, and —"

She tsks and tries to turn away, but I grip her jaw. "Sophia, listen to me."

"I'd rather not."

"That's too bad." Her hostile little glare has my dick perking back up, but I concentrate on what needs to be said. "You're a distraction that I've never had to deal with before, and today ended up being about proving to myself that I'm still the same man with or without you in my life." Now that I've got her attention, I let my hand drop. "I didn't want the guys to see me differently. I got caught up in myself and I hurt you. I —" I swallow my distaste. "I'm sorry. I guess if we're going to do this, I can't expect you to be the only one to compromise."

Her eyes shine with tears in the dim light and something wrenches in my chest. "God, why is this so hard?" I hold out my hand to her, and hesitantly, she takes it. As soon as our palms meet, the tears spill over. I nudge Bruce out of the way and pull her onto my lap. Thank fuck she comes willingly.

With my arms around her, that constant nagging restlessness I've been putting up with all day fades away. The relief is short-lived though as she nuzzles at my neck and then freezes.

"Why do you smell like . . . a bar?" Her entire body seems to deflate. "You were out drinking?"

I grunt. "I was."

She tries to push away from me, but I hold her tight. "What a freaking cliché," she whines. "I've been wringing my hands all night and you've been out with your friends?"

"Appears so. It was a strip club too."

"What the hell, Alejandro?" She struggles harder, but I don't relent. "Let. Me. Go."

"I wanted to punish you."

That stops her. "What? What _for?_"

"I was pissed that you tried to leave without protection."

"You complete ass," she seethes. "I did that because I was worried it would reflect badly on you that I'm a love-sick fool who was waiting for you to come home so we could eat together. And of course, what's the first thing Jeremy says when he sees me? _You haven't eaten yet?_ God, I hate you right now."

She goes back to straining against my grip on her, but I hold her tighter. "Settle down."

"I won't. You can shove your strippers where the sun don't shine. Let go of me."

After a bit of a battle, I get her immobilized. "I haven't touched another woman in a very long time," I hiss in her ear, my dick now hard as stone.

She's not appeased. Not even a little. "So the strippers were to prove *what?* What a big man you are? How irrelevant I am to you?" She tests her bonds again.

"Probably," I tell her truthfully. "In hindsight, it was juvenile."

"You think?"

Her wriggling has turned her back to my chest and with my arm clamped across her torso, pinning her arms, she's helpless. Scared she's going to throw her head back, I use my other hand to capture her throat and pull her head back against my neck. Feeling her pulse thunder under my fingers is a rush like no other. "Fuck. All I've thought about all day is being inside of you." I grind up into her.

But the rush, the heat, the lust instantly evaporate as she pulls in a shaky breath that sounds a lot like crying. Immediately, I let her go, but she doesn't move away, just lies against me, a sob breaking from her chest. My heart stops. *"Mi amor?"* I whisper, fear cascading through me.

She twists, curling herself into my chest. Hesitantly, I support her weight as the sobs continue, each one cutting me deeper and deeper. "I'm so sorry."

Nodding against my shoulder, her arms go around me, trying to pull herself closer. Still she cries. Oh, Jesus. I've finally done her real harm. "I didn't mean to hurt you," I murmur uselessly. "Please tell me you're okay."

"Alejandro?" she says with a hitch in her breath.

"Yes."

"If you ever step foot in a strip club again, I won't stay." She sits up. "Do you hear me? I won't stay."

"Strip club?" I ask, dumbfounded.

"Yes!" I flinch at the volume of her voice.

"Sophia, I –"

"No! I mean it." Her voice warbles. "You want me to respect you, then you respect me. And you going to strip clubs is the very definition of disrespect. And it makes me feel like shit."

Her earnestness seers into me while relief soothes the burn. "Mariposa, I thought I hurt you. I don't care about the strip club –"

"Well, I do." Her hand wipes at her tears angrily.

It all seems so petty now. So completely selfish. I don't know how I lost sight of what's important, of who's important. Who cares if my men think I'm pussy-whipped? Am I really so weak that I'd let them dictate my life? Because I've wounded her. A thought that turns my stomach and fills me with self-loathing.

"Okay," I tell her gently. "I promise I'll never go back if I don't have to."

She's obviously trying to decipher my meaning, but I've had enough of us lashing out at one another with partial-truths. I'm not leaving anything open to interpretation anymore. "I might have to go for work, but I won't hang around, okay?" She's skeptical and who can blame her. "You're the only woman I want. Don't ever doubt that."

I tentatively fold her back into my chest and nuzzle her, whispering, "I love you, Sophia, more than anything in the world."

"I love you, too. So much."

"I'm sorry for being an asshole," I tell her, confounded that I've had to use the S-word two or even three times in two days. "I don't mean to mess everything up."

She pushes a kiss to my throat. "Hopefully, we'll figure each other out soon."

"Hopefully," I echo. "If not, I'll go gray."

She giggles and then her stomach grumbles loudly, making her giggles increase. "And I'll starve."

"You haven't eaten?"

"No, it's still in the fridge . . . actually," she says, hesitating for a second. "I got you a surprise."

"You did?"

"Yeah. Do you want to see it?" I hate that she sounds unsure.

"Of course I do."

I help her to her feet and she leads me out to the kitchen, where she makes me stand on the far side of the island. She turns the light over the stove on. Then, with her hand on the fridge door handle, she says, "Close your eyes."

"Really?" I drawl before I can check myself. Thankfully it doesn't dim her growing enthusiasm. "Fine."

I hear the fridge door. "No peeking," she admonishes, knowing me too well.

"Now?"

"No, I'll tell you." She scrattles around a bit more. "Okay, now."

I open my eyes to her smile, then look down.

"I got you pie!" she says happily. "I wasn't sure what kind to get, so I ended up with two. Cherry and coconut cream . . ." Her face falls at my neutral expression. "You don't like them? I know coconut was pretty risky, but you seemed to like the smell when we were at the lake, and I admit that cherry is *my* favorite, but . . . I should have gotten apple, right? Apple is the —"

"Soph," I interrupt.

She bites at her thumb nail. "Yeah?"

"Get over here."

Coming around the island, she's surprised when I abruptly pull her into my arms. "I fucking love you," I tell her, a jagged sensation piercing my chest.

"Yeah?" This *yeah* is full of pleasure. "So you like the surprise?"

"I do. No one's ever bought me pie before." I don't tell her that I don't remember anyone doing anything like this for me – ever.

She pulls back to see me. "You want a piece?"

"Damn right."

Her smile tells me she's pleased as she searches the cupboards for what she needs, then cuts me a piece of coconut cream pie. But instead of getting one for herself, she goes back to the fridge and pulls out a Subway bag. I frown at it as she sits beside me.

"What's with the Subway for dinner?"

She laughs softly. "What are you, a snob?"

"Maybe," I grumble, cutting into my pie. "Couldn't you have found something better?"

"Well, someone – and I won't name any names here," she says, pausing to make sure I get that she's talking about herself. "Is still learning how to manage her money and she may have impulsively spent an obscene amount on gourmet pies and screwed up her already tenuous budget. I mean, I could dip into the money for my cell phone bill or Amelia's cable, but I *have* learned that causes problems down the line. Did you know that Ellie once . . ."

With the incredible taste of the pie in my mouth it takes a moment for her words to register. *She's broke? She's eating crap for dinner because she's counting pennies?*

I swallow, then stop her mid-anecdote with, "Whoa, whoa, whoa." If I didn't feel like a heel before, I do now.

"Yeah, I'm serious," she says, thinking I'm listening to her story about her sister living off Ramen. "But –"

"Soph, are you telling me that . . ." I let my fork clatter to the countertop. Something that feels suspiciously like shame starts to creep up on me.

"You okay?" she asks.

"Not really. I'm trying to come to terms with just how far my head is up my own ass."

"What?" she laughs.

It's been *years* since I've worried about money. Even before Javier was killed, he, Niner and I were making bank. We had side hustles apart from *Los Santos del Diablo* and we'd already started investing in property. Then when I firmed up leadership about seven, eight years ago, the money poured in. And it did not even occur to me to provide for Sophie. Even though I know exactly how much money she makes, how much money is in her bank account, how much she owes on her credit cards. *What is wrong with me?*

"Come here." I pull her off the stool and tow her down the hall.

"What's going on?"

In my office, I turn on the lamp next to my laptop.

"Alejandro?"

In the built-in shelving unit behind the desk, there are cabinets at the bottom. "The left side is a gun safe," I say, opening the cabinet door to show her. "And the right side is a regular safe. This one's never locked if you ever need anything, okay?" Pushing down on the heavy handle, I get the door open. Her predictable gasp echoes in the room when she sees the cash stacked almost to the top. Grabbing a bundle, I peel off a reasonable amount and hold it out to her.

"I'm not taking that," she says, edging away like I'm offering her a dead animal carcass.

"It's clean. Nowadays, I have more legitimate businesses than illegitimate." Our eyes meet. We've never talked about this and I can see wariness reflecting back at me.

"No one uses cash anymore."

My sweet, innocent girl. "It's just to hold you over. By Friday, I'll have a debit and credit card for you."

"I don't need your money."

I laugh and her lips purse into a thin, disapproving line. I'm about to open my mouth and probably say something stupid when I suddenly change tack. "Jeremy said you guys went out for lunch today." Her eyes flash so I quickly continue. "They shouldn't have to pay for their own meals." This is total bullshit. I pay them plenty, but exactly like I thought, Sophie's demeanor changes. She worries her lip at the corner.

"I guess," she says, tentatively reaching for the money. "But this is too much."

I shrug. "Keep it for emergencies."

I should feel like a ripe bastard for manipulating her like this, but I don't. Keeping her safe isn't always going to involve the morally right thing and I'm good with that.

Back in the kitchen, as we re-take our seats at the island, I tell her, "You know, you should have had pie for dinner."

She laughs softly. It has a resigned ring to it, but it's tinged with happiness. "Believe me, I thought about it. But how would that . . ." I barely listen to the specifics of what she's saying, basking in the knowledge that a talkative Sophie is a content Sophie and that's all I really need.

CHAPTER 13

Sophie

The next morning, Alejandro kisses me goodbye and then re-plants his face in his pillow. After a rough night, I'm tired too, but I have a counselling appointment at ten in Palo Alto I have to get to. I'm also hoping to pick up some of my things from my parents' house afterwards. Life with Alejandro is proving to have some extreme highs and lows, but I'm optimistic that we'll eventually find a smoother playing field. The man is not completely unreasonable, and we're still learning the ins and outs of each other. I can work with that.

I pull open the penthouse door and find Jeremy and Aaron waiting for me in the hall. "Morning!" I give them smiles, which they return. In the parking garage, our Tahoe is already warmed up and waiting for us. It's pouring rain today, so I can't say I'm sad that I won't be driving myself. More I can work with.

When we stop for coffee, I hand Jeremy a fifty dollar bill and he takes it without question. Easy. Piece of cake . . . or pie. Life is good.

I spend the hour with Tina, my therapist, talking about Alejandro. Though I have to use a lot of hypotheticals and skip over some stuff completely, it feels good to voice my reservations and my hopes. In the end, she warns me about his bulldozer-like behavior and I duly note it.

The guys and I go for lunch, then we get lucky when there's no one except the housekeeper at my parents' house. We're able to fill the back of the SUV with the rest of my clothes and shoes, as well as some of my keepsakes from over the years. I don't quite trust my mother not to dispose of everything. She's been sour ever since I moved out and made a deal directly with my dad to support myself if he'd continue to pay for my counselling.

While we're unloading my stuff, Alejandro texts, asking me how my session went. It may be pathetic to be so delighted, but I melt with happiness anyway. An hour later he calls, informing me he's taking me out for a late dinner. Someplace fancy that requires a dress and the shoes with the red soles, he tells me.

"You're taking me on a date?" I tease.

"Well, I'll be there for a meeting anyway, so –"

I laugh, cutting him off. "Wow, you really are bad at this. You're supposed to say, *yes, dear, I am.*"

One of those noises that tells me he's disgruntled fills my ear. "You know I'll never be that guy, right?"

"I'm aware. But you make up for it in other ways."

Silence greets my attempt to flirt. How embarrassing. I'm about to change the subject when he finally says, "Mariposa," in a low voice that sends a bolt of lust through me.

I clear my throat. "Um, yeah?"

"We definitely have a date tonight." And somehow I know he's not referring to the restaurant.

· · · · ·

I wear my favorite black wrap dress that hugs me in all the right places; the neckline plunges but isn't vulgar and the hemline hits me in the perfect spot an inch above my knees. I decide I look amazing, especially with the Louboutins that Alejandro asked for on my feet.

Jeremy and Aaron are dressed in suits, and when my eyebrows go up, Jeremy laughs. "Don't worry, we won't be right at the table with you. Gotta blend in, that's all."

The drive to the restaurant, *Analena,* doesn't take long. I'm a bit surprised when we pull up in the back alley, but I brush it aside as unimportant.

It's raining hard, so Aaron holds an umbrella in one hand and offers me the other so I don't slip on the uneven cobbles. We go through the kitchen and I feel a little on display as I follow Jeremy's tall frame across the restaurant with Aaron at my back; the attention we attract is a bit unnerving. That is until I catch sight of Alejandro in a booth in the far corner, deep in conversation with someone seated across from him. His posture reads as casual menace, so I know he's all business right now.

The moment his predatory gaze lands on me, I feel it down to my very bones. I've learned not to let these moods of his daunt me though; they're about work, not me.

He stands to greet me, kissing me on the cheek, just hitting the corner of my mouth. "Hey," I whisper, but I don't get a response as he helps me out of my coat and hands it to the hostess. I turn to his guest and I freeze.

"Sophie," the man says. "This is a surprise."

Of all the rotten luck. "Mr. Findley," I say, managing a small, forced smile.

"You two know each other?" Alejandro asks, the cruel edge in his tone almost making me wince. He gestures for me to get in the booth.

Mr. Findley, seemingly oblivious, pushes his gray hair away from his forehead and smirks. "Oh, we spent a weekend together a few years ago."

I'm pretty sure I do an extremely poor job of hiding my utter revulsion. The man is such a worm, always has been. He's the current mayor of Palo Alto and a good friend of my ex-boyfriend's father.

Alejandro slides in beside me and places a possessive palm on my thigh. "That so?" he intones.

"Oh, yes," Findley says, all smarmy charm. "Sophie's quite entertaining."

This time, I can't hold back a soft sound of loathing and Alejandro's hand squeezes gently above my knee.

"Are you implying you have some kind of carnal knowledge of my girlfriend, Don?"

I don't know if it's the word *girlfriend* or the malice radiating from Alejandro, but Mr. Findley realizes he's made a tactical error. Maybe he thought to ingratiate himself with Alejandro by objectifying me.

"Wha . . . no, of course not! I was just . . ." He flounders, searching for a word to save the situation. My haughty disdain further rattles him, but he finally comes up with, "I was teasing."

Alejandro leaves Mr. Findley to squirm in an icy silence. Even I'm a bit unnerved by the time he tries again. "I thought —"

Alejandro's hand lifts from the table, stopping him. "I'm going to need that approval on Laney's desk by the end of the week."

Mr. Findley sputters. "But we just discussed this and —"

"Friday morning, nine a.m.," he says darkly. He makes a gesture and Rolando materializes, lifting his arm, inviting the mayor to leave.

With both outrage and horror on his face, the man gets to his feet and straightens his suit jacket before he turns on his heel and stalks away.

A soft giggle slips out of me, drawing the attention of an unamused Alejandro. "How do you know that sleazy asshole?"

"A few years ago I went to a golf retreat with Stuart and his family, and he was there."

"A golf retreat?" he says, clearly unimpressed.

I shrug. "Stuart wanted me there to stave off the boredom. How do *you* know him?"

"Mutual acquaintances," he says dryly.

Okay then. "Do I get a proper hello now?"

There it is, a crack in his façade. A lip twitch and then a flash of warmth as he pulls me close and kisses my neck below my ear. *"¿Cómo estás, mi amor? Te ves increíble."*

I flush with pleasure and lean further into him. "Thanks," I murmur. "Are you done with intimidating people for the day?"

Against my skin, I feel his lips form a full-blown smile. When he pulls away, though, all trace of emotion has been erased and I shiver with the knowledge that I get to experience an Alejandro that no one else does.

We make a bit of small talk and he asks me a few questions about my counseling appointment. It takes a moment to understand that he needs reassurance.

"You don't have to worry," I tell him. "I'm careful with what I say. I would never do anything to put you at risk."

He nods solemnly. "I know you wouldn't. You always think of others before yourself." His tone is tinged with disapproval, probably because he sees it as a character flaw. I'm repressing a grin when he continues, "It's not a great situation for you to be in, though. I can see that."

Oh, this man. *Is he trying to empathize?* I didn't think I could love him any more if I tried. I lean in and stroke his jaw and give him a simple, "thank you," before I kiss his lips gently.

"I hope you'll forgive the interruption," pierces our bubble and Alejandro turns to glare. I'm assuming the guy standing at our table is the chef by the way he's dressed. "Jefe," he says.

"Jerry," Alejandro responds, doing his best to remain civil.

"I brought the wine," he says, signalling a man to come forward. "And I was wondering if you'd allow me to prepare you and your guest something special tonight."

I almost laugh out loud at the flat expression on Alejandro's face. "I like special," I say facetiously, sticking out my hand. "I'm Sophie."

We shake and the guy relaxes. "Jerry Fowler." And it turns out he's not only the chef, but the owner as well.

Once the man is gone, I tease Alejandro, "I don't know how you have any friends at all with all the glowering you do." His expression doesn't change, so I take that as my cue to change the subject.

"So I've been thinking about Daniela's birthday," I say. The mention of his goddaughter gets his attention. "And I had some questions about her mother."

He frowns. "Gina? What kind of questions?"

"Well, you're really Daniela's only link to her and I was wondering if you had any old pictures of her and Javier."

Daniela's father, Javier, was his best friend for a long time before he and Gina were killed in a drive-by shooting when Daniela was only a few months old.

He rubs at his beard, looking slightly uncomfortable. "Uh, yeah, maybe. Why?"

"I think maybe Daniela would like to have a scrapbook and maybe you can talk to her about them." He's quiet, almost pensive and I wonder if I've made a mistake. "Did you know Gina well? I've always wondered where Daniela gets her, uh, zest for life."

That pulls him out of his thoughts and he chuckles softly. "Daniela is just like her."

"Yeah?" I smile brightly.

"Yeah. Gina was always giving us shit. The woman made her opinion known about everything." He thinks it over. "She was a lot of fun."

"Were they together long?"

"Gina and Javi? Yeah, four years . . . five maybe. We went through a lot together and then . . .'

And then they were shot and killed. Kicking myself, I try to re-direct the conversation a bit. "Do you know anything about Gina's family? Why they don't see Daniela?"

"Gina was a foster kid. As far as I know, she didn't have any family. I do remember she had a foster mom . . . maybe she has some photos too. I'll get Jc to find her."

"That would be wonderful."

And from there, we spend the night with our heads together; the company is wonderful, the food and wine delicious, but nothing is quite as divine as the sexual tension that begins as a low hum and builds on itself until it runs like a live wire between us.

By the time he's helping me on with my coat, I'm tipsy and awash in dirty thoughts. The walk through the restaurant and the kitchen passes by in a blur with his hand at my back. It's still pouring rain and this time Skippy holds the umbrella for me.

Alejandro wants me next to him in the middle seat. He's trying to kiss me and I giggle happily as I fumble with the seat belt. I just hear the click of the latch when Skippy slams on the brakes and I'm jerked hard against the belt.

"What the –?" Skippy says. "Is that Nicky G?"

Showcased by the headlights in the downpour, a man is blocking the alley. His eyes are wide, almost manic and his chest is heaving.

"Do *not* open that door," Alejandro commands and it takes a second to realize he's talking to Skippy, who's undone his seatbelt. "Inch forward, he'll move."

He will? Alejandro must feel the tension running through my body. "It's fine," he tells me. Then to Rolando, he says, "Tell Jeremy to standby."

Skippy rolls forward and Alejandro's right, the guy moves. Except instead of off to the side, he jumps on the hood of the SUV.

"Stay put, Skip, until this is dealt with." He pulls my head to his shoulder and says quietly, "Don't watch this idiot."

Before I do as I'm told, I see the guy yelling something, though I can't hear what it is through the thick glass or over the downpour. Alejandro seems more put out than concerned, so I take my cues from him and try to relax.

"What the hell are you doing?" Skippy demands, his voice loud in the small space.

Alejandro tsks. "That's not helpful."

Through Alejandro's window, I see Jeremy pass by and I immediately sit up.

"Don't worry," Alejandro soothes. "He knows what he's doing."

I watch Jeremy exchange words with the guy splayed across the hood. After a minute or so, Jeremy loses patience and with one firm yank, he topples the guy over the edge and onto the ground.

It's not long before Rolando, who's watching out his window, says, "Clear," and Skippy drives away like nothing happened, chuckling under his breath.

I keep my head on Alejandro's shoulder and let my mind ricochet through my emotions. Though conflict usually sets off my anxiety, I think I'm fine. Maybe mildly fazed, but with Alejandro beside me, completely calm and unshakable, I'm not feeling anything stronger coming on. Truthfully, it's wonderful not to have to face stressful situations alone.

Mere minutes later, we pull into the underground at the penthouse. I undo my seatbelt but Alejandro puts a quelling hand on my thigh. "That's all for tonight, Skip."

"Sure, Jefe. Bye Soph."

"Bye," I call after him as he slips out.

"Rolando, you'll handle things with Nicky?"

"Of course."

The door slams, leaving us cocooned in silence. He unbuckles himself and turns to me, his eyes taking my measure. "You all right?"

I inspect my still dark gray nails for a moment. "Yeah, I am."

"There are a lot of people who want my attention," he says. "And not all of them are as civilized as Don Findley."

My grimace sparks a soft laugh in him. "I'll always do my best to shield you from this kind of thing, but contrary to popular belief, I don't control the universe."

My head tilts. "Was that a joke?" His good humor starts to smooth out any of my feathers that may have been ruffled.

He fails to suppress a grin. "Sometimes I just have to roll with all the weird shit that goes on around here."

"Life with you will never be boring?"

"Never," he says with a chuckle, taking my hand and helping me out.

He hits the elevator call button then unties the belt of my coat. "Have I mentioned how much I like this dress?" he asks, holding the coat open, his eyes roaming over the curves of my body.

"Only once, and from you, I'll never tire of hearing that sort of thing." I lift my arms to his shoulders and he moves in to take my mouth, the hunger behind the kiss thrilling me.

The elevator dings and he carefully walks me backwards. Pressing me into the wall next to the panel, not letting up on the kiss, he punches our floor and awkwardly enters the code into the reader. His fingers span my waist then wander up my sides to my breasts and I moan into his mouth. I'm not too proud to admit the anticipation is almost killing me. I want him inside me like I want my next breath.

We get off at the penthouse, but he stops in the hall. A bit dazed, I let him slip my coat off, but I don't like that he brushes my hands away from his shoulders once they're free. "I want you to walk," he says, his dark eyes lit with lust.

I blink at him in confusion. "What?"

He takes hold of my hand and brings it to the front of his pants. He's rock hard and all thoughts except the ones of him pushing into me flee. Squeezing him, I try to get my lips on his again, but he leans away from me. "But I want –"

"Oh, I know exactly what you want," he says, cutting me off. "But first you'll walk this hall."

The hand that's covering mine over his dick lifts and like we're dancing, he slowly twirls me until I'm facing in the direction of his door. Then he swats my ass. *"Camina."*

Finally understanding that he wants to watch me in my dress and heels, I throw him a smirk over my shoulder and do as I'm told. I put some sway into my hips, grateful for the buzz of the wine. By the time I've covered the twenty feet, he's on me, pressing my front into his door, grinding himself into my ass. "I'm gonna fuck you in these shoes."

Before I can tell him how much I like the idea, he snakes an arm around my waist and gets the door open.

"Bruce," I laugh as he wiggles and squirms around our feet in greeting. I bend down to give him some love. "How's my boy?" I coo. "I'm sorry you can't go out right now. First your daddy's going to fuck me silly in these shoes. Yes, he is."

With Alejandro chuckling behind me, I straighten and notice a soft glow of light coming from the main room. Curious, I take a few steps and gasp, my hands rising to cover my mouth. Lit tea-light candles cover the kitchen island and surround a crystal vase filled with perfect red roses.

"Oh, wow," I breathe, turning to Alejandro.

"You like it?"

"I love it." I throw myself on him. With arms around my waist, he lifts me and moves us over to the flowers. I look again and this time I see there's a package of gummy worms at the base of the vase and my heart soars higher. *And is that . . ?* Holy crap. There's a velvet box that can only contain jewellery.

"Oh, Alejandro, what did you do?" The words comes out laced with emotion and I feel tears prick at my eyes.

He frames my face with his palms. "I wanted to give you some hearts and flowers stuff." In the warm glow of the candles in the dark room, he looks so earnest as he wipes at my cheek with his thumb. "Don't cry, okay?"

I nod jerkily and as I take a deep breath, I feel the urge abate somewhat.

"Do you want to open it now?" he asks.

"Of course I do." I reach for the package of gummy worms and peel it open, very pointedly skipping over the jewelry.

"You know," he says, laughing softly, shaking his head. "There's a special place in Hell reserved for women like you."

Around my own laugh, I bite a gummy worm in half. "I'm sure I'll get a prime spot right next to you."

"I can always return it if you're not interested." He reaches for my present, but I beat him to it, plucking the box off the counter and holding it to my chest.

"I don't think so." I crack the box open and almost choke on the gummy worm. It's a tennis bracelet, one that practically blinds me in the candlelight. "Alejandro, I . . ."

He dips his head to catch my eyes. "You what?" he asks, sounding the tiniest bit unsure of himself. "You like it?"

"It's beautiful." I can't stop staring at it. "But . . . but it's too much. I –"

"It's not too much. You should see the one Niner chose. He called me a cheap bastard."

"What?" I giggle.

"Yeah. But I got this one because the clasp is like a butterfly. It reminded me of you."

The clasp *does* look like a butterfly even if I think it's supposed to be a flower with four diamond petals. Suddenly I can't hold back my tears. This man, for all his faults, *loves* me. And heaven help me, I don't think I'll ever get my heart back from him. If there's one thing life has taught me in twenty-seven years, it's that this depth of feeling doesn't come along every day.

"I thought you weren't going to cry," he admonishes gently, taking the box from me.

I watch him free the bracelet. "Thank you for this," I tell him. "For all of it."

He gestures with the bracelet for me to hold out my hand. "You're welcome, mariposa." The clasp makes a satisfyingly solid click as it catches and we both stare down at it. "Now, let's see what it looks like without the dress."

I giggle while he slowly pulls on the tie that holds my wrap dress together.

His only answer is a groan at the sight of the black lace bra and panty set I wore for him. "Goddam, you're better than any fantasy." The dress slides off my shoulders on its way to the floor and our mouths pick up where they left off in the hall.

CHAPTER 14

Aléjandro

"Alejandro?"

I burrow further into the blankets, ignoring the whisper.

"Alejandro? *Mi amor?*"

Mi amor? A grin tugs at my lips as I crack an eyelid. The light coming in around the blinds is enough for me to take in Sophie leaning over me.

"I'm sorry to wake you, but I have to go to work," she says. "And I can't get the bracelet off." She holds up her arm so I can see it's still circling her wrist . . . exactly where it's going to stay.

"Just wear it," I mumble.

"To work? No! What if I lose it? Or it gets stolen?"

I snort into my pillow. "No one's going to steal it." *They'd have to have a death wish to do something so stupid.*

"No, come on. Tell me how to get it off. I can't figure out the clasp."

"It needs a special tool. It'll take forever to get it off."

"Ugh. I'm going to be late."

"Hey," I call as she heads for the door. "Where's my kiss?"

She rolls her eyes, but gives me a smile as she rushes back to lay a quick one on my lips. "I'll see you later, right?"

"Yeah."

Once the quiet settles around me again, I realize my body's decided it's awake. *What a pain in the ass.* I may sleep better when she's beside me, but as soon as she's gone, my mind can't resist running on its hamster wheel. Reaching for my cell, I check the time. 6:52. *In the fucking morning.* I launch the new and improved tracking app JJ installed and it shows Sophie's location is a mere six blocks away in the coffee drive-thru line. *Do I feel bad about the tracker in the bracelet?* No. *Do I have plans to tell her about the tracker in the bracelet?* That's unclear. We're supposedly on this new *I respect you, you respect me* thing, but telling her is going to mean a fight, one that will probably involve tears and rage and guilt. None of which I'm fond of. But there'll be make-up sex . . . hopefully.

Before the *tell her/don't tell her* conundrum can really get spinning, I head down to the gym. I've got a full day in front of me anyway, starting with finding out what Nicky G was up to last night.

I'm at the Garden before nine thirty, Niner in tow, bitching about the ungodly hour. After sending Skip on a coffee run, we go down to the basement where Luis is sitting with his feet up on the desk outside his little dungeon setup. Nicky G is sitting on a chair in the corner, clean and wearing new clothes, scarfing down something out of a bowl like it's the first thing he's eaten in a month.

"What's all this?"

"Jefe," Luis says, his feet falling to the floor. "Got some news."

Luis, Niner and I go back upstairs to the parking garage. We keep our voices down, even if we're far enough from anyone that we won't be overheard.

"Seems Nicky G had a visit from Harvey Sharkane a couple days ago," Luis starts.

"What?" Niner sputters.

"You heard me."

"He's here in the Bay area?" Anticipation runs down my spine at the idea of getting my hands on the rat bastard.

"Yeah. As far as Nicky knows . . . though he's not the most reliable of sources."

"But he's not stupid," Niner says. "Otherwise he'd never have lasted on the streets as long as he has."

Luis nods. "That's what I thought too."

"Can we get to the specifics?" I demand. "Like what Harvey wants with a lowlife like Nick?"

"Offered him money for every time he reported on your location."

"What?" I feel my face screw up. "I'm right fucking here!" I hold my arms out, pissed off now, probably at the implication that I've been hiding.

"I'm only telling you what Nick told me. He wanted you to know about it."

I nod even if irritation is still scratching at me like a bitch. "You took care of him?"

"That's why he's eating."

"How does Harvey know someone like Nick anyway?" Niner asks.

"Says Harvey repped him on a drug charge back in the day."

I start pacing. It's true that both Harvey and Nicky G have been around longer than I have, and that's saying something. But still, it begs the question, "Is Harvey really so desperate that he needs the help of a long-time addict and nickel-and-dime thief?"

Niner tilts his head. "Apparently."

"I say we put a bounty on Harvey's head and be done with it," Luis announces.

"And have every asshole in the Bay Area trying to collect?" I grit out with sarcasm. "The cops would get wind of it in two seconds." Unlike the cartels, we operate in a world with consequences.

"Then we put out the word we'll pay for info," Niner says.

"Fine," I mutter as I walk away. "But an amount that makes it clear I don't give a shit about Harvey Sharkane." What a joke. *How can a man who's so insignificant be such a thorn in my side?*

Upstairs, Laney can't believe we've shown up this early. "Has Hell frozen over? Or are you two still confused by Daylight Savings Time?"

Like he always does, Niner takes the bait. "Actually, we heard you got a makeover, but I don't see what all the fuss is about."

She gives him a smirk, indicating, I'm sure, that her insult was superior to his and that she really doesn't care if he likes the new, very noticeable, bright pink bangs.

"So," Laney says to me. "I've received two calls from Mayor Findley's office already this morning. Do I want to know how he pissed you off?"

"Nope," I call, heading down the hall to the kitchen to make one of those awful coffee pods before my head splits open from the lack of caffeine. Unfortunately, Laney follows me.

"You know the building permit can't be approved by Friday, right? It's literally impossible."

"Yeah, I know. Let the fine Mayor sweat it out a bit longer, then tell him you convinced me to change my mind. Just make sure he knows I'm annoyed as fuck with him."

She grins. "Will do."

"Is JJ in?" I ask before she can go back to her desk.

"Is it noon?"

"How about Roberta?"

"It's barely ten o'clock, Jefe. I'm all you've got."

I huff. "Is there anything that needs my attention? Something that involves some knee-cap breakage maybe?"

She laughs. "Feeling restless?"

"Yeah," I admit.

"There's been a couple complaints from the girls working for the Mirran brothers down in San Jose. I was going to send Rolando this afternoon."

Perfect. I fucking hate pimps. Since prostitution is inevitable, I put up with it, but in Northern California, girls know that Laney will always take their calls. "Niner and I will handle it."

• • • • •

All in all, the day proves to be productive. We pay the Mirran brothers a visit and then, on the way back, we stop in at the house in East Palo Alto where I remember Gina's foster mom lived. What seemed like a long shot actually pans out. The woman is still there, and even better, she's kept a small box of Gina's stuff: report cards, a couple of art projects from middle school, her high school graduation picture, and a couple of candids. When I explain that they're for Gina's daughter, the woman gladly hands them over with a teary-eyed smile.

It's a lucky break that I plan to take full advantage of. It should soften Sophie up for the blow about the tracker. I figure if I come clean now, I can manage the fall-out, maybe even avoid another of those unnerving doll references she likes to throw at me.

"Soph?" I call out, bending down to greet our mangy mongrel.

"Hey, you're home," she says happily, appearing from down the hall.

To say that she's thrilled with the box of Gina's old stuff would be an understatement. While I change into a pair of jeans, she sits on the bed and goes through it, gushing about how happy Daniela is going to be.

In the closet, I pull down an old banker's box to see what I've got left over from the days when Javier was still alive. Lifting the lid is like opening a can of snakes. The memories come at me hard and fast. On top is the framed picture Gina gave me for my twenty-seventh birthday, or maybe twenty-eighth. Javier and I are so young. I barely recognize myself without the beard.

Sophie finds me a few minutes later, sitting on the floor, my back to the wall, going through everything with wistful longing pulsing in my gut. Joining me, she glances at the loose picture I'm holding and gasps. "Is that you?"

I chuckle softly and pass it to her. "It is. Feels like a lifetime ago."

"You look so different," she says, wonder in her voice. "How old are you here?"

"I don't know, maybe twenty-four."

"Who's this?" She points to the kid sitting on the couch next to me. "Is that . . . is that Scott?"

"Yeah, he was maybe eight or nine."

She's completely delighted by this. "What a skinny little shrimp."

I pass her the next one, and again, she gasps. "Oh my god, is that Niner?"

"Yeah, and Javier." We've got beers in our hands, laughing about something that Niner's said, I'm sure.

"Niner hasn't changed much, has he?"

"Nope." The next pic is more recent, one of Gina and Javier, his arms filled with a tiny Daniela. "Shit," I mutter, trying to absorb the punch of emotion the image brings.

Sophie lays her head on my shoulder. "You guys were close." It's not a question.

"Yeah." I check the picture out again. Javi is so happy, sitting with his two girls. "We were getting out," I admit, hating the familiar sick feeling that always assaults me when I let myself remember those months around the time of their deaths. "We were going to leave it all behind. Gina was pregnant and Javier was getting antsy. I wanted to be a part of my boys' lives. We had a good chance too. *Los Santos* was in a lot of turmoil in those days."

"Really?"

"Yeah, but before we could go through with it, everything came down around us. Well, came down around *me* because they were gone."

She picks up my hand and laces our fingers together, which reminds me I shouldn't be sharing this with her. One day she may find herself in the FBI's crosshairs and the less she knows, the better. Yet the will to stop isn't there.

"After it happened, I couldn't bring myself to walk away," I say hoarsely, my gaze caught on the obvious pride in the picture, the newly-minted parents. "Instead of sticking to the plan, I pushed myself deeper. Because someone had to answer for their deaths."

Quiet rises up between us and the sudden irrational fear that she's disappointed in me begins to mingle with the nausea in my stomach. It's not that I regret my decision to seek revenge, but it was a pivotal moment in my life, and looking back, I'm not at all sure I made the right choice.

"And did they?"

"Did they what?" I echo harshly. Too harshly, I realize as she flinches.

"Did someone answer for it?"

"You're damn right they did." I drop the picture and rake a hand through my hair, waiting for her condemnation. When it doesn't come, I lash out. "I'm not a good man. I didn't get to where I am today by doing the right thing."

"Maybe not," she says quietly, lifting my hand to her cheek. "But I know the other side of you, the one that lights up when you see your goddaughter, the one that helps Scott when he needs it." She must sense what I think of her examples, because she hurries to add, "And the one who holds me together when I'm about to shatter into a million pieces."

That pulls me away from the self-recrimination. "That'll never happen, Soph. Not if I have anything to say about it. And anyway," I go on, peeved with *her* now. "You've come so far."

She kisses my shoulder. "And why is that? Because your love has filled in all my cracks."

I snort with amusement, unsure if I should call her out for underestimating herself or for being so cheesy.

She returns to the box for the next picture and I realize she was just distracting me with something that would help me pull myself together. Maybe this is the heart of what it means to be in a relationship; it's not the push and the pull, but a steadying hand when it's needed.

We're packing it all away when she comes at me with a question that I would've seen coming if I hadn't been caught up in my little epiphany. "So, um, the getting out thing? Is that still an option?"

My heart sinks low in my chest. "Not really," I say gently. "Well, maybe in the future. But right now, with you in the mix . . ." I shake my head. "I don't think removing us from the structure that keeps us safe would be in our best interests." I take hold of her left hand and arrange the tennis bracelet so the butterfly clasp sits atop her pulse point. I brace myself for what has to come next. "About this," I say, caressing the soft skin that frames the diamonds. "I need you to wear it . . . always." Her eyes flicker between mine and I watch understanding slowly dawn in them.

Unlike the indignation and wrath I was expecting though, she finally gives me a solemn nod as she covers my hand with her own. "Okay."

"You promise? It's important."

"Yeah, okay," she says with more certainty. "I promise."

Relief overwhelms me as I pull her to my chest. "Thank you," I tell her earnestly, completely disbelieving that she's let me off so easily.

CHAPTER 15

Sophie

The amount of subterfuge needed before we can arrive at my sister's place for Daniela's birthday doesn't bother me. Alejandro is only being cautious and I'm pleasantly surprised that when we change cars in a public underground parking garage for the second time, it'll just be me and him, no driver and no security.

"A word of warning," he says as we walk up the front steps. "I'm not sure how long we can stay."

I pull my hand back from the doorbell. "What?" He looks incredible in dark jeans and a thin, black crewneck sweater that clings to his chest in all the right places. I catch sight of the sliver of tattoo that's visible on his neck because for once, he's not wearing a shirt with a collar. "Why?"

"Scotty's grandmother will only tolerate me for short periods of time." At my confusion, he adds, "Javier's murder hit her hard . . . she, uh, blames me for what happened to her son."

Uncharacteristic remorse clouds his features and I don't like it. My man's sense of responsibility has always extended well beyond the pale of what's reasonable in my opinion. But there's no point in worrying about any of this now, so I give him what I hope is a reassuring grin. "Don't worry, she likes me fine and you're with me."

Ringing the doorbell, I listen to the stampede of feet and the loud, excited voices of the girls as they race for the door. Rosa, the youngest, is the one to wrench it open, followed closely by Carmen. "Aunt Sophie!" they cry happily, throwing their arms around my waist.

Daniela's not quite as interested in me when she sees who I've come with. "Tío Alejandro!" she squeals, throwing herself into his open arms.

We get swept into the house for hugs and kisses with Scott and Ellie and Scott's sisters.

"You're late," my sister murmurs, bumping my shoulder good-naturedly. Thank goodness she's in a good mood.

We watch Scott and Alejandro talk with Daniela still perched in his arms across the foyer. "Yeah, well, you can't give either of us the third degree with a house full of people, can you?"

"Chicken," she accuses, but then gives me a rueful smile. "You look good. Things are working out then?" My smile must be enormous because Ellie laughs.

"Yeah, they're working out."

"You know I'll eventually corner you, right? You can't avoid this conversation forever."

"Oh, I don't know. I've been doing a pretty good job so far. Forty-five days and counting."

Rosa saves me by plucking at my sleeve. "Aunt Sophie?" Her gaze is glued to the four gift bags I'm holding. "Are those for us?" We brought Daniela a birthday present, plus something for each of the three girls.

"They are, but first Daniela has to open her birthday present, okay?" To my amusement, her sweet little face screws up with a bit of displeasure. She must not like taking a back seat to her big sister. I know the feeling well. Taking her hand, I pull her in Daniela's direction, throwing my sister a triumphant look over my shoulder.

Scott doesn't let Daniela open her gift bag right there in the entryway. We end up at the back of the house in the family room where Desiree and Mari, Scott's sisters, are talking with their grandmother. I watch the old woman's eyes narrow on Alejandro as we approach.

"Señora," I say, infusing my voice with as much charm and sweetness as I can. I lean down to kiss her cheek. *"¿Cómo está?"*

I get a warm smile and a, *"Muy bien, mija, y tú?"* She doesn't fail to notice that I don't let go of Alejandro's hand or that Daniela continues to stand sentinel on his other side. She addresses him in a cool tone that doesn't contradict Alejandro's assessment of their relationship, but Daniela smoothly finds a spot in the Spanish conversation to extricate us from the awkwardness. Leading us to the other side of the room, she sits between us on the couch.

"This is technically from both of us," I tell her as I hand over the gift bag, "but mostly it's from your Tío Alejandro, okay?"

Daniela's deep brown eyes gleam with delight. "You guys are together, aren't you?" she whispers conspiratorially.

"Yes," I whisper back.

"I knew it! My mom and dad have been gossiping about you guys since Christmas." She reaches into the gift bag, fishing the scrapbook out from the tissue paper.

I watch her brow furrow. It takes a very long minute for her to figure out what she's holding, but then she buries her face in my side.

I wrap my arm around her. "Do you not like it?" She sniffles quietly and my heart seizes in my chest. "I'm so sorry. I thought you might like to have some pictures of your parents." Then it hits me that maybe she just wants Scott and Ellie to be her parents. I meet my sister's eyes across the room as she makes her way over, her brows lifted in question.

I exchange places with Ellie who hugs her daughter. When Daniela realizes I'm moving away, she clutches at my hand. "No, wait. I love it, Aunt Sophie."

"You do?" I ask skeptically.

"Yes, don't go."

Alejandro pulls me down onto his lap as Daniela wipes at her tears with the sleeve of her dress and reopens the book. My sister inhales sharply. "You look just like her, Daniela."

"Do you think?" she asks, studying her mom's high school graduation picture. "She was so pretty."

"I thought so too," I tell her. "You're both so very beautiful."

"Where did you get this?" Ellie asks, looking at me with wonder.

"Alejandro got it." I lay my cheek to his temple.

"I went to see Gina's foster mom," he tells Ellie, and my sister blinks at him in surprise.

Daniela turns the page and starts to giggle. "Who's this?"

With Alejandro's help, I did my best to put the pictures in chronological order.

"That's me," Alejandro says, pointing. "And that's Javier, your dad, and that's your *papá*."

She shrieks with laughter. *"Papá, ven."*

In the picture, Javier and Alejandro, only teenagers themselves, are holding a toddler-sized Scott upside down, each by an arm and a leg and they're making funny faces for the camera. Scott comes over, and from there, everything goes better than I could have hoped. Everyone *oohs* and *awws* at the pictures as Alejandro tells the stories behind them. Even Scott's grandmother is pulled in by all the joy.

Halfway through the book, Ellie and I have a silent conversation.

This is a wonderful thing you've done.

I grin. *I know.*

Then her eyebrows lift. *And well played.*

Now you know how important he is to me.

Reaching for my hand, she squeezes it and a rush of relief has tears welling in my eyes. My sister means the world to me. I'd be miserable if I had to choose a side. Alejandro, always aware, kisses my forehead, something that doesn't go unnoticed by Ellie.

Later, the ten of us are sitting down to eat dinner when the doorbell rings.

"I'll get it," Daniela says excitedly, sliding from her chair. All three girls go running with Scott in tow.

I hear murmured voices from the foyer, but I'm too busy loving how it feels to have Alejandro sitting beside me at a family gathering to pay much attention. "The book went over so well," I say in a low voice only for him.

"It did." He smiles at me lazily. "But you knew it would, didn't you?" I try to hide my satisfaction by pressing my nose to his shoulder and he chuckles. "I'll have to remember never to underestimate you."

"Good evening, everyone."

My heartbeat stutters painfully as I sit up properly to behold my mother standing in the doorway, imperious as ever in one of her trademark Chanel suits.

"Mom," Ellie says, the brittleness of her voice subduing my instinct to accuse her of setting me up. She's obviously as horrified as I am. "You said you couldn't make it."

My dad brings up the rear, appearing sheepish. "Our event ended early, so we decided to stop by. It smells wonderful in here."

"We're having pozole," Rosa chirps, weaving her way through the adults to re-take her chair next to Ellie, oblivious to the sudden tension. "It's Daniela's and my dad's favorite."

Ellie takes a deep breath, then says, "Have you eaten? There's plenty for everyone."

"We'd love some," my dad says.

Oh, shit. This is not going to end well. My mother is already examining Alejandro like he's an insect she's about to squash.

"Okay," Ellie says. "Scott, can you get the extra leaf for the table, please?"

Scott needs Alejandro's help with the table, so I don't get a chance to warn him. He seems to know what's coming, though, because once the table is ready and everyone has retaken their seats, he murmurs, "Don't worry. I'll be fine."

"So, Sophie," my mother says, examining her soup like it's already left a bad taste in her mouth even though she hasn't tried it yet. She very primly puts her spoon back on the table. "Aren't you going to introduce us to your . . . guest?"

The patronizing tone of her voice immediately fortifies me. It's one thing to come at me, but quite another to come at Alejandro. If she thinks I'll roll over and let her insult him in any way, she's sorely mistaken. "This is Alejandro, my new boyfriend," I say evenly. "Alejandro, this is my mother, Janine, and my dad, Jonathan."

"I see," she says before anyone else can say a word. "Is he the reason you haven't been taking my calls?"

Ellie cuts in. "This is hardly the time, Mom." She tries to change the subject. "How was the mayor's fundraising luncheon?"

"Oh, quite informative. It seems he knows more about my youngest daughter's dating life than I do."

"What?" Then it dawns on me. Mayor Findley. The world is smaller than one might expect – unfortunately. My parents and Don Findley definitely move in the same circles. I don't know why it didn't occur to me.

"So," my dad breaks in, probably sensing his wife is on the verge of saying something very unpleasant. "Alejandro, what is it that you do?"

Scott chokes on his dinner, but Alejandro very casually wipes his mouth on his napkin and answers. "Real estate development, mostly."

"Oh." My father is surprised and I decide the mayor must have painted a pretty dark picture. "Anything I've heard of? What's your latest project?"

Alejandro sits back in his chair, eyeing my father carefully. "Well, I was going to do Findley's new golf course, but clearly, he's decided to back out of the deal."

The spoon in my father's hand pauses halfway to his mouth.

"Oh, please," my mother drawls. "I can see the tattoo on his neck from here."

I pull in a breath to defend him, but Daniela beats me to it. "What's wrong with tattoos?" She sounds distressed. "My mom had a tattoo on her arm."

"There's nothing wrong with tattoos, Dani," Ellie says, directing an angry stare at our mother. "Mrs. Summers is being judgmental and drawing attention to her biased view of the world."

A pall settles over the room and I feel my chest begin to tighten with a tinge of anxiety. Then Carmen asks into the silence, "What's biased?"

"Well," Ellie says. "It's when you only look at something from your own, narrow point of view. It's important to consider things from all angles *before* you speak."

The urge to throw a *burn!* at my mom like a little kid rages inside of me, but instead, I say, "Thank you, Ellie."

But my mother is unaffected by the insult. "Sophie," she intones, "you'll come home with us tonight."

"What?" I squeak out.

"If you think I'll allow you to continue gallivanting –"

"Mom, I'm twenty-seven years old!"

She raises the volume of her voice. "– around with this common criminal, you've got another thing coming."

I stand, my chair scraping against the hardwood. I lean forward on the table to give her a piece of my mind despite the further tightening in my chest, but Alejandro places a restraining hand on my arm.

"*¿Está borracha la señora?*" Scott's grandmother says, causing titters of laughter to break out around the table. Not liking that she doesn't know what was said, my mother presses on.

"Don't think for a minute that I haven't noticed that bracelet, Sophie. Has he bought your acquiescence in this charade?"

I'm pretty sure my mouth has fallen open as I sink back into my seat. "Have you lost your mind?"

Ellie can't believe she's said that either because she adds, "I think she *is* drunk."

My mother's head swivels in Ellie's direction. "You won't speak to me like that."

"Uh, no, you won't speak to her," Ellie gestures at me, "like that, in *my* house."

"You can't possibly condone this relationship. Your sister can't date the likes of him. People are already talking."

"The likes of him? Really, Mom? You're such a hypocrite."

"What's that supposed to mean?"

Everyone's eyes are ping-ponging up and down the table between them, including mine.

"It means that people who live in glass houses shouldn't throw stones."

The effrontery on my mother's face would be hilarious if the circumstances were different. "You *cannot* be implying there is some kind of comparison to be made here."

"Did you or did you not buy the house in Palm Springs with the money Dad got for defending Arnold Lipton?"

My father lifts his hands as if to indicate that cooler heads would be advisable, but my mother scorns the idea with, "That has no relevance to this conversation."

"Doesn't it?"

"I don't see how. Arnold Lipton is a genius."

"No, Mom, Arnold Lipton is an intellectual property thief who made millions off of someone else's work – thanks to Dad." My father's law firm handles a lot of Silicon Valley's cases.

Outrage sparks in my mom's expression and I have to choke back a laugh, which gets the glacial glare I grew up watching my sister receive turned in my direction. "What are *you* laughing about? This is all your doing. Mark my words, Sophie, we won't pay for this preposterous nursing degree you asked about if this continues."

It's Ellie's turn to laugh. "Good thing Scott already agreed to finance it with his inheritance."

Alejandro stiffens beside me. Good grief. I made that deal with Scott back in November before Thanksgiving.

"But what about Tía Mari's MIT?" Rosa asks, watching this farce with worry.

And that does it. We're at a child's tenth birthday dinner for god's sake. "Okay, this stops now," I order. "If you can't keep your petty prejudices to yourself, Mom, you can leave. I don't know why you thought they would sway me in the first place. I love Alejandro. Alejandro loves me. End of story."

Down the table, Scott's sister, Desiree sighs out, "Awwww."

And Daniela claps gleefully beside me. "I knew it!" She leans forward to see Alejandro on my other side. "Tío, are you going to *marry* Aunt Sophie?"

My face goes up in flames as I slump back in my chair. "Daniela," I say weakly, then rest my head on the back of my hands on the table in front of me. What a disaster. This is what I get for feeling so smug over the success of the scrap book.

Alejandro's hand lands on my back and its warm weight has me leaning into his side.

But of course my mother's not done yet. "She is certainly not going to –"

"I believe Sophia's had the last word," Alejandro says in that ice cold tone of his.

I look up in time to see my mother's head rear back, incensed at his insolence. Finally, my father steps in. "Janine, that's enough. What is this?" he asks with a flourish of his spoon. "It's delicious."

"It's pozo—" Ellie tries.

"Hang on," my mother says, looking directly at Alejandro even though I'm silently begging her to shut up. "I didn't hear you confirming my daughter's little profession of love."

Alejandro scoffs. "You think I'd be sitting here, listening to *this* if I didn't love her?"

That elicits another, "Awww," from Desiree and I sit up to look at Alejandro.

Everything in my heart must be clearly displayed on my face because he places a soft kiss on my mouth. As I melt into his side, his arm a reassuring weight around me, I realize the building pressure in my chest has subsided and I'm able to pull a normal breath into my lungs.

"Hey, Daniela," Alejandro says. "Did I tell you that your Aunt Sophie and I got a dog?"

She gasps. "No!"

"Yeah, I bet she's got pictures you can see after dinner."

That ignites a flurry of questions from the girls and a contemplative détente with my parents. I'm not sure if it was Alejandro's confirming that he loves me or the permanence implied by our having adopted a dog together that does it, but I'll take it.

CHAPTER 16

Alejandro

I deserve a gold star.

No question.

Sitting here, letting that nasty piece of work take shots at me like I belong in the dirt beneath her stilettos.

To be fair, busting the boyfriend's balls is any decent mother's job. But damn, she came at me with a sledgehammer. I was more prepared for the subtle disdain that my own mother employs. Lesson learned.

At least I was able to divert the conversation before I lost my cool. Once the girls got talking about dogs, there was no stopping them. Not even the well-heeled *Karen* could get a word in edgewise. Though I feel bad for Scotty and Ellie who are inundated with pleas from the girls for a dog of their own.

When we finish eating, Sophie's parents make a quick exit. Surprisingly, her father shakes my hand and says he hopes we can get to know each other better in the future. I'd bet every penny I've ever earned he's hoping this is only a phase his daughter's going through. Whatever. He'll adjust. He has no other choice.

Once the door closes behind them, Ellie breathes an exaggerated sigh of relief and everyone laughs. Up and down the table, Spanish breaks out, gossiping about *'la señora'*. I grin to myself at the crack Scott's grandmother made earlier, asking if the woman was drunk, probably because she had the nerve to call me a criminal to my face.

A few minutes later, Carmen goes around the table with a little bag. Everyone has to pull a token out to see who'll be helping with the clean-up; yellow for safe, red for dish duty. Only Scott and his *abuela* are exempt because they cooked, and Daniela because it's her birthday. When it's my turn, Carmen hesitates, but I smile at her as I stick my hand in. We both see it's yellow at the same time and laugh.

"*Ah, sí*," Scott's *abuela* says, "*desde chiquitos, Javier y Alejandro siempre tuvieron la suerte del diablo.*"

"*Igual que yo*," Daniela adds with delight.

"*Sí, igual que tú, mija.*"

Everyone understands except Sophie, so I pull her close and explain. "She says Javier, Daniela and I have the luck of the devil."

"Is she being nice to you?" she asks in a whisper, looking hopeful. "Or is the devil thing an insult?"

"Since she included Daniela, I'm going with nice."

"That's great."

I kiss her before Rosa comes to take Sophie's hand, leading her into the kitchen like it's a life sentence and not a half hour of dish washing.

Scott comes to sit beside me. "I'm so sorry, Tío."

I wave his apology away. "Apparently, we won the mother-in-law sweepstakes."

Chuckling humorlessly, he rubs at the back of his neck. "No shit. You got off easy though."

"She called me a common criminal," I say dryly.

"Yeah, the first time I met her, she accused me of being a *laborer,* and to her mind, that's the same thing."

We laugh, but it's a bit grim and it withers out as his grandmother appears at his elbow.

"Mijo, let me talk to Alejandro, please," she says in Spanish.

Shooting me another apology, this one silent, he vacates Sophie's chair so his *abuela* can sit down. Once she's settled, she trains her uncomfortably penetrating gaze on me. "I blamed you for Javier's death."

I almost grimace. She's never been one to beat around the bush and as I run the backs of my fingers along my beard, I resign myself to another round of bashing. Rough night, all in all.

"I was so heartbroken. I still am."

"I know," I say, because I do. Javier had a special relationship with his mom.

"But over the last couple of years," she goes on, "I've remembered that my son had a mind of his own."

"Señora," I start, feeling the familiar nausea rise in my gut. "You've never wanted my apology, so I won't offer another one, but you know that I've always taken full responsibility for what happened."

She stares at me. Too long and too hard, and I'm about to look away when her lips purse. "You needn't."

I blank. "Needn't what?"

"Take responsibility. Javier wasn't a child when he was gunned down. He was a thirty-year-old man who knew exactly what he was involved in."

"Señor–"

172

She silences me with a look. "When I cut ties with you, Alejandro, I was blinded by my grief. I lost a son. But you lost a brother. You were hurting too."

I swallow hard because emotion is starting to get the better of me. My next words come out a bit strangled. "It was a terrible time and I wasn't fit company for anyone." She knows exactly what I'm talking about. My attempts to burn down the world to avenge Javier are the stuff of legend on the streets of the San Francisco Peninsula. "And I owe you an apology as well for not recognizing you were struggling financially on top of everything else. Like you say, grief can be blinding."

A sheepish grin appears on her lined face. "I probably would have starved before I accepted your money."

"No," I say gently. "You had mouths to feed. You would have taken the money and then slammed the door in my face."

Attempts to hide her amusement fail miserably and she shakes her head like she can't believe she's sitting here joking with me. I can't believe it myself.

"I want to thank you for giving Daniela the gift of her parents today," she says, changing the subject. "That was incredibly kind."

"That was all my mariposa's idea. I won't take credit for it."

Her head cocks, considering me. "Fair enough. Your . . . *mariposa* is a gentle soul, no?" I hear what she leaves unsaid, that Sophie is far too gentle for *the likes of me*, but before I can agree, she continues. "This name you've chosen for her, it fits. Like a *Monarca*, she, too, is fragile, but those delicate wings are capable of carrying her across the entire continent if need be. You will treat her with the respect she deserves."

It sounds more like a decree than a suggestion and I feel my lips tip up at the corners. "I'm doing my best."

She makes a noise best described as a harrumph. "You are the reason she was so sad a few months ago?"

"Yes," I admit, sobering immediately. "I wanted a different life for her than the one I can provide."

"But?"

"But I couldn't stay away."

Instead of disapproval, I get . . . joy? The lines on her face deepen with a genuine smile. "I'm glad to hear it, *mijo*."

Mijo is what she *and* my mother used to call me and I'm suddenly hit with a wave of sorrow, one that this old woman notices right away.

"You'll come to visit me some time," she announces. "You can bring the other one . . . the funny one."

"Niner?"

"Yes, *Noveno*. Such a ridiculous name. And of course, bring your *mariposa*. I'll make some *chiles en nogada* if you call ahead." She pats my hand as she rises from her chair.

• • • • •

On the drive home, I'm more at peace with myself than I have been in years. I'm happy to be the one driving, my girl beside me, my playlist on the speakers. I can't imagine life getting any better.

"Alejandro?"

"Hmm?"

"Will you teach me some more Spanish? I hate being the only one who doesn't know what's going on."

I smile over at her, watching the city lights slide over her lovely features in the dark. "Sure. What do you want to know?"

Tonight was nice. I don't remember the last time I spoke so much Spanish, and from there it dawns on me that I've lived in America for almost thirty years. That's three quarters of my life.

"I don't know."

"Okay, how about this? *Mi novio me ama y hará lo que sea necesario para tenerme segura y contenta.*" I barely manage to keep a straight face. Somehow I doubt she'll ever need to know that for casual conversation.

"*Mi novio me ama,*" she echoes, doing a pretty decent job. "*Y* . . . what was the rest?"

I repeat it for her, and as she says it back, I finally crack. "You give it a French accent," I laugh.

She giggles with me. "I'll have to work on that. What did I say?"

I laugh harder. "*My boyfriend loves me and he'll do whatever's necessary to keep me safe and happy.*"

She whacks my arm, but then says, "That's actually kind of romantic."

I pull her hand to my mouth and kiss it. "*Te amo mucho, mi mariposa.*"

Sighing happily, she answers me in English. "I love you, too."

Seems the lesson is over because she changes the subject. "So, hey. I've decided to get a tattoo."

Thoughtlessly, I snort with derision and then feel like a jackass as she pulls her hand from mine, crossing her arms over her chest, radiating offense.

"You're not one of those hypocrites who think they look tacky on women, are you?"

"No!" How do I tell her that I'm covered with them because I like the oblivion of the slightly painful process? That the discomfort reminds me of all the things I need to make up for? A kind of penance. She's got nothing to repent for.

"Well, then what?"

"Well, for one, it hurts."

"I can handle it."

Fearing she'll see my doubt, I don't take my eyes off the road. "What do you want to get?"

"It's a surprise," she says, excitement now coloring her tone.

"You don't need to do it for me, Soph."

"Please," she says with sarcasm. "I want to do it for me, but if you're too busy, I can always get Jeremy to take me."

"The hell you will," I retort, again without thinking.

"Great. It's settled then. When should we go?"

Groaning, I send her an accusing look. "I walked right into that one."

"You did."

"So your genius can be used for good or evil?"

"What?" she says, a sweet smile playing on her lips.

"Well, that book you made for Daniela worked like a charm, but you also just manipulated me into doing what you want, so . . ."

"So, women are tricky?" she says, her voice dipped in an eye-roll. "Don't be such a baby. It's not my fault you're so predictable."

God, I *am* predictable, I think, a bit dismayed. But then another thought hits me. "My tattoo guy is never touching you."

"I'm sure he knows *someone* you'd approve of."

"You're serious about this?"

She perks up again. "Yeah, I'm serious."

"Fine," I grumble. "On one condition."

"You mean on *no conditions?*"

I ignore her. "I want to know why you didn't tell me about going to nursing school."

"Oh." There's a pause and I glance over to see her biting at her lip. "I haven't even finished my application yet. There was nothing to tell."

"Sophia," I press.

"Fine. I wanted to wait until I got accepted before I said anything."

"What? Why?"

"I don't know. What if I don't get accepted?"

Her reasoning escapes me. "And that would matter because . . ."

"Well, as you like to point out, I'm already working for minimum wage. I guess I don't like the idea of you being . . ." she waves her hand in a circle, searching for the right word, ". . . disappointed in me."

We come to a red light and I'm able to face her. "That's not even a possibility."

"No?"

The hope contained in that single syllable is irksome. "No."

"Well don't get pissy. We don't all have an iron-clad sense of self like you do."

I ignore that and move on to more pertinent concerns. "And Scotty's not bloody well paying for it," I inform her.

"He was only going to loan me the money."

"You really think I'd let you be indebted to another man?"

She laughs. "Is this more of your inner caveman banging his club around?"

"Yes."

Still chuckling, she surprises me with, "Well, thank you, because I'm not sure Scott and Ellie can afford the loan since his sister, Mari, got into MIT."

I just grunt, still annoyed with her.

"So, what kind of an interest rate are you going to give me?"

I narrow my eyes at her. "What?" She's twirling her hair around her finger and I'm distracted by the way she parts her lips. She doesn't say anything, and it finally clicks. My little minx wants to play. "I'm sure I can come up with something that weighs heavily in my favor."

"Oh, I bet you could," she says, good-naturedly shoving my shoulder. My mood begins to slide back into the debit column at her reaction. Not even the guy honking at me to go when the light turns green makes a dent in how good it feels to be with her.

· · · · ·

Turns out Sophie wasn't throwing out idle comments. By Tuesday, she has JJ set her up with an app to learn Spanish, and by Friday, she's gone over my head and enlisted Niner's help to go to a preliminary appointment at our tattoo guy's shop. She claims my vague promises to make the appointment weren't good enough.

"When you said you had something to take care of yesterday," I gripe at Niner, who's in the front seat next to Skip. "I thought you meant something to do with Ben."

He shrugs. "The queen asks for help, she gets it."

The mulish look Sophie's wearing becomes one of pride. I admit the comment even softens me up a bit . . . until he keeps talking.

"Chill out, Jefe. I kept all the dogs from drooling on our precious *Rosita Fresita* yesterday. Same as I'll do today. Nothing to worry about."

"Nothing to worry about?" I mutter darkly. It's actually not the guys I'm worried about. Unless they're looking for a hole in their foreheads, nobody would ever approach her. No, I'm worried because she doesn't want me with her while she gets the work done. The thought of her *enduring* the process without me has my teeth on edge. I make a last ditch attempt to convince her as we pull up at the shop.

"You sit with me, I'll sit with you."

"No, I want it to be a surprise." She can see how put out I am, so she undoes her seat belt and comes closer. "If I need you, you'll be right down the hall."

Closing my eyes against the urge to disagree with her, I finally nod. Because I'm acting like an overbearing, little bitch.

We go in and Hannah, the only female artist at the shop, is waiting at reception for Sophie. "You ready?" she asks my girl. I gesture impatiently for Niner to follow them and because we're in public he doesn't give me shit about it. At least that's something.

CHAPTER 17

Sophie

I'm a wrung out sponge by the time it's over. Two and a half hours of . . . not torture, I won't be that dramatic, but it wasn't pleasant. I have no idea how Alejandro has covered himself in tattoos. The amount of hours he's put himself through boggles my mind.

"I told you to choose a different spot for your first time," Niner says blithely, helping me back to the front of the shop with an arm under my elbow. "Along your ribs is sensitive."

I direct a dirty look his way and he has the gall to laugh.

In the reception area, we find Alejandro talking to a few of the artists. He's visibly relieved to see me so I give him a smile, albeit a weak one.

"You survived?"

I nod as he carefully folds me into his arms. I just want to go home and sleep.

"I cannot wait to get you naked," he says quietly in my ear, but my only response is a sound that conveys just how unlikely that scenario is.

On the way home, I fall asleep on his shoulder, so I feel a little better as we ride the elevator upstairs. Alejandro ushers me into our bedroom and sits me on the edge of the bed, going to work on getting my boots off.

"We're not having sex," I announce.

"I'm not an animal," he retorts with exasperation.

Bruce Wayne jumps up beside me, but Alejandro makes him get down and takes his place. When he starts pulling my sweater up, I try to swat his hands away.

"I have to see it," he says. "It's a life or death situation."

"What?"

"I'm serious. I'm going to die if you don't let me see it." He pulls the sweater up over my head and the slight wobble in my belly tells me I'm nervous about his reaction.

Carefully, he peels back the bandage to expose the enflamed skin. On my left side, along my ribs is a Monarch butterfly that's about the size of a silver dollar.

"I know, it's cheesy," I say, my cheeks heating. "But I wanted something that reminds me of you." I finally gather the courage to look at him, but his unreadable gaze is glued to the butterfly.

"It's not cheesy," he says hoarsely. "But why there?"

My cheeks get hotter. "Because that's where your hand sits when you hold me at night."

He nods slowly, then leans in to rest his forehead on my shoulder for a moment. "God, mariposa," he whispers. Then he sits up again and pulls off his own T-shirt.

The skulls on the fronts of his shoulders with their blacked out eyes glare at me as usual. "I thought you were getting Doom and Gloom touched up. They don't look any different than they did yesterday."

A soft laugh sounds between us as he shakes his head. "You and your names, woman." He twists to show me his back, reaching to peel a small bandage away.

I gasp. "Shut up! You got one too?" The only space not covered by ink on his back surrounds the two cranes that sit on the lower left. They're standing in water, one with its head raised and the other staring off in the opposite direction. The image seems to have special meaning to him but he's always been vague with the reasons. And now a small Monarch butterfly sits in the sky above them. Wonder begins to replace my initial excitement, but not before I say, "Does this mean we're going to start wearing matching T-shirts?" I mean to tease him, but all the choked emotion ruins the effect.

Re-sealing his tattoo under the bandage, he says, "No, it means I'm not letting you go – ever. You're mine." As if to emphasize his point, his gaze collides with mine, intense and searching. He means it. And maybe if I weren't so in love with him, the possessiveness would scare me, maybe even suffocate me. But I like the feeling of belonging, of knowing my place in the world is at his side.

He takes one last, long look at my butterfly before he covers it again. "Do we understand each other?" he demands. "I love you and there's nothing you can do to change that."

I wish I had it in me to come back with something flirty or flippant, but the delicious weight of his words has me pinned down. "I wouldn't change it for anything," I whisper before his mouth covers mine.

We kiss and kiss, our love tasting of rapture and care and safety. There's no urgency or desperation. We have our whole lives ahead of us.

· · · · ·

I've been both dreading and looking forward to the sorority alumni luncheon. A month ago when I'd talked to Bea, she'd been as happy as I had to reconnect. But I haven't heard from her since. I briefly considered skipping it altogether to avoid this low-level hum of anxiety, but I figure it's a fairly safe opportunity to take another step toward claiming the old me, the one who was stolen by a man who didn't even remember me.

On a daily basis, I swallow back the knowledge that Paul Gallagher is dead . . . not exactly because of me, but close. I haven't come to terms with it yet – I'm not sure I ever will – but his murder doesn't haunt me the way it probably should. If that makes me a bad person, I think I'm okay with that. The man crushed me, physically and mentally, without a second thought. And I'm not the only one. Surely the world is a better place for his absence.

As Jeremy pulls up at the hotel in Palo Alto near my alma mater of Stanford, Aaron jumps out, glowering at the valet who reaches for my door. The three of us, Jeremy, Aaron, and I, have bonded over the last six weeks, and Aaron's protectiveness makes me smile. He extends his hand and helps me down from the vehicle.

Our arrival attracts some attention, people probably wondering who's important enough to need security. Lately I've noticed how much more relaxed I am in public. It seems that being El Jefe's girl has been good for me. Wanting to meet any standards, either real or imagined, that come with the position has nudged me out of my self-obsessed corner. I can now walk into an expensive restaurant, wearing a fabulous black sheath dress and tall heels with my head held high despite the gash across my neck. Of course a lot of the new self-confidence stems from the presence of my bodyguards, but I'll take it. Progress is progress.

The maître d' shows me in, and Jeremy and Aaron melt away toward the bar. Approaching the long table of women, most of whom I haven't seen in years, rattles me a bit. But then, Bea stands and rushes forward to meet me. "Sophie!" she exclaims, pulling me into an embrace. "You look incredible."

"Oh, you too." It's so good to see her. We were college roommates all through our undergrad and I didn't realize how much I missed her until this very moment as she pulls me toward her end of the table.

"Here, I saved you a seat."

"Thanks," I whisper as I sit down, waving to the rest of the table. My reception is lukewarm at best, but that's to be expected. I haven't been active in the group for a long while. Plus, I was never part of the clique that ruled the sorority.

The decision to come is a great one. Besides Bea, Alexis and Julie are here. The four of us used to be inseparable in college and it's wonderful to catch up with them. Bea and Alexis are still working and living in LA and they sometimes see Kathy, who was with us at the gas station holdup. But Julie doesn't live that far away in Sacramento and we decide to make lunch together a monthly occurrence.

As the meal winds down, Julie and Alexis head to the restrooms, but Bea stops me from getting up. "Soph," she tells me in a low voice. "I wanted to tell you how sorry I am about what happened." Her eyes drop to the scar on my neck, but I don't feel the usual anxiety-tinged horror. "I should have been there for you afterwards, but I wasn't sure how to go about it."

"Bea, I'm the one who dodged your calls, remember?"

"Yeah, but I should have tried harder."

"It doesn't matter anymore," I tell her truthfully. "We should focus on the future."

"Agreed. So, you were pretty vague about this new boyfriend of yours." She picks up my wrist to examine the tennis bracelet. "It's more serious than you let on, isn't it?"

I smile widely. "It is. I'm completely head over heels."

She starts in with the third degree and I positively revel in being able to gush about my new boyfriend.

By the time we pull our heads apart, we're the only ones left at our table. With a hug and promises to keep in touch, we say goodbye. I signal to Jeremy that I'm going to the restroom before we go.

The restaurant is mostly deserted in the lull between lunch and dinner so I get the bathroom to myself. Coming out of the stall, I set my purse on the marble counter and wash my hands, examining my reflection. I decide I look as happy as I feel.

The door swings opens and a woman comes in. "Ms. Summers?"

Frowning at her, I answer cautiously. "Yes?"

"My name is Patricia Hinkley. I'm with the FBI."

CHAPTER 18

Alejandro

"What is it, Sophie?" I say sharply into my phone. My day is not going well and I've got a roomful of men waiting on me and Niner to start a meeting that's apparently not going to yield good news.

"Uhhh."

The hesitance in her voice sets off alarm bells. "What's wrong?"

"Um, are you coming home soon?"

"No." My feet stall out. "Did something happen?" I snap my fingers at Niner, but he's already got his phone out, hopefully calling Jeremy. I can't imagine what could go wrong at a sorority alumni luncheon. Fuck, if this is some angsty drama-rama friend bullshit, I'm going to be . . . I take a deep, calming breath. "Sophia, are you okay?"

Instead of answering me, she goes with a soft, "Can you come home?"

"What? Why?" I demand. My knee-jerk reaction is to end the call. I've got shit to do. But I hold off. We're coming up on two months together and she's never done anything like this.

Niner ends his call and shrugs, then reports in a low voice, "Nothing out of the ordinary."

"Please?" Her voice wavers.

"It's important?"

"Yes," she whispers.

"Okay." I organize my thoughts "We're forty five minutes out, maybe an hour with traffic."

"Thank you." The line goes dead.

Did she hang up on me? "Oh, for crying out loud."

Niner laughs. "Trouble in paradise?"

Ignoring him, I march back down the stairs of the warehouse, thrusting open the door at the bottom with a loud bang. Through the towering shelving units filled with office supplies, I get glimpses of Skippy and Rolando arguing near the open bay doors. I'm not close enough to hear any of it – thankfully. I've got enough problems without listening to the brothers' squabble.

"Skip," I snap and he jumps. "Let's go."

"Yeah, okay." He hits the fob and moves to get in the driver's seat, but Rolando takes hold of his arm.

"I mean it," he tells his brother. "Don't fuck around with this."

Roughly shaking him off, Skip gets in and starts the SUV. I slide in the back and slam the door, indicating that Niner can ride in the front since I'm not in the mood for his jokes.

"Where to, Jefe?"

"The penthouse."

I get out my phone and call John Boyd, telling him to hold the meeting without me.

"Everything okay with Sophie, Jefe?" Skippy asks, glancing over his shoulder with concern.

"Why wouldn't it be?" I accuse, my suspicious nature kicking in. *Does this little punk know something?* Though his attitude has improved since the attack in Oregon, he's still beyond annoying most of the time.

"Uh," he sounds confused. "Because we're going to the penthouse even though we just got here?"

My rancor settles a bit. "She's fine," I grunt, hoping it's true.

The hour it takes to get home in the rain and the rush hour traffic is torture with my brain obsessing over what could have possibly gone down. Did she mention my name and someone recognized it? Sure my reputation is common knowledge in certain circles. But Stanford sorority alum circles? I doubt it.

By the time I'm unlocking the penthouse door, I'm wound pretty tight. Bruce Wayne greets me with a furiously wagging tail, but I ignore him and head for the bedroom.

"Hey," I hear and my head jerks around in surprise. Sophie's in the living room, sitting on the edge of the couch, radiating tension with her hands clasped between her knees. Whatever this is, it's not good.

I approach, sitting on the coffee table in front of her. Her body language isn't inviting me to touch her, something that chips away at my irritation. "What's going on?"

Chewing her lip, she pries her hands apart and hands me a half-crumpled business card. I take it from her sweaty palm and flatten it out. The first thing I notice is the government seal and I blow out a breath. *Fuck*. The FBI.

They must have come at her hard for her to be so shaken. Though I suppose a civilian isn't accustomed to any contact with law enforcement, let alone with a federal agency trying to bring pressure to bear.

Tentatively, I lay a hand on her knee. "You okay?" Her demeanor tells me she's not and my heart hurts for her. "Will you tell me what they wanted?"

She swallows hard. "The lady," she whispers, gesturing to the card, "found me in the restroom, like in the movies." Averting her eyes, which are filling with tears, she wrings her hands. "She said you do terrible things, Alejandro."

Scratching at my beard, I consider that statement from her perspective. But I can't imagine what's got her so spooked. I'm not an upstanding citizen by any measure, but neither am I out murdering little old ladies in their beds. And Sophie knows I did her attacker in . . . doesn't she? Or does she think I let him go after a stern talking to? She's never asked me about it.

And then a sick realization hits me; everything I now say to Sophie could be going to the Feds. Shit, everything I've *said* could be going to the Feds.

I get to my feet. "Stand up."

Taken aback by my harsh tone, she blinks up at me, loosing a single tear that slides down her cheek. "What?"

A flash of dread almost has me second guessing myself, but I push it down and take hold of her upper arm, pulling her up. "Turn around," I command, not giving her a chance to comply. She teeters on the heels she's wearing and I steady her by grabbing the top of her dress near the zipper pull.

"What are you doing?" she cries as the zipper comes down, trying to swat at my hands.

I ignore her and drag the dress down. The short sleeves effectively trap her arms as I scan over her back. Nothing. I spin her around again and this time she's not so cooperative.

"Get your hands off me!" Her knee comes up, but the dress catches the movement and a loud rip follows her shrieked words. She jerks her arms, frantically trying to free them and my instincts to subdue her kick into overdrive.

Threading my fingers into the hair at the back of her head, I yank her forward to put my mouth to her ear, but not before I get a good look at the horrified betrayal on her face.

Oh, fuck. Fuck, fuck, fuck. What am I doing?

"Just . . . just let me check you over," I rasp.

"For what?!"

I breathe in a lungful of her calming scent and then wrap my free arm around her back, pulling her against me. "Forgive me," I say, not caring that she can feel my body's want for her, no matter how inappropriate. "But this has to be done."

Slowly, I loosen my grip on her hair and pull back. She doesn't struggle, but her eyes are filled with rage and shimmering tears as I tug the dress down over her hips and get her to step out of it.

While I feel the seams of her dress for a wire, I scan her over in the matching lace bra and panties. There's nothing. She holds out her arms belligerently. "Satisfied?"

"No. It all needs to come off."

Her lips form a sneer, something I've never seen on them before, and I know this is going to cost me, cost us. With trembling hands, she reaches back and undoes the clasp, dropping the bra on the floor. Then she does the same with the panties once they're off.

She's a few paces away when something close to shame rises inside of me. "Mariposa."

Turning, she lifts a foot and pulls a shoe off, chucking it at me. First one and then the other. "Go to hell," she spits as the last one bounces off my arm and clatters against the table. At least she wasn't aiming for my head, I think as she disappears down the hall, her naked ass cheeks taunting me.

I sink back down onto the coffee table and go over every stitch of her clothing all the while ignoring my heavy heart and my raging hard-on. When I'm done, I find her sitting in an armchair in our bedroom, wearing sweats, staring out the windows, Bruce Wayne snuggled beside her. She refuses to look at me, but the dog watches me with contempt as I take off my suit jacket and the gun holster.

Crouching down in front of her, I try to catch her eye. "It had to be done."

"Not like that, it didn't."

"I —"

"No. Two months ago you stood in Amelia's kitchen and promised you wouldn't be cruel."

"You're right."

She gives me the creepy smile, the one I hate so much. "You think because you cop to it so easily that I should let it go."

Lowering my forehead to her knee, I attempt to form a strategy to get back in her good graces, but who am I kidding? I go with the straight-up truth. "I got scared. I don't know what I'd do if you betrayed me."

"I'd *never* betray you, you stupid man."

I lift my head and see sharp anger and earnest sincerity written all over her. Blowing out a long breath, I say, "I know you wouldn't. I guess I panicked, all right?"

"All right?" she says, her voice brittle and on the edge of cracking. "I get accosted by the FBI and then come home to be accosted by you? How is that all right?"

"She touched you?" This idea is like gasoline being poured on a fire.

"No," she says, exasperated. "You know what I mean."

"Was there just the one woman?"

She glares at me long and hard as if deciding if she's going to let me change the subject or not. Finally, she nods.

"Did she tell you not to tell me about this?"

She nods again and this time her brow creases like the memory is something she'd rather forget.

"Did you . . . tell her anything?"

"No!" she cries. "Of course I didn't."

"Okay, okay. I had to ask."

She sniffles a bit. "She showed me pictures . . ."

My thoughts come to an abrupt halt. "Pictures?"

"Of women . . . who've been . . ."

All my brain comes up with is a big question mark. "Who've been what?"

"Abused," she whispers, looking haunted by whatever was shown to her.

Another wave of temper burns through me. *Motherfucker*. Internally scrambling to keep a lid on my wrath, I say as gently as I can, "Sophia, I've never 'abused' a woman in my life."

"Not even for profit?"

"Jesus," I hiss. "No." Fury shakes my resolve to never tell Sophie anything about my business. *"Los Santos* does not run girls, not for *years*. There's plenty of money out there that's . . ." I struggle to come up with a word. "That's not as messy to collect."

I push to my feet, unable to stay still any longer. "Prostitution is way more trouble than it's worth." I pace, gripping a hand in my hair. "Do I profit indirectly from it? Yes. I 'tax' it. Because it's impossible to stop. But Laney keeps track of the girls. And I really have to shut my mouth now."

Her curiosity only amplifies my utter disgust with the situation. "I can't fucking believe they'd manipulate you like this!" I'm about to kick the accent table that's beside her chair, but she can't tolerate sudden noise or movement, and I've done her enough damage to last a lifetime.

Sophie leans down and kisses Bruce Wayne's head as if to fortify herself. "She said I could go to jail."

"For what?" I demand.

She flinches. "She didn't say."

"What did she want from you? Information?"

Nodding, she sets sombre eyes on me, which immediately cools me down. None of this is her fault.

"What kind of information?" I ask, trying to sound more civilized.

"Times and places, your schedule mostly."

I frown. "She thought you would have that kind of information?"

"She said if I didn't get it that I'd go to prison, and so will my dad."

"Your dad?"

"Yes," she whispers desperately. "She said they already have enough to send my father to prison for the rest of his life if I don't cooperate."

My disbelief grows. I doubt very much that a federal prosecutor is sitting on a case that's ready to go in order to blackmail Sophie into providing information that would be next to impossible for her to get. Unless they think we're complete fools. I grab my suit jacket and pull out the creased business card from my pocket. *How would I even know if it's real? How would Sophie?*

Slowly, I sink down on the arm of the chair beside her. "These pictures she showed you, how did she link them to me?"

"What?"

"How do you know they weren't random images pulled off the internet?"

"I guess I . . ."

I give us both a second to consider my question, and then, almost thinking aloud I say, "Maybe she was using them for their shock value. I haven't even seen them and my first reaction was outrage."

Sophie follows my train of thought. "So I wouldn't ask any questions?"

"Exactly." I dig out my phone and text JJ.

When I'm done, I feel drained and a bit unsteady on my feet. I reach for her arm, urging her up. She glowers at me before she capitulates and slowly gets to her feet so I can sit in the chair. Once she's settled on my lap, I tuck her head under my chin.

"You know what kind of man I am, mariposa." She doesn't jump to defend me like she would have only yesterday, but that's fine. Blind loyalty is never a good thing. "But whatever pictures she showed you had nothing to do with me. I promise you. I'm never unnecessarily brutal or unfair in my business. If I was, I'd be dead within a year." She stiffens at that so I pull back to see her. "In my line of . . . work, a tyrant doesn't last long. Does that make sense?"

Despite the situation still clearly weighing on her, her lips pull into a weak smile. "You're a gangster with a heart?"

"No. I can safely say that's not something I've ever been accused of."

"Then what?" she asks in a more serious voice. "What have you been accused of?"

"That I'm a ruthless bastard. But there are no surprises with me. The rules aren't a mystery."

"And these rules are . . ."

"None of your business." Her expression morphs into a mask of censure, but it doesn't sway me. "You don't need to know more than that."

She adds a raised brow. "You can't pat me on the head and send me on my way."

"I can if it keeps you safe."

"You mean if it keeps *you* safe," she accuses. "I can't believe you thought I betrayed you."

God, I handled this all wrong today. So very wrong. And it comes to me just how shaken this afternoon has left her. Maybe I could offer her *something* to help repair some of the harm both the FBI and I have done to her.

"Fine," I relent. "I'll tell you this much. There's no unnecessary bullshit under my watch." I give her a pointed look. "And that includes no coerced, abused or missing women."

She lays her head back on my shoulder and I'm not sure what causes her relief, that I've given her some information or that I've convinced her I'm not a pimp. Either way, I'll take it. The world now feels like it's been nudged back onto its proper axis.

My phone buzzes in my hand and I glance at the screen. "JJ's here. Do you feel up to talking to him?"

Nodding, she wearily gets to her feet. We go out and JJ's leaning on the kitchen island, scrolling through his phone. I really need to start locking my door.

"Hey, Jefe," he says, then smiles at Sophie.

"Take a look at this." I toss the business card onto the counter.

"Damn. Where'd that come from?"

"Sophie was approached today."

JJ whistles low. "You want me to check it out?"

"Yeah," I say, instead of the blunt *obviously* that's on the tip of my tongue.

"All right. I can't be digging around in the FBI database from here, so I'll be at the Garden."

As he heads for the door, I have a thought. "Hang on. Soph, were you supposed to call this woman? Or was she going to contact you?"

JJ makes a scornful noise. "No way. No one's *contacting* her. I've got her number locked down tight."

Sophie nods her agreement. "I'm supposed to call the number on the card before tomorrow night."

The more I think about it, the more I'm convinced this is a setup. "Okay, I'll meet you over there," I say to JJ.

When he's gone, I text everyone to gather at the Garden. If my suspicions are correct, we may be able to put a lot of our problems to rest in the next few hours.

• • • • •

Sophie doesn't want to stay by herself in the penthouse and I can't, in all conscience, make her. This involves her directly. So we bundle a thrilled Bruce Wayne into the backseat of the Tahoe between us and then head out to set up shop at the Garden.

Bruce causes a stir with the admin staff who are packing up for the night. The mangy mutt preens under their attention like a peacock, which cheers Sophie, so I keep my sarcasm to myself. It would be false anyway. The little bastard has wormed his way so far into my heart that I barely remember what life was like without him.

Niner shows up ten minutes later. *"Fresita,"* he calls jovially. "Heard you got propositioned."

Sophie can't help but smile at him from where she's sitting with Laney at the conference table.

"Was she hot?" Niner continues. "I bet she was. Those buttoned-down, power-suit types always give off the kinkiest vibes, don't they?" He jerks his head my way and Sophie giggles, a flush turning her pink.

Though it irks me that I'm pacing and running heart-burn inducing scenarios in my over-taxed mind while Niner's being a clown, I appreciate his natural ability to make things better for my girl.

"Sophie," JJ calls from his bunker. "Come check this out, please."

We all crowd in and JJ pulls out the chair next to him for Sophie. "So," he says, touching one of the many screens a few times to bring up an image. "Patricia Hinkley does indeed work for the FBI. This her?"

Sophie visibly recoils with surprise. "No."

"It's not?"

"No, the woman I met was much younger and she was a natural redhead."

On the screen, a very middle-aged woman with streaks of gray in her short dark hair stares out at us.

"Not surprising," JJ says, "since Ms. Hinkley is definitely not a field agent. She works in human resources."

"So," I say to the room in general. "Someone chose a name from the FBI directory. If Sophie checked, it would have some authenticity, but they didn't expect her to dig any deeper. Have you checked out the phone number on the card?"

"I'm still hunting it down. Some effort has gone into disguising it."

"How long will it take?"

"Another half hour maybe."

"Okay. Can you pull up a picture of Harvey?"

He bangs away at his keyboard and the picture appears.

"Soph, did you see him anywhere today?"

"The lawyer guy? No, but I wasn't watching for him."

Niner huffs with annoyance. "You think this is Harvey?"

"Yeah, I do. It fits his m.o. On the surface, there's some logic to it, but underneath, it's amateur and desperate."

"But what would he be able to get from our *Fresita?*"

"Opportunity to put a bullet in me, I'm guessing. If he knows where I'm going to be beforehand, when I'm not working, I might be more vulnerable."

A soft beeping noise fills the room. "Okay, so not a half hour," JJ says. "Looks like the number is currently pinging from Oakland. In the north. Bushrod Park maybe."

Luis immediately turns to go, but I signal him to hold on. "Will you be able to narrow it down?" I ask JJ.

"Not to a single address no, but close. Give me a few more minutes."

I pull Luis aside. "I don't want any of this getting out."

"I'll go alone."

"Nah, I don't like that either." Oakland is not a place you want to be caught out alone, no matter how tight our death grip is on the local gangs.

Luis smirks, as close to amused as I've ever seen him. "You worried about my well-being, Jefe?"

"I'm worried," I deadpan, "that some asshole is going to decide his claim to fame will be popping Luis Morales. What then?"

"I can take care of myself." I follow him out into the conference room where Skippy is setting a box of Chinese takeout on the table. "Call me with the info," Luis adds as Laney buzzes him out.

"Where's he going?" Skip asks, starting to unpack the food.

Suspicion flares in my gut. I take a good look at Skippy. Niner's nickname for him is *chamaco*, and it fits him. He is a *kid*, always eager to please and always wounded by criticism. *Does he have it in him to betray me?* I don't think so. He may not be the sharpest stick out there, but he's not clueless either.

When no one answers his question about Luis, he doesn't miss a beat. "I got Sophie an extra egg roll. Last time she said she liked them."

I give him a nod and his young face breaks out in a smile.

CHAPTER 19

Sophie

Chinese food is my favorite, but I have zero appetite tonight. First the run-in with the non-FBI agent and then Alejandro's reaction to it. Good grief. Alejandro. I should have known he'd have some kind of visceral response, but I'd been too caught up in those images to see it coming.

That fucking woman.

I feel violated, foolish, and livid all at the same time. I almost wish I could turn back the clock to laugh in her face.

I hate that I was so easily duped, that I even considered Alejandro may have caused the injuries in those horrifying pictures, either directly or indirectly. Of course he didn't. It's so obvious now. But in the moment, I was left reeling. A little like Alejandro . . .

I'm not okay with how he treated me, but I think I understand it. We're still learning. And we still have a long way to go.

As if sensing my inner turmoil, Bruce Wayne paws at my foot under the conference table. I smile down at the expectant cock of his head. Okay, so maybe he's not picking up on my mood so much as just begging for more dinner, but his presence is still comforting.

Tossing him a piece of beef, I watch him catch it mid-air only to come close to spitting it out. "Sorry," I tell him. "I don't have any chicken left." Our dog may be a bit spoiled.

"Jefe," JJ calls from his office and everyone around the table looks up.

Alejandro gets to his feet, squeezing my shoulder briefly before heading in with Laney and Niner, closing the door solidly behind them. I go back to pushing my food around on the plate.

"Hey," Skippy says from beside me. "Have you seen this?" He shows me the screen of his phone.

"Is that Desiree?" Scott's sister is out with her friends, having a lot more fun than I am tonight. "I didn't know you knew her."

"Yeah, we went to the same high school. She never gave me the time of day though."

At Skip's bitter tone, I have to repress a scoff. *Why are you following her then?* I want to ask, but hold it back. I've had more than enough conflict today.

"You okay?" Skip asks. "You seem a little out of it tonight."

"Eh, a visit from the FBI will do that to a girl."

His eyes widen. "That's what all this is about?" He appears to appraise me. "Wow, I've never rated any attention from the Feds."

He uses that same tone that gives the impression of bitterness, or maybe resentment. Skippy really does need to grow up. "Seems neither do I. The woman was a fake."

"What? Seriously?"

"Yeah, they think it was set up by the lawyer guy."

"Harvey?" he says, sounding shocked.

Nodding, I search for something to give Bruce from Alejandro's plate on my other side.

A minute later, out of the blue, Skip glumly says, "I always liked Harvey. He was the only one who gave a shit about my brother."

I frown. "Rolando?"

"Nah, my oldest brother, Victor. The one rotting in jail."

Flinching at the bitterness he now seems entitled to, I murmur, "Oh, I'm sorry to hear that. I didn't know."

"Yeah, well, I'm not surprised. No one ever talks about him anymore. Sometimes I think I'm the only one who even remembers him."

"I'm sure that's not true. Is there a chance he'll get out soon?"

He snorts. "His appeal has been postponed so many times. Whenever I ask about it, El Jefe brushes me off."

I sympathize with him. Alejandro is dismissive with a lot of people. "Do you want me to ask him about it?"

Skippy's expression wars between hope and defeat before he goes back to his phone. "Yeah, that'd be great," he mumbles.

I've finally decided to call it quits on dinner when a crash comes from the other side of the door, followed by Alejandro's bellowed, "God dammit."

Some of the guys sitting at the other end of the table exchange nervous glances, then jump when the door bursts open and Alejandro barks, "Skip, let's go."

Bruce, who gets up to see what the fuss is about, approaches Alejandro cautiously. As if just remembering our presence, Alejandro's eyes cut from the dog to me. "Mariposa," he says, with low, intimate intensity.

Under the weight of everyone's stares, I have a quick debate with myself; submission or sarcasm? It's not a tough call since poking a grizzly bear when it's already worked up wouldn't be smart, especially not in front of an audience. He intercepts me on my way to him and then corrals me against the wall in the furthest corner of the office.

"I have to go out," he says.

"Okay." I stroke my nails through his beard, feeling the muscles in his jaw clench before he relaxes into my touch. "You didn't catch the guy?"

"He got away," he growls, the intensity back. "He slipped out right before Luis got there, but we've got all his stuff now. It won't be long until I get my hands on his scrawny little neck and this will all be over."

Not going to lie, his intensity sends a nice bolt of lust right between my thighs. "Can you drop me off at home before you go?"

"Of course I can."

Taking my hand, he turns and we find everyone in the room quickly averting their eyes. "Nosy assholes," he mutters, but I hear the note of satisfaction in his voice. He likes that they know I'm a priority. And so do I.

• • • • •

In the morning, Alejandro is falling into bed as I'm getting up for work. By the time I get out of the shower, he's fast asleep. I kiss his brow before heading out with Aaron and Jeremy, a bit disappointed I won't get an update on the lawyer situation.

Work is good; a litter of golden retriever puppies is brought in for shots – so cute – and there are no horrible medical emergencies – thank goodness. And then on the way home, Julie and I are *Snapping* back and forth like we used to in college.

I'm laughing at Julie's last Snapchat when I get a text. A video message. Maybe because I'm feeling so upbeat, or maybe because I know JJ filters my messages, but I hit play without thinking. A heavy baseline fills my ears and I immediately turn the volume down on my AirPods, then use my free hand to block the light because the image is so hard to see. I think I'm watching something from a night club until the camera angle changes slightly, bringing the image into sharper focus. *Ugh.* It's not a nightclub, it's a strip club. A woman in only a thong is giving a lap dance to some guy –

Pain drives into my chest.

Alejandro. The guy is Alejandro. I scramble to stop the video with clumsy fingers. *What the fuck?* Like a hot knife through butter, betrayal sinks deep. *Is that what he was doing last night?* The urge to puke assails me.

No, I don't believe it. I don't. I swear I don't. He wouldn't do that to me. I check the number it came from, but I don't recognize it.

Dread twisting through me, I hit play on the video again. My fingertips tingle with adrenaline as Alejandro comes onto the screen again. He's sitting there, his composed, smug self, suit jacket gone, wearing his shoulder holster, a glass of amber liquid in his hand, as the woman moves. She's graceful and sensual and my gorge rises when she undoes a button on his dress shirt. I can't see her face, but I can see his. It's obvious he's had a few drinks and his eyes are at half-mast; he wants her.

I'm almost grateful that the angle doesn't allow me to actually see him toy with her breast, but as soon as he reaches for her pussy, I can't watch anymore. I'm not fast enough finding the pause button, though, and I get an eyeful of his arm's motion and Tony coming right up to them in the background.

The SUV heads down the ramp into the underground parking garage and the nausea sloshes in my stomach. As Jeremy is waved through security, I clear my throat. "Hey, you guys," my voice wavers and Aaron turns. "Did I hear you say that Tony's back?"

"Uh, yeah," he says. "He got in last night."

With jerky movements, I stuff my phone and my AirPods into my purse. Jeremy opens my door and I slide out onto unsteady legs. He catches my elbow. "You okay?" I give him a terse nod.

We ride the elevator in silence, my dismay growing as the image of Alejandro with another woman etches itself deeper and deeper into my mind. At the penthouse door, I give the guys a weak smile and watch them exchange quizzical looks before I go in.

He didn't do it, I tell myself, but my hand is still shaky as I turn to re-lock the deadbolt. Thankfully at three o'clock on a Friday afternoon, there's no chance Alejandro will be home. Before we come face-to-face, I need to pull myself together, to think about this logically.

"Hey."

My already distressed heart lurches up into my throat at the unexpected voice. I turn and find Alejandro leaning against the kitchen counter eating a sandwich, Bruce Wayne begging at his feet.

"You're jumpy," he says, throwing a piece of sandwich meat to the dog.

I can only stare; his hair is shower-wet and the only stich of clothing on his body is a pair of sweat pants that hang low on his hips, letting me see the V of his abdomen and the tattoos that cover his arms. Under different circumstances, I'd be all over him, but today, my heart feels like it's been laid out on a bed of nails.

His brows rise when I don't say anything. "What's up with you?" He pops the last bite into his mouth, studying me while he chews, then swallows. "Bad day?"

"Where were you last night?" The unplanned words fall from my mouth, but I gain courage when they come out strong and unyielding.

He's not particularly pleased with the question if the way he folds his arms over his chest is anything to go by. "Where do you think? I was working."

It's the same vague answer he always gives if I ask him anything about his day . . . or night. I lift my chin. "That's not good enough this time."

He's even less impressed now. "What's up your ass?"

The last of my patience breaks apart. "Is that necessary?" I retort, then mimic, *"What's up your ass?* I don't talk to you like that."

His eyes flash with something unnameable, but it's not good. "Let me rephrase then. What up your ass, your highness?"

I don't feel the gulf between us very often, but it's never been more evident than this very second. Even after what happened yesterday. Suddenly, I want to chuck every one of our differences into the abyss; the vulgarity, the orders, the security, the death threats, the guns, the violence, the fake FBI, the disgusting video. It's all too much.

I match his defensive posture. "You really want to know what's up my ass? *You are.* With your secrecy and weird hours, expecting me to sit around like a good little pet, waiting for you to show up when you feel like it."

"Don't you mean like a doll?" he tosses back. "I prefer the creepy doll references."

"You're mocking me?" The outrage in my voice rings in the air between us. He doesn't get to be the sarcastic one in this scenario.

"Yeah, I'm mocking you. How about you quit with the dramatics and tell me what *the fuck* is going on."

"Stuart *never* swore at me," I cry. "Why do you –"

"Stuart? You're bringing that mealy-mouthed, little weas–"

"Don't you dare!" Somewhere in the back of my mind, I know this is illogical, but I can't seem to stop myself. "Stuart at least had the decency to –"

"Decency?" He stalks toward me with menace, but I'm not afraid of him and I stand my ground. I'm tall enough that I don't have to crank my neck to see the fierceness of his glare. "You want decency? When I already told you I have none?"

"You never said that," I retort, then my voice betrays me by wavering as I go on, "And you *promised*." To cover the weakness, I poke his chest with my index finger.

His face pinches. "Promised what? You've lost your ffu– you've lost your marbles."

Shame nips at me as he censors himself, but I can't shake the repellent image of that woman grinding on him.

"No. Actually, my marbles are all present and accounted for. It's yours that are missing if you think I'll accept that lame-ass answer you're always handing out like it's a 2-for-1 coupon on the Vegas Strip."

He looks baffled. "What answer?"

My outrage grows. *How dare he be obtuse?* "Where were you last night?" I repeat.

"All right. Enough. I'm done with this conversation." He goes around me and heads down the hall to the bedroom and I scurry after him.

"So you won't tell me? You're basically admitting that you did it?"

He whirls on me and I have to pull up short or crash into him. "What, exactly, are you accusing me of, Sophia?" I hear the warning in his tone, but also the lust, and sure enough, I look down and his dick is starting to tent the loose pants. He likes it when I challenge him.

My eyes travel back up his bare chest to linger on his lips, before they collide with his. Something cutting is on the tip of my tongue when I catch a flicker of vulnerability under all the vexed bravado. He really has no idea what I'm talking about. My stomach lurches because of course he doesn't. This is Alejandro. He doesn't play games and he's never once checked out a woman in my presence.

As we stand there, my ire bleeds away and the balance of power begins to shift back in his favor. "I'm waiting," he says, his tone low and clipped.

When I only bite at my lip nervously, he comes closer, forcing me backwards until I hit the wall. Bracing an elbow next to my head, he leans in. "Do we need to talk before we do this?"

"Do what?" I whisper, blinking up at him, his nearness stirring up the lust that's always simmering right below the surface between us.

"Before we put that mouth of yours to better use."

Desire flares inside of me, hot and intense, but then I remember the lap dance and my gaze lowers. He immediately forces my chin up and his eyes bounce between mine, searching for something. "I asked you a question, mariposa. Talk now or later?"

The thought of showing him the video is about as appealing as admitting that I started this argument knowing he didn't do it . . . or at least didn't do it recently. Yeah, I'm going to go with the orgasms that seem to be up on offer instead. "Later," I tell him, my voice well above the meek whisper I was expecting. I think it surprises him too because his brows lift slightly.

He leans in again, running his nose along my neck to my ear. "I was going to spank you for this little display, but I think I've come up with a better punishment." He places an open-mouthed kiss below my ear and then pushes away. "Strip."

"What? Right here?" My mind is still fumbling with the word *punishment*.

His expression says, *yeah, right here* as he props himself against the wall across from me. "You're dressed like a nun anyway."

"A nun?" I work my jeans down my hips.

"Is there an echo in here?"

"Very funny." My scrubs top comes off, then the long-sleeved turtleneck that I'm wearing underneath it.

"I don't think you'll find much to laugh about soon enough, *mi amor*."

Down to my bra and panties, I pause, but he gestures for me to keep going. It comes to me that I have every intention of putting all my trust in him, so I get rid of the underwear as well.

"Gorgeous," he murmurs, coming forward to meet my lips in a bruising kiss, his tongue pushing into my mouth, setting off white-hot sparks behind my closed eyelids. He encourages me to hook a leg up on his hip and I hum with anticipation when he puts a hand between us. I'm expecting his touch, but he surprises me with his cock as he dips down and shunts himself deep.

We both groan, mine a lot higher pitched and laced with shock than his deep rumble. To relieve some of the awkward angle, I wrap my arms around his neck and lift my other leg. He takes my weight with ease and I become putty in his arms as he carries me down the hall to the dimly lit bedroom.

By the time we reach the bed, I'm trying to ride him, impatient for the glorious feel of him moving in me, but instead of helping, he slides himself out and sets me on my feet.

I make an unhappy noise, but he pins me with a look that shuts me right up, jerking his chin at the mattress. "On your knees," he says. "Ass in the air, face on the bed. Eyes closed."

I'd protest, I swear I would if I didn't love his ordering me around so much. Every word out of his mouth when he gets like this is a blissful contradiction; physically, he ties me up in knots, but mentally, he unwinds me until every trace of worry has been dissolved.

From my position on the bed, I can hear him, first in the bathroom, and then rummaging in the bedside table drawer. I should probably be more apprehensive about his definition of *punishment*, but I'm happy to let him worry about it for me.

He gets on the bed behind me. "Spread your knees more," he commands, his voice stern but his touch gentle on my calf. He traces a line higher, smoothing up my thigh then along my ribs to the butterfly tattoo. He usually never misses an opportunity to obsess over it, but right now it just gets a cursory brush of his fingers before they're sliding back down across my ass. He squeezes a cheek and I suck in a quick breath as he lifts and pulls, exposing me to the cooler air. "Quit your squirming, Sophia, and remind me of your rules."

My mind blanks. *Rules?* My mouth opens to ask him what he's talking about when he brushes his fingertips along my crack, grazing my asshole. Surprise has me jerking away from him, lying myself flat on the bed. Over my shoulder, I see the heated look on his face before he follows me down. The feel of his body covering mine is divine. I love how he presses me into the mattress, his very hard length nestled against my ass.

"Mmmm," he hums next to my ear, his beard tickling my neck and sending delicious shivers rolling down my spine. "You're going to look amazing with my dick in your ass, aren't you?" He curls his hips into me as if to punctuate his point. *Oh, shit.* Those rules.

"Answer me," he whispers. "Tell me how much you want me to work my way into that little hole of yours."

All I respond with are whimpers as his words ricochet inside of me, leaving me hot and cold and desperate all at once.

"Now, we were discussing your rules. There were two if I remember correctly." He pushes up and a waft of air slides across my back. A protest dies in my throat as he bites my shoulder. "The first was lube," he says, now trailing kisses down my spine. "Right?"

I manage a thin noise of agreement, clutching at the duvet in an attempt to ground myself.

He nuzzles the hollow of my lower back, breathing me deep, then licking a path to my tail bone where he places a kiss. "And the second, I believe, was something along the lines of *you go there, you stay there.*" Suddenly his fingers are sliding between my cheeks and I almost come out of my skin as he again brushes against the sensitive nerve-endings, teasingly gentle at first, then with more intention. *Oh my god, oh my god*, starts looping through my head as I try to absorb the sensation.

An arm goes under my hips and lifts me back onto my knees. "Stay there." His fingers haven't even breached me yet and I'm quivering with arousal and nervous restlessness, something that escalates when I hear the pop of the cap on the lube. "Spread your knees again. That's it." His fingers are pulled away for a moment but come back with lube and I let out a half-groan, half-whine as he gently pushes a finger forward.

"Oh, fuck," he says, echoing my very thoughts as I clench around him.

"Alejandro?" leaves my strangled throat.

"*¿Sí, mi amor?*"

Except I have no idea what I want to say, what with all the drowning in anticipation I'm doing.

"You're fine," he reassures me. "And if you behave yourself, I'll even let you touch that hot little clit of yours." I gasp as he adds another lubed finger and pushes in ever so slowly. It doesn't hurt, but it's foreign and not comfortable and the contradictions it evokes are so confusing; yes/no, go/stop, more/less . . . but I *want* the soaring climax it promises.

When he pulls his fingers away, my mind does a tug of war between relief and disappointment. It's all moot, though, as he replaces them with his well-lubed tip, which sinks in and has me sucking in a ragged breath. A scorching-hot, full-body rush of heat races over every inch of my skin, making me break out in a sweat.

"Easy," he soothes, but the strain in his voice is obvious with me clamping down on him. "Oh, fuck, Sophia." He grunts, sliding deeper by an inch. "Just fuck." Another inch. "So much better than I imagined."

But I block him out, my mind struggling with the stretch. He keeps inching forward and little whimpers start falling from my lips. "Okay, okay," he whispers, trying to comfort me. "Come here." An arm crosses my chest and lifts me to vertical. Panic makes an attempt to unmoor me from the decadent confusion until he's able to stabilize me with his other hand between my shoulder blades. I grip the arm across my chest. "Ssshhh," he hushes, slowly sitting back on his haunches and taking me with him. "Almost there."

We get to the point where he has to continue easing into me and another wave of heat burns like wildfire across my skin. I'm about to let out a *stop* when finally his thighs meet mine and the reassuring feel of his chest meeting my back has me releasing the breath I was holding. He wraps his other arm around me and I relax as best I can into his warmth as he whispers endearments that I can't quite hold onto with my mind spinning so hard.

I turn my head, needing to be closer to him and he catches my lips with his own. Our tongues tangle and desire surges in me again. Wherever this is going . . *desperate* barely come close to describing it.

A familiar low hum has me wrenching my eyes open. Before my mind catches up, he puts my vibrator to my clit and immediately cracks me open into a million little pieces of euphoria.

CHAPTER 20

Alejandro

Holy fuck.

Dropping the vibrator, I hold her against my chest as she chokes on a scream, her entire body convulsing with the climax, the rhythmic clenching like a velvet vise around my dick.

Over the years, there's never been a shortage of women willing to let me fuck them any way I please. But this is different. This is my mariposa trusting me when I'm not at all sure I've earned it. This is me about to be overwhelmed with how much I love her. How much I need and want her.

She finally stops coming and hangs almost limply in my arms, trying to catch her breath. Jesus, I'm all the way up her ass and if the urge to move gets any greater, my head will implode. Holding her more tightly, I give an experimental curl of my hips. While she only manages a soft huff, I almost pass out with how good it is.

I've got just enough of my sanity left to go slow, to keep my strokes short and easy, to savor every single second. When Sophie's writhing and mewling re-intensifies, I force myself to still and put the vibrator to her clit again. It takes a little longer to lure this climax from her than the first, but when it comes, it's spectacular with her shuddering and straining in my arms. I surge up into her once, twice, and then let myself follow her headlong into a mind-numbing orgasm.

Her trembling is the first thing that registers with me as I come back to myself. Shit. As gently as possible, I pull my softening dick from her and turn her in my arms. She's dazed all right, but more in a loopy way than an *I'm about to cry* way.

Her head lolls on my arm, but I pull her chin back and she finally focuses on me. "Are you trying to kill me?" she whispers, and my heart soars at the little grin on her lips.

"You okay? Did I hurt you?"

She snorts out a laugh. "I may never walk again, but it was so worth it."

Relief, sweet and true, sweeps away the worry as I push up on my knees and then carry her to the bathroom. I set her down on her feet to get the water started in the shower. Turning back, I see her wincing and get hit with a big helping of guilt.

"Don't look at me like that," she teases. "I'll feel better once I'm cleaned up."

Closing the shower door behind us, she groans under the heat of the water, while I wonder how I got so lucky. I grab her shower gel and get my ass to work taking care of her.

"Soph?"

"Hhhmm?"

"You'll tell me if I'm messing things up, right?"

She cracks an eyelid to study me as an ache starts behind my sternum. The thought of losing her because I'm an asshole seems not just likely, but probable. Look what I did to her yesterday. And now today. Instead of coaxing what's wrong from her, my instincts told me to bring her to heel, and I listened.

"I don't think things through sometimes," I tell her, gliding my soapy hands down an arm. "As soon as I feel like things are slipping from my control, I . . . I hold on tighter."

"Can I assume that *hold on tighter* is your euphemism for . . ." She waves her hand in the direction of the bedroom.

Rinsing my hands, I frame her face. Her glorious blond hair is plastered to her head, her eye makeup is smudged, and the apples of her cheeks are splotched with red while the rest of her complexion is too pale. And she's the most painfully beautiful woman I've ever seen. Not because of genetics, but because her sweet, gentle nature has swallowed me whole. No matter how ill-matched we are, I'll always love her.

"It's not a euphemism . . . it's who I am."

"I know," she says simply, pushing up on her toes to kiss me. "And it was you who told me that's why it's so good between us."

I feel a smirk creeping up on me. "Did I say that?"

"You did."

"But that doesn't mean it's always healthy." As soon as I say the words, I hear how true they are. "We haven't even talked about what got you so upset."

She grimaces.

"I'm not going to like it, am I?"

"Someone's trying to screw with us. At least I hope that's what it is. If not, I'll have to castrate you."

The malice on her face has me seriously wondering what could have happened. "All right. Let's finish up here and we'll deal with it."

When we're done, I give her some privacy and pull on my discarded sweats and a T-shirt. In the kitchen, I find my phone on the island counter. Before I can even unlock the screen, it lights up with Niner's name. I sigh as I answer. "What is it, *güey?*"

"Why aren't you answering? We've got a problem."

"When do we not?" He must hear something in my voice because in a very un-Niner-like way, he's quiet long enough for me to say more. "Can it wait a half hour? I've got shit going on here."

"Uhhh," he considers. "Not really."

"Let me put it this way," I say sharply. "If the world isn't ending, I need at least thirty minutes."

"Fine. But no more."

The bastard hangs up, but my irritation fades when I see how many calls I've missed. Five from Niner. One from Luis. And three from Rolando. *For fuck's sake.* But I don't care if the world *is* ending. Nothing is more important than Sophie.

I flop down on the sofa and let that thought roll around in my head. *Nothing is more important than Sophie.* It's the truth. I can't think of anything or anyone that means more to me. My actual family mostly ditched me long ago, and sure, my team are my chosen family, but compared to Sophie? And when I look down at the *Los Santos* tattoo that takes up the entire inside of my forearm, I feel so much weight. I think I keep the organization fisted so tightly because I'm convinced if I let go, everything will go to hell and we'll all end up in jail or dead. A prison cell or a pine box, isn't that the saying?

Sophie appears from the hall, barefoot, wearing yoga pants and a loose tank top over a sports bra. Finishing up the second of two braids in her wet hair, she stops in front of her purse on the floor, where she let it drop earlier, and exhales loudly.

"What?" I ask.

"You've rendered me incapable of bending down that far."

"Huh?" Then I realize what she means. "Oh." Guilt pricks at my conscience again. "I'll get it for you."

"Thanks."

Passing it to her, I say the first thing that comes to mind to distract us from what I've done. "My mother believes if you leave your purse on the floor, you'll always be poor."

She gingerly lowers herself onto the couch and says in an exhausted voice, "Good thing my one true love knows how to cheat the system and won't let me starve."

More guilt. She sounds so unlike herself. Watching her dig through her purse, I hope she's upset by what she has to show me and not me *punishing* her. She pulls out her cellphone, swipes at the screen few times, and hands it to me.

At first, the image is too dark to make anything out, but as soon as I see what it is, my molars feel ready to splinter with how hard I'm clenching my jaw. "What. The. Fuck?" I grind out. "Who sent you this?"

"Those are my questions," she says dryly.

No wonder she was in a rage. If I saw her with some guy, I'd lose my shit, no question. Regardless of when it took place . . . *son of a bitch*. "You thought this is what I was doing last night? I've *told* you I haven't even looked at another woman almost since the day we met."

"Yeah, I know. I didn't –"

"I mean, my beard's way shorter here and that's Crystal. She's been –"

"Stop talking immediately! I do *not* want to hear about *Crystal*."

I snap my mouth shut.

"And I *didn't* believe you'd done it," she goes on peevishly. "I was in shock. Surely you can understand that, especially since you never give me any real information."

I start to protest, but she cuts me off.

"Let's not go around that bush again. I just need you to make sure this never happens again."

Holding back a few sullen words, I look back at the video and fury starts to reboil my blood. "You didn't watch the whole thing, did you?" I don't give her a chance to answer before I move on to a more relevant question. "How did it get on your phone in the first place?" I check, but the number the video came from seems to be random. "JJ's software doesn't allow . . . unless . . ." I grab my phone off the coffee table. Unless it's from someone who's cleared to send Sophie a message, but who's not in her contacts yet. Sitting next to her, I type the number into my phone.

And it comes up with a name. *Mother fucker*.

"Skippy?" Sophie scoffs.

My brain starts to pinball. That dumb little shit. I'll kill him. What in the *hell* did he hope to achieve? There's zero logic here. Did he think there wouldn't be any consequences? "I want to know where he got the video. It's at least three or four years old. He was a kid back then."

"You mean *more* of a kid?" Sophie retorts.

There's a loud knock at the door. Damn. I forgot about Niner. "Yeah," I yell, almost annoyed I've told everyone to stop walking into my place now that Sophie's living here. Niner tries the door, but of course it's locked, and we hear him swearing on the other side as his keys jingle.

"Niner has a key to our apartment?" Sophie asks with a raised eyebrow.

I can't even summon a smile though. What are the chances he's here about the video? Not good, I think tiredly. And then, worse, it's not only Niner who walks through the door, but Luis, Rolando, Skippy, and Jeremy too. Unease churns in my gut. "No one said this was going to be a fucking party."

Niner sits on the end of the coffee table, facing me, jaw shifting from side to side. Luis, then Skippy, then Rolando file in to stand in the space between the table and the flat screen on the wall, while Jeremy stays at the door, like a sentry. Unease becomes foreboding. I don't like this – at all.

"Sophie," I say in a low voice. "I need you to go to the bedroom."

"No," she says, zeroed in on Skippy. "I want to hear this."

He must catch what she says, because he announces, "You deserved to know."

Okay, maybe this *is* about the video.

"Know what?" she grits out. "That he had a life before me?"

Skip's brows draw down in confusion. "Try last week."

"You're *such* a moron," she says.

"Okay, hold up," Niner interrupts. "Entertaining as whatever this is." He gestures between Sophie and Skip. "It can wait. Rolando's got a few things to get off his chest."

Rolando? I eye them all again and realize Rolando looks like he's going to be sick and Luis is stiffer than usual. *What is going on?* I don't like that I'm not armed. And Sophie is still in the room.

"Mariposa," I say, doing my utmost not to be harsh. "I asked you to leave."

"Jefe," Rolando says, his voice rough. "Can *La Mariposa* stay? Please?"

I rise to my feet, because he has no right to even speak her name, let alone her nickname. Niner catches my attention with a shake of his head, warning me to hold off.

"Start. Talking."

Rolando takes a shaky breath. "It's not . . . I just . . . I . . ."

"What the hell is this, Rolo?" Skippy demands, which confuses me more. *He doesn't know?*

"Shut it, *chamaco,*" Niner snaps.

"You shut it! You're the *chamaco,* following El Jefe around like a little kid."

Almost before Skippy can finish his sentence, Luis takes a step and has his gun to Skip's temple. "Not. Another. Word." Everyone in the room freezes except the dog who's on his feet now, not liking the energy in the room. "Agreed?"

Skip nods faintly, clearly stunned. Luis lowers the gun but doesn't holster it.

"Someone better tell me what's going on," I bite out.

Rolando's shoulder slump. "It was me, Jefe. I take full responsibility for all of it."

"What the fff –" Skippy starts, but Luis cuts him off by half-raising the gun again.

"Responsibility for what?" I despise not knowing what's going on.

"For . . . for feeding the lawyer information."

"I'm sorry, *what?*"

This is about Harvey Sharkane?

And Rolando Arraya has been feeding him information?

My thoughts stumble over the idea, and then I snort with derision. "I don't think so. Try again." Rolando is not stupid and only a complete idiot would betray *Los Santos* from the inside. My gaze slowly moves to Skippy.

"Bingo," Niner says softly.

"No, Jefe," Rolando pleads. "It was me."

A pin dropping could be heard for how silent the room is until I say, "Is that right?" I plant my hands on my hips. "You got anything to say, Skip?"

"I don't know what he's talking about," the kid says shakily.

"You don't? Where'd you get the video then?"

His head jerks back and the deer in the headlights expression would be comical if the repercussions of what he's done weren't reverberating through my soul. *Oh, Skip.* The world we inhabit is not a forgiving one. Not even for a kid with two big brothers near the top.

"You already admitted you sent it . . ." I let that hang there as if to imply the game is up, he may as well confess.

No confessions though. All I get are a litany of desperate denials and claims of innocence that get old very quickly. "Shut the fuck up, Skip." I turn to Rolando, whose brow is dotted with sweat. "How and when did you find out?"

"It was me, I swe–"

"*How* and *when* did you find out?"

The defeat on his face is almost painful to look at. "A few days ago," he whispers, lowering his gaze to the carpet. "JJ asked me if I'd met Angela."

"Rolo!" Skip cries and when my glare isn't enough to silence him, Luis raises the gun again.

"Who's Angela?" I ask.

"She doesn't exist," Rolando says, defeated. "I went through Skip's phone. They were hiding their text messages in between dick pics and pussy shots. Anything important was sent in between raunchy sexting so JJ wouldn't look too closely."

"That's pretty smart, Skip. I'm going to go out on a limb and say it was Harvey's idea, because you've obviously got the brains of a fence post. I mean, why would you help a guy who arranged hits that would have included you?"

"Oh my god," Sophie says in a horrified voice and everyone turns. *"That's* why you ran?"

Ran? When did Skippy run? She gets to her feet and goes around the coffee table, surprising us all by throwing herself toward Skip, pushing him hard. "Coward!" She shoves him again and the dog starts barking. "You brought them to the cabin and then you ran!"

"It was Laney's fault!" he says as Sophie goes for him again, but this time, I reach for her because it's obvious that Skip's about to retaliate.

"Touch her," my tone cuts through the disbelief in the room as I haul Sophie back against me, "and I'll kill you right now." I snap my fingers and Bruce Wayne quiets and comes to stand next to us.

"No, *I'll* kill you," Luis says, lifting the gun once again. "If you don't explain yourself. What about Laney?"

Skip backs up, but hits the TV, running out of room like the cornered rat he is.

"What about Laney?" Luis repeats, losing patience.

"She was complaining about some veterinarian in that town in Oregon who wouldn't give you an appointment right away."

My mind goes back to our time at the cabin and yeah, we had to wait a few days to take Bruce Wayne to the vet. "So what?"

"So, nothing. I heard the name of the town and the appointment time."

Luis narrows his eyes at Skippy. "How the fuck is that on Laney?"

"Well, she should have been more careful with –"

The safety is off and Luis has the gun pressed to Skip's gut before anyone can blink.

"Luis," I say softly. *"Ahora no es el lugar, ni el momento." This is not the time or the place.*

He backs off, but there's hatred in his eyes and a nasty sneer on his lips as Rolando moans, "Oh, god."

"This is all your fault!" Skippy bursts out.

"They were always going to find out!" Rolando yells back, his fear boiling over. "This isn't a game. You'll end up at the bottom of the Bay."

And there it is, reality giving Skip a nice, solid bitch-slap. His eyes dart between me, Luis, then land back on his brother. "But I stopped! Harvey kept pestering me about Sophie, so I stopped giving him anything. I swear I did."

"So then it's okay?!" Sophie shrieks, trying to break from my hold.

"Ssshhh, mi amor," I soothe, refusing to let her go.

Watching us, Skip's face screws up with disgust. "He doesn't give a shit about anyone except himself! I don't know why no one else sees that. He always treats me like trash, and –"

Niner laughs. "You have *got* to be kidding me. Are you for real?"

"Apparently," Luis drawls.

"– and," Skip yells over Niner and Luis, sounding outraged and triumphant now, like he's playing a trump card. "He doesn't want Victor to come home!" He turns a beseeching look on Rolando. "How can you be loyal to him? Harvey told me he's never made Victor's appeal a priority."

It's my turn to laugh, because I truly can't believe what I'm hearing. "Harvey told you this? The guy I've paid *hundreds* of thousands of dollars to in legal fees? The guy who's been missing for almost a year, forcing us to postpone Victor's appeal?"

Skip's mouth opens, then closes, not sure what to say to that.

"Please, Jefe," Rolando begs. "Harvey was snowing him. You gotta believe me. He applied all the right pressure to all the right buttons. Let me take responsibility. For all of it."

"That's not how this works and you know it." I contemplate the older brother for a few moments. "Harvey got away last night."

Rolando gives a tight nod. "I know. That's why I'm here. Skip won't listen to reason."

"And this garbage with the video?" I ask, turning to Skippy.

He fidgets on his feet, but continues with the bluster. "Like I said, she deserved to know."

"I'm going to be sick," Sophie announces, tugging at my arm and I let her go. She heads down the hall, the dog following her.

Luis gives me a nod, letting me know he'll handle the initial stages of this cluster fuck. Before I can follow my girl though, Niner is asking, "What I don't get, even if you don't *like* your boss, is how you could you let our own guys get hacked up? You knew Damon and Chuey almost your whole life."

Naked confusion sketches itself onto Skip's features. "What've they got to do with it?"

"Who," Niner says with false calm, "did you think was responsible for their deaths?"

Watching Skip realize how far out of his depth he is is just sad.

"Harvey wouldn't do that."

This time, it's Niner who loses it and he's a lot stronger than Sophie. Fury has him up and planting a foot in the middle of the coffee table to launch himself at Skip. His fist comes down squarely on his jaw. "You stupid fucker!" Skip's head snaps back, hitting the wall and he crumples to the floor.

I leave them to it. Skippy has dug his own grave; now he's going to have to lie in it.

"Soph?" I call as I reach the bedroom. She's opened the blinds and is standing directly in front of the floor-to-ceiling windows, watching the traffic below. "You okay?"

"Not particularly. I can't believe I ever felt sorry for him."

Leaning my back to the glass next to her, I wait for her to look at me. It takes a solid minute, but she finally relents and shows me her big, blue eyes. They're full of conflicting emotions.

"What's going to happen to him?" she whispers.

"I don't know yet."

"You're not a very good liar, you know that, right?"

I search her features for condemnation or censure, but I don't find it. I'm actually surprised she's not coming down on the side of mercy. "I never want you to worry about something like this." I wouldn't wish the weight of this burden on anyone, let alone her. And this one is going to be a heavy one to bear.

She only nods and lets me pull her into my arms. "It's not always like this, is it?"

"Honestly," I say, laying my cheek on her head. "There hasn't been this much going on since the first few years after I took over. Once we get Harvey, it will all calm down. You'll see."

Now I just need to get my hands cn the traitorous bastard, I think darkly as she leans more fully into me. Closing my eyes, I soak up the feel of my woman putting her trust in me.

CHAPTER 21

Sophie

Though it feels like it should, Skippy's betrayal doesn't stop the world from turning. Life continues, day by day. I still go to work, I still go to therapy. Alejandro still comes home to me most nights. Everything's the same – on the surface. Underneath, however, there's a lingering sadness. Skippy wasn't an insignificant part of our lives and Alejandro has known him since he was a boy. If events have hit me hard, I can only imagine the emotional toll they're taking on him.

For my own peace of mind, I haven't asked many questions about Skippy or Rolando. All I know is that they're not around anymore. Maybe I'm a coward . . . or maybe I'm worried that I'm not who I thought I was. I'm grieving, yes, but I can't forgive. Is this me now? Pitiless and hard? After puzzling it over, I conclude my problem is Alejandro's involvement. If Skippy had tried to kill me, I feel like I'd have an easier time finding some forgiveness. But attacking the man I love? Turns out I'm fine with pitiless and hard.

The only positive outcome has been how Alejandro and I have grown closer, as if our shared sorrow has wrapped our souls more tightly together.

Two weeks after the scene in the penthouse, on a Friday night, or I guess a Saturday morning now since it's almost two in the morning, and Alejandro and I are on the bed, making out after a date night at Analena. It starts off languid and slow, all deep kisses and wandering hands, but with every piece of clothing that comes off, the urgency grows.

When his phone rings from the bedside table, it takes a moment for our lips to come to a halt. Alejandro's phone almost never actually rings since only a select few have direct access to him. And considering the time of night, it can't be good news. He groans as he rolls over to reach for it.

I watch him check the screen before he jackknifes into a sitting position and accepts the call.

"Char?" he answers in an odd tone that my wine-buzzed brain needs a second to identify as fearful. It's not something I've ever heard from him. My concern doubles down on itself as it clicks who *Char* is. I search the duvet for something to put on. It doesn't seem right to be sitting here, naked, while Alejandro talks to his ex-wife and the mother of his children.

"Okay," he finally says after listening for quite a while. "So you need a lawyer?" Pause. "Don't worry. I'll handle it." Pause. "Just don't say anything until you talk to the lawyer." Alejandro's normally guarded expression grows uneasy. "I don't think that's necessary."

Charlene's voice gets loud enough that he pulls the phone away from his ear, wincing. "Okay. I . . . I'll be there by morning." He listens some more "I promised you I would." Pause. "Okay, bye." He hangs up and presses the end of the phone to his forehead as if in thought.

"What's going on?" I ask.

Blowing out a heavy breath, he takes my hand in one of his while he works on the phone with the other. He calls Laney, putting it on speaker.

"This better be important, Jefe," she gripes. I hear her close a door somewhere to muffle the noise of a party or a nightclub.

Alejandro doesn't bother with pleasantries. "I need a criminal defense lawyer in Denver ASAP, one who specializes in young offenders."

"For real? Tyler or Samson?"

"Tyler," he says. "It's serious, so we need someone with connections. Throw as much money at it as you need to."

My mind races. *Tyler? Tyler's only in ninth grade.*

"And we need a plane. We leave for Denver as soon as possible. You, me, Soph, Niner, I guess Luis if he's willing, Tony if he's not, Jeremy and Aaron."

"All right. I'll start on the lawyer, then arrange transport."

Laney hangs up and Alejandro drops the phone like it's a hot coal.

"What happened?"

"Apparently, the kid left the scene of a car accident."

I frown. "That's not a crime, is it?"

"It is if you were driving. And the car is stolen."

"What?! Isn't he only fifteen?"

"Yeah," he says gravely. "The woman in the other car is in serious condition, but it looks like she'll pull through, so there won't be any manslaughter charges."

I gape at him. "And your . . . Charlene wants to you to go to Denver?"

"She says they can't handle him anymore."

Watching him rub a hand over his beard, I grapple with what that means. "And?"

"And I have no clue." His eyes swing in my direction and narrow on his dress shirt I've pulled on. "What the hell is this?" He doesn't give me a chance to say anything, just fists the hair at the back of my neck and pulls me to his mouth. Soon all coherent thought has fled and I'm nothing but a panting, climaxing mess as he drives into me.

I'm not sure if the orgasm helps him to calm down, but it works like a charm on me, probably because it's combined with the wine in my system. I must doze off for a bit, because the next thing I know, he's waking me. It's five a.m. and we'll be leaving in thirty minutes.

He hasn't left me much time and I'm soon doubting his claim that it's okay for me to go in jeans, a hoodie, and my Chucks because he looks like a million bucks, as always, in his perfect suit. But he ushers me into the elevator regardless. Downstairs, two Tahoes are idling and everyone is assembled. Laney is still in a glittering black mini-dress from last night, her cell phone pressed to her ear and I notice Luis is more dressed up than usual. *Were they out together?*

Niner is abnormally quiet on the way to the airport, but I suppose everyone is. Jeremy is yawning behind the wheel and Alejandro is lost in his own thoughts. I know he hasn't slept.

The quiet continues on the two and a half hour flight with most people trying to catch some more sleep. Laney is up and working on her laptop though and Luis is on his phone beside her. Niner and Alejandro exchange a few words here and there in Spanish, probably about Charlene if they don't want me to understand. They can't think I'd be jealous of a woman who left Alejandro fifteen years ago, can they? But with them both on edge, I keep my thoughts to myself.

The sky has brightened to full morning by the time we step off the plane and find two SUV's waiting for us. Even though it's mid-March, it's cold and windy in Denver and there's still snow piled up at the sides of the runway. I wish I'd thought to bring a coat.

Alejandro and I share a small, knowing smile when Laney, who's now wearing Luis's leather jacket over her dress, gets into the front seat of the SUV he's driving. Since New Year's they haven't really been seen together, but it seems like that's changed.

We slide into the other vehicle, with Jeremy driving and Niner riding shotgun. Twenty minutes later, we reach the precinct where Tyler is being held. Street parking is readily available since it's Saturday morning.

Laney gives us an update on the sidewalk. "Okay, there's a meeting between the assistant district attorney, the lawyer, and Tyler's parents that should be wrapping up about now." She scans our little group before saying, "The riff raff all stays out here, which means only El Jefe, Sophie, and I are going in."

Niner laughs. "You'll be lucky if you don't end up in lock-up with the hookers in that dress."

She gives him a cutting smile. "If the patriarchy wants to take me on, I'm always willing."

"Is that how you seduced Luis here, with your *willingness?*"

Luis doesn't appreciate that and counters with something in Spanish that's obviously a threat. Alejandro just takes my hand and starts walking, grumbling something about imbeciles under his breath. Laney falls into step with us as we cross the street.

"Never thought I'd walk into a cop shop voluntarily," he says.

"Yeah, no shit," Laney says absently, checking her phone. "Charlene says they'll meet us in the lobby."

"You know her?" I ask.

"I arrange her child support payments, so no, not really. Let's get in there and see what's going on."

On the other side of the doors is a run-of-the-mill lobby. It's empty of people except for the cop behind the reception desk and a small huddle of people, who turn as we approach. One of them I recognize from the picture in Alejandro's home office. His son, Tyler. A son who looks even more like him in person.

"Oh, wow," I whisper and I feel Alejandro's steps falter alongside my own.

"Alex," one of the women says and it takes me a second to associate the name with Alejandro.

We cross the last few feet and I come face to face with his ex-wife. Charlene is quite a bit shorter than I am, but that's where the differences end. *Holy crap*. Like me, she's a slender, natural blonde whose blue eyes blaze in the natural light coming in through the windows.

"I wasn't sure you'd come," she says in a slightly peevish tone.

"I said I would."

To that, she makes a noise that would have rivalled my *babcia's* harrumph were she still with us. I've already decided not to be a cliché and despise the woman, so I don't take offense when her eyes slide over me dismissively and move on to Laney.

"I'm Elaine Ng," Laney says to the lawyer, shaking her hand and ignoring Charlene. I have to repress a smile at the silent rebuke; I guess she didn't like the way Charlene spoke to Alejandro. "You must be Whitney Rodalno. Thank you for coming on such short notice. Please tell us what you know."

Ms. Rodalno is a middle-aged woman in a power suit whose brusque demeanor matches Laney's. "So the child," she starts and Tyler scoffs.

"Quiet," Charlene scolds, making her son look mutinous.

"So the *child*," the lawyer says again, unkindly emphasizing the word. "Has been released into the care of his parents for now. Charges have not been laid, but they will be. The offense is serious enough that the ADA is looking to make an example of him."

"Of course they are," Alejandro mutters.

Ms. Rodalno nods. "Exactly. Children of color are disproportionately represented in the system for a reason. What we want to avoid is a transfer hearing which could lift him out of juvenile court. Having him tried as an adult would not be to our advantage."

"So you'll take the case?" Laney asks.

"Of course. The retainer you provided will cover expenses for now. I'll be in touch."

"Thank you," Laney says and the lawyer leaves with a quiet goodbye.

Attention turns back to Charlene . . . and her husband, who I barely noticed until now. He's an older guy with thinning red hair and a very fair complexion. It couldn't be more obvious that he's not Tyler's biological father. If I remember correctly, his name is Doug.

"Why am I here, Char?" Alejandro asks.

"Because we can't do this on our own anymore."

"What does that mean?"

"It means that I'm at the end of my rope. He's completely out of control."

"I'm standing right here, Mom."

She turns to Tyler. "Yes, you are, in the middle of a police station, after spending the night in jail because you almost killed a woman. You've gone too far this time, Tyler. You're going to stay with Alex for a while."

"What?" father and son say at the same time and my heart flutters in my chest.

"It's either that," Charlene says. "Or military school."

"That's not even a real thing," Tyler retorts.

"Oh, it is. Believe me, I've checked."

"You can't make me go," he explodes.

"Son," Doug says, placing a hand on his shoulder, but Tyler jerks away.

"This is bullshit!"

The yelling has the police officer at the reception desk getting to his feet.

"Enough," Alejandro says in that cutting, authoritative voice of his, drawing everyone's attention, especially his son's. "We're not discussing this here."

"At home then," Charlene says, pulling out her phone. "I'm texting Laney the address." She starts to go, but as if she's just remembered something, she turns back. "Thank you for coming, Alex," she whispers before she's followed from the building by her husband and her son who takes at least three curious peeks over his shoulder as he goes.

• • • • •

Charlene and Doug Russell live in a very upscale subdivision that features cookie-cutter mini-mansions, perfectly manicured lawns, and expensive SUV's in every driveway. It's the picture of suburban bliss and trying to picture Alejandro living his life here has me drawing blanks.

"Welcome to the land of minivans, the PTA, and DILFs in running shorts," Niner announces, craning his neck to watch a guy who's probably training for an Ironman run by on the sidewalk.

Jeremy fails to fully stifle a chuckle as he parks behind Luis on the street in front of the house. "You want me to wait here, Jefe?" he asks.

"No. I'm not leaving you guys out in this cold."

On the ride over, Niner tried his best to grill Alejandro, but my man wasn't very forthcoming. Probably because he's as shell-shocked as I am. A teenager living with us? Ridiculous. The only thing either Alejandro or I know about teenagers is that we used to be one. Which I think may be Charlene's point since Alejandro has walked in some very similar shoes in the past.

We've all arrived at the same time, and as we get out of the vehicles, I see that Tyler is examining us as closely as everyone is examining him.

"He looks so much like you," I say only for Alejandro as we walk up the drive.

"He does . . . what do you make of all this?"

I chew my lip before I tell him the truth. "I think maybe you could help him see his life from a different angle."

As we go up the steps, I catch a glimpse of a grimace which could stem from so many different places, but now is not the time to ask him about it.

Inside the front door is a cavernous foyer, complete with a chandelier that glows in the morning sunshine. Despite the size of the entryway, we fill the space quickly and Charlene frowns at all the people. I actually feel sorry for the woman. She's obviously had a really rough night.

"That scowl's not for me, is it?" Niner asks, stepping forward. "Because I sure as hell didn't do anything to earn it."

A grudging smile tilts the corners of Charlene's mouth. "How is it you look the same, Niner?"

He pulls her into a hug. "How do you think? I have incredible genes, just like you. You don't look a day over . . ." he pauses for dramatic effect, ". . . twenty-five."

Charlene pulls back, now sporting a full-blown smile. "Flatterer."

Laney makes a noise of disgust. "Not that this isn't riveting, but we have a plane to catch. Let's move this along."

"Yeah, okay," Charlene says wearily. "We can talk privately in the kitchen if the rest of your people want to stay here in the front room." She gestures to a room off the foyer and then heads down the hall.

I make to join the others, but Alejandro gives me a look of exasperation as he tows me along with him through to the back of the house.

There's a bit of an awkward pause in the kitchen until Alejandro takes control like he always does, extending his hand to Doug. "I didn't do this earlier," he says as they shake. "It's good to see you again."

"Yeah, same. I wish it were under better circumstances. Thanks for coming."

"This is my girlfriend, Sophie.'

"Hi, nice to meet you," I say, shaking his very limp hand. I remember Alejandro describing Doug as being everything he's not. If he meant mild-mannered and overly-polite, he wasn't wrong. I get the feeling Doug would give me his last nickel if I asked for it and would thank me for taking it. Which isn't a bad thing, it's just the very opposite of Alejandro.

Charlene invites us to sit around a large rectangular, farm-style dining table and Alejandro doesn't waste any time. "Tyler, come and sit down. This concerns you."

From where he's skulking in the doorway, he drags his feet like he's about to line up for a firing squad and slouches in a chair at the far end of the table.

Charlene lets out a sigh and puts it as plainly as she can. "We can't handle him anymore. He didn't even have permission to leave the house last night. Short of locking him in his room, I have no way to control him."

To someone who doesn't know him well, Alejandro appears perfectly at ease. But I do, and he's anything but. "What does that have to do with me?"

"Are you serious right now?" Charlene's voice raises an octave.

In contrast, Alejandro's voice lowers. "Are you?"

Doug clears his throat. "She –" He winces, probably because Charlene's grabbing his leg under the table. "*We* thought maybe it would be a good idea for you to take him for a while, even if it's only for the duration of Spring break . . . or maybe for the summer." It's obvious that Doug doesn't like the idea, but if the dark circles under his eyes are anything to go by, he's at the end of his rope too.

"I know exactly jack-shit about being a parent. You know this, Charlene."

"Well," she snaps. "Maybe it's time you learned."

"Don't make it sound like it's all on me that I don't know my kids."

Poor Doug flinches, but Charlene shoots back with, "You made your choices." Her hostile tone elicits one of Alejandro's trademark glares, the one that intimidates almost everyone.

His ex-wife, however, is unaffected. I can't say the same; the escalating tension doesn't sit well with me.

"Okay," I say. "This isn't helpful."

Charlene shoots me a dirty look. "Nobody asked you. Flavors of the week don't get a say."

"Charlene," Alejandro growls in warning, but I defend myself.

"Actually, I'm more of a permanent fixture. And don't make me regret my decision not to hate you on sight, all right? Let's just stick to the problem at hand." I turn to Tyler. "Would you like to come stay with us for the rest of spring break?"

"You can't leave it up to him," Charlene says, verging on outraged now.

Before Tyler can respond, a voice from the doorway says, "Mom, what's going on?"

Beside me, Alejandro stills as his other son walks into the room.

"What's with all the people in the living room?" he asks, going to the fridge and coming out with a carton of orange juice, scanning over us briefly before getting a glass from the cupboard.

Charlene heaves a long-suffering sigh. "Your brother got arrested last night."

"Again." He doesn't sound surprised. "What'd you do this time?" he asks Tyler.

On closer inspection, Samson appears worse for wear and I realize he's just come home from being out all night.

"It's much more serious this time," his mother answers. "And Alex and *Sophie*," she draws my name out as she gestures to us, "are going to take him back to California with them."

"I haven't agreed to that," Alejandro declares in a voice that doesn't allow for contradiction. "I'm not sure dumping your kid with strangers is a good idea."

"What's he talking about, Mom? Who is this guy?"

"This is Alejandro—"

"Whoa," Samson interrupts. "Alejandro? *The* Alejandro?" His eyes clamp onto his biological father as he takes a few steps forward.

"Yeah," Charlene says reluctantly. "*The* Alejandro."

"Really?"

I don't think Alejandro knows what to expect. So far, Tyler hasn't approached him, but Samson comes around the table and Alejandro gets to his feet. There's nothing aggressive or even put out in the son's approach, but the father seems to expect him to lash out somehow.

"Wow, this is totally surreal," Samson says, surveying Alejandro up and down again then sticking his hand out. "Sam Russell."

Cautiously, Alejandro shakes his hand. "Alejandro Bernal-Acosta."

"You're the one who's giving me the . . . uh, scholarship for Harvard, right? I can't thank you enough." Though Samson favors his mother in many ways, including his skin tone, side-by-side, it's obvious that his height and build are all Alejandro.

"You're thanking me?" Alejandro says, incredulous.

Samson's unsure now. "Should I not? Is Mom blackmailing you or something?"

"Good grief," Charlene says. "Of course I'm not blackmailing him. I've always told you that he was more than generous, but he couldn't be in your lives." She looks to Alejandro. "And I always said I wouldn't poison them against you."

Alejandro sits back down as if defeated and I cover his hand where it sits on the table. "I know," he says. "And I'm grateful." He looks up at Samson. "You shouldn't thank me. You're the one who did all the work. The least I can do is pay for it."

"Oh, please," Tyler says, making gagging noises. "Everyone already knows what a hero you are, Sam."

He's getting up from the table when Alejandro's voice cuts through the room. "Sit down."

Even Tyler seems surprised that he obeys, but that doesn't stop him from moaning some more. "Why? I already know you won't take me. I've been asking about you for years, but Mom never gives me a straight answer."

His words catch Alejandro off guard for a second, then, "Stop the martyr routine and answer Sophie's question. Do you want to come stay with us for the rest of spring break?"

I don't miss the spark of interest in him. "Really?"

"It'll be my rules, though. I doubt you'll like them."

Tyler shrugs like only a teenager can, nonchalance and disdain at full volume.

"And you can't bring your phone," Alejandro adds.

That gets Tyler's attention. "Why not?"

"Because you don't need whatever asshole friends got you into this mess."

He considers that. "I can really go?" he asks his mom.

"Yes, sweetheart," Charlene says, some emotion finally bleeding through the rock-solid façade she's been trying to maintain.

"Go pack some shit," Alejandro commands and I swear I see Tyler brighten more with every curse word used. "We're leaving as soon as possible."

CHAPTER 22

Alejandro

From the backseat of the SUV, I watch the kid . . . *my kid* say goodbye to his family on the front porch. His mom tries to smother him with a hug, which he endures, looking like he's just eaten a cockroach. Little does he know those will dry up if he continues the way he is, and he'll miss them when they're gone – like I do.

Fucking regret. I hate it. Almost as much as I miss the affection of my mother.

Tyler approaches the vehicle with caution, lugging a duffel bag on his shoulder.

"Ayúdale," I tell Niner who gets down from the driver's seat and *helps* him stow his stuff in the back. I sent Jeremy to ride with Luis because I wanted Niner here with us as a buffer. If anyone can work out what fifteen-year-olds talk about, it's Niner.

But once we're on our way, I find out the kid's not shy.

"So you're my real dad?"

"Obviously."

"Why'd you never come visit us?"

"I had work."

"What should I call you?"

"Alejandro, or Alex if you want."

"Why do you have so many people with you?"

"Work."

"What time does our flight leave?"

"When I get there."

He doesn't appreciate my terse answers, so he starts asking Niner about his tattoos, which even in forty degree weather, are on display.

"Are those gang tatts?" he asks.

"Some of them."

"You ever been to jail?"

"I haven't. I heard you spent the night though. How was it?" That's Niner all right. Tactless to the end. Though I'm curious about the kid's take on the experience.

"Uhh, it was uhh . . . shitty. They wouldn't let me have my phone."

"Well, you gotta learn how to not get caught."

"Niner," Sophie exclaims. "Don't listen to him, Tyler. You can't get caught if you don't do it in the first place."

"Actually," Niner starts, but I head him off.

"Ya cállate." I tell him to *shut up*.

"Fine," Niner says, sounding hard done by. "I'll change the subject. Did you know I knew your mom back in the day when she was married to this old man?" He jerks his thumb at the backseat.

Tyler frowns at him, then twists around to look at me. "You were married to my mom?"

Niner laughs. "She didn't tell you she was married before? Nothing says *guilt* like keeping secrets."

I blow out an obnoxiously loud breath, but Niner doesn't take the hint.

"You know," he goes on. "I could probably be persuaded to dig up some blackmail material on your mom for the next time she pisses you off."

Tyler's eyes widen comically. "Okay. How do I persuade you?"

After that I tune them out, rubbing at my temples, trying to ease the strain. I haven't slept at all and this whole situation has been a head trip. Jesus, I met my kids; one is a little punk, who spent the night in jail, and the other is apparently a complete angel, who was up all night at a friend's house cramming for an AP Biology exam . . . whatever AP is. Plus, seeing how much Charlene resembles Sophie threw me for a loop. How did I not realize I have such a specific type? And now I'm responsible for another human being. Well, I guess I'm already responsible for a shit-ton of human beings, but this one is different because he probably wouldn't survive if I left him on a street corner somewhere.

"No way!" Tyler exclaims, pulling me from my asinine thoughts. "We're going on a private plane?"

"Well, yeah," Niner says like the kid's daft. "El Jefe doesn't fly commercial."

"What's El Heffay?"

"Don't you speak *any* Spanish?"

"Okay," I interrupt the incessant chatter, thoroughly annoyed that Tyler talks as much as Niner does. "Let's shut up for a while."

We pull up on the tarmac and Jeremy is already waiting to open my door. I extend my hand for Sophie's and we get out into the cold wind and head for the plane. The pilot is waiting at the top of the stairs and wants a word. I gesture for Sophie to take a seat, and while the pilot talks, I glance out and see

Tyler coming up the steps behind Laney, openly ogling her legs and her ass. Next I'm treated to Luis's death glare. Right, I guess I'll be having a *conversation* with the kid about that.

I join Sophie, Niner, and Tyler at the four person table.

"So," Tyler starts.

"No," I cut him off. "I want at least five minutes of silence."

Giggling softly, Sophie laces our fingers together and leans on me. Some of the tension drains away and I rest my cheek on top of her head. But then I notice the kid's eyes all over us . . . well, all over Sophie, appraising and . . . hungry. My jaw sets. In the kid's defense, he's pretty manic right now; he spent the night in jail, met his biological father, and now he's on a private jet with strangers. At fifteen, I'd have been wired too. But some things just aren't done.

Once we're in the air, Sophie excuses herself to the bathroom, and for some reason, Tyler takes that as a signal to start up again.

"So, are you rich or something? Is that how you got her?" Her jerks his chin toward the back of the plane. "She's a seriously hot piece of ass."

Niner chokes on his disbelieving laugh as I grit out, "Leave us."

"You got balls, kid," he says, pushing out of his seat. "I'll give you that."

"What?" Tyler says with a sly grin, watching Niner move to sit with the others. "What'd I say?"

"Your dad never teach you anything about women?"

He sneers. "My dad doesn't talk about *women*, or anyone. That would go against his belief system. He's a pacifist." He says *pacifist* like it's a dirty word.

"Well, you'll be wishing *I* was a pacifist if you ever look at or speak about Sophie like that again."

The defiance on his face dims as I stare him down. "You're not into that pacifist stuff?" he asks hesitantly, like he's never met an adult who isn't.

"Fuck no." A few beats pass as he absorbs that. "In my world, the attitude you just displayed tells me three things. One, you're stupid. Reducing women to objects shows a fundamental lack of understanding of the real world. Two, you're weak. Only the insecure target those who've done nothing to deserve it. And three, you're looking for a fight, which brings us back to *stupid* if you think I'll give you a pass because we share blood, and *weak* because you couldn't take me even if we were alone, let alone with four of my men around."

His mouth hangs open, reminding me of a fish. Maybe I should have gone easier on him, but I'll be damned if my own son goes out into the world unprepared for the consequences of his actions.

After a long moment, he asks, "So, I shouldn't look at girls?"

If I thought he was being sarcastic, I'd smack him upside the head, but the question sounds genuine. "I didn't say that. No man is ever not going to look, but there's a difference between that and what you were doing."

He nods as if he's actually taking in what I'm saying. I notice Aaron trying to stay a respectful distance away in the small space, so I gesture for him to approach. "Jefe, Laney had food delivered," he says. "Would you like some?"

"Yeah, thanks."

I make sure to get coffee and a breakfast sandwich for Sophie as well, and I'm glad to hear that Tyler says please and thank you. When we're alone again, he says, "So, you're Heffay? It means boss right?"

I nod. "You do know some Spanish, then?"

"Nah. Well, kinda. I took it last year in school, but I didn't do too good. I hate that as soon as someone looks at me, they assume I already know it. People are jerks. I mean, my last name's Russell for god's sake . . . hey, how come my name's not Bernal-Acosta?"

"Well, it wouldn't be. You'd be Bernal-Falchuk."

His nose wrinkles. "Falchuk? That's mom's old name."

I almost cringe at his ignorance of his roots. It's not his fault though, it's mine. "That's how it works. Your dad's last name and your mom's last name."

"Huh." He takes a bite of his breakfast. "Will you teach me some Spanish?"

"If you want. You can learn with Sophie."

After that, he finally quiets down, and by the time we reach the penthouse, he's clearly fried and running on fumes. He revives a bit when Bruce Wayne comes to meet him, but I get Sophie to show him to the guest room on the far side of the apartment so we can all crash.

Before I fall asleep, though. I get hit with the insane realization that *my* fifteen-year-old son is down the hall.

• • • • •

We sleep most of the day. Sophie and I get up around dinner time, but Tyler stays conked out in his room. I figure he'll get up when he's hungry. After we eat, the events of the past day start catching up with me and I have to go down to the gym.

Still the kid sleeps.

I try to do the same, but by two in the morning, I can tell it's a lost cause. Maybe I'll take Bruce around the block a few times, he'll appreciate that. But when I get up, my rotten sidekick isn't on my bed where he usually slinks up after we're sleeping, or on his own bed in the corner near the closet. I pull on some sweats and go in search of him.

I hear them before I see them; Tyler is saying something to Bruce Wayne. Sudden nerves have my stomach twisting as I come into the main room.

"Hey," I say, startling him. He's got a piece of cold pizza in his hand and he looks guilty as fuck in the light thrown by the lamp over the stove.

"Oh, hey. I hope it's okay I raided the fridge."

"It's fine. Pass me the box, would you?"

Shoving the slice into his mouth to hold it, he grabs the box out of the fridge and pushes it toward me on the island. The resemblance between us is more than a little uncanny. It's like looking into a mirror when I was his age. He's about Sophie's height right now, and a touch of humor comes to me at the memory of myself being all elbows and knees. I'm sure he's got a few more inches in him yet and then he'll grow into his frame. At least he's settled into his voice already. I remember my oldest sister, Nora, teasing me mercilessly about my voice cracking.

"You've got a ton of tattoos."

I pause mid-chew, realizing I should have put a shirt on.

"And you're, like, ripped."

Well, here's an opportunity I'm not going to pass up. "You know why I spend so much time in the gym?"

"Because you gotta hold on to your girl?"

I bark out a laugh. I can't help it. I guess everything comes down to sex at that age. "No, *güey*. Because it's one of the only things that keeps my anxiety levels down."

His brows pull together.

"And I picked up the anxiety when I did seven months in lock-up around the time you were born."

His eyes cut away and down. "You did?"

"Yeah. Two hundred and eighteen days. And I think you have an idea of how shitty that was since you got a taste yesterday."

"It wasn't great, no." Clearing his throat, he examines his pizza like it's no longer appetizing. "Is this the part where you lecture me?"

"Nah, every man's gotta learn for himself."

He seems surprised, or maybe confused. "I don't think that's what Mom wants you to tell me."

"Yeah, well, your mother and I rarely got along. And I'm sure you're not interested in me telling you what to do anyway."

His lost expression tells me I've gone too far into reverse psychology territory, but he bounces back before I have a chance to recalculate my approach.

"So, you're in a gang or something?"

I sigh. "Or something."

"Is that why you were never in our lives?"

"Yeah, for the most part. Listen. You may see all this," I say, gesturing at the room. "And the plane and think everything is great in my world, but I paid some very steep tolls to be here."

He's skeptical and not shy about wanting some proof. "Like what?"

"Well, for one, I didn't get to watch you grow up." I almost laugh – again – at how unimpressed he is by that statement. "Maybe that doesn't mean much to you now, but it will one day."

Shrugging like he's used to this kind of adult posturing, he goes back to his pizza. Fine, I'm not done yet.

"My parents disowned me when I was nineteen. I've only seen my mother a handful of times in twenty years."

That gets more of a reaction, so I hit him again. "My best friend got murdered, a guy I spent almost every day with from the ages of twelve to thirty." I let that sink in for a second, but I think it's harder on me than him because I can feel a lump forming in my throat. Shit, moving on. "There are a lot of places I can't travel to, including the country of my birth. I'll probably never see any of my extended family again. And I'm always, *always* worried that my life will blow back on the people that I love, including Sophie. I doubt you can imagine what it's like to worry that your woman will be taken, tortured, raped, and murdered."

I'm not sure who's more aghast at my words, him or me. "But if you keep going the way you have been, you may not even be as lucky as I am."

"Lucky?" he echoes. "How are you lucky?"

"Well, I'm not rotting in a prison cell or in an early grave, am I? Which is where a lot of guys like me – and maybe you – end up."

Aghast becomes outraged. "Did Mom tell you I was hanging with gang-bangers? Because I'm not!"

"Then how'd you end up boosting that car?"

"I didn't boost anything. It was Corwin's dad's car. Those ass-wipe, preppy, rich kids from school dared me! What was I supposed to do?"

Real anguish pours off of him and it shakes things loose inside of me; memories of being bullied when I was a teenager, feeling helpless and worthless and empty. And how I came back swinging, harder, stronger, crueler, more ruthless . . . all of it leading me down a path I never wanted, the same path my kid could end up on.

"These —" I clear my scratchy throat. "These kids, they white?"

"Yeah, most of them." The defeat in his voice pisses me off.

"They a problem in and out of school?"

Throwing Bruce a piece of pepperoni, he gives me a sullen, "Yeah."

"Your parents been in to see the principal?"

He shrugs.

"Nothing was done," I guess. "What does your dad say?"

"I told you, my dad's a pacifist. He thinks I need to engage in constructive dialogue with these dick-wads. He doesn't understand. And Mom thinks that because Samson's never had any problems that I shouldn't either."

"But you're not your brother, are you?"

"No! I'm not. He's good at *everything*. Academics, sports, he hangs with the cool kids in his grade. The homecoming queen is his girlfriend for god's sake." He rolls his eyes and I have to contain a smile. "I'm never going to measure up to him, but my mom and dad want me to try anyway."

"Well, that's their problem. You don't need to measure up to anyone's standards but your own. You think you can work around these kids or is this a permanent thing?"

More half-hearted shrugging.

"Tyler, I asked you to assess the situation."

His eyes sharpen on me. "You really want my opinion?" He sounds baffled.

"Well, yeah. As we've established, I know fuck-all about your life."

At first he doesn't react, but then slowly a grin starts to crack his carefully schooled expression.

And from there, I learn a lot about my son, standing there in my mostly dark penthouse at the kitchen island, eating pizza and drinking Coke in the early hours before dawn. I find out he wants to make films and that it was his YouTube channel that originally caused the friction with the *in-crowd*. The gratitude on his face when I tell him we'll find him a new school for his sophomore year, one that focuses more on the performing arts, is something I won't ever forget.

CHAPTER 23

love lazy days around the house. I don't get them very often, though, because my man is mostly incapable of sitting around and doing nothing. So when I wake early on Sunday morning as Alejandro is coming back to bed, the idea of a cup of coffee in the quiet pulls me to my feet.

Day is breaking over the horizon as I slide one of the armchairs across the hardwood to face the enormous windows. Armed with my coffee, I enjoy the view, scroll through my social media until I get bored, and then get back into the thriller I've been reading on and off.

A couple of hours later, Bruce Wayne makes an appearance, punctuating his full-body stretch with a groan.

"Where've you been?" I ask him, giving him a snuggle. "Hmmm?"

"He slept with me," says Tyler from the edge of the room.

I smile up at him. "I figured. Do you know if Alejandro took him out when he was awake earlier?"

"Uh, no he didn't."

I type out a message for the desk downstairs so someone will come up to take the dog for his morning walk. I wish I could take him, but I've found my new life is much simpler if I go with the flow of reality instead of constantly swimming against the current.

"Um, Sophie?" Tyler says, sounding awkward and hesitant.

My head snaps up from my phone. Yikes, I'm being rude.

"Is it okay if I take a shower?"

"Oh, yes, of course." It suddenly occurs to me that I'm the host here. He's not quite an adult and I need to be more proactive. "Does your bathroom have towels?"

His shrug makes me laugh. "That's my answer too. I don't think I've ever been in that bathroom before."

Bruce follows us down the hall and Tyler asks, "You haven't lived here long?"

"Nope. Only a few months."

"Really? You and Alex seem pretty tight."

In his en suite, I mull that over as I pull open the first cupboard in the vanity. "We are," I finally say, handing him a towel. The next cupboard provides some body wash and shampoo.

"Thanks," he says and I leave him to it.

Back in the hall, Bruce chuffs out a soft bark when a knock comes at the door and goes racing ahead. Alejandro is already clipping the leash onto the dog's collar by the time I get there.

"Morning," I murmur as soon as the door is closed, sidling up to him and kissing the corner of his mouth. Like always, first thing in the morning, he only grunts at me like a caveman. A morning person he is not. I get his usual pod going in the coffee machine. "So, what should we feed Tyler for breakfast? I'm decidedly lacking on the providing-nourishment front."

His expression pinches, falling into a category somewhere between confused and annoyed.

"Hey," I tell him, half-laughing. "I'll have you know, not every woman comes with a full set of maternal instincts." I can't hold back a grimace. "We're lucky he's old enough to mostly fend for himself or he'd probably get eaten by wolves."

Giggling at my own joke, I head for the fridge, but he takes hold of my arm and hits me with a full-blown frown. "What?" I say with feigned innocence. "By accident of course. It's not like I'd invite the wolves to take him."

"What do you mean?" he asks. "You don't mix with kids or something?"

"Definitely not."

"But you're good with the girls."

"Yeah, but it's pretty easy to be the fun aunt for a couple of hours. That doesn't mean it would be in anyone's best interests to leave me in charge for a prolonged period of time." I grab the milk from the fridge for his coffee.

"So you don't want kids?"

I'm in a good mood and fully caffeinated, but I still feel a wiggle of unease in my belly at the question. We've talked about a lot of things, but this isn't one of them. "Umm, not really?" The wiggle becomes more of a twist. *What if he does? Holy shit.* I've never gotten that vibe from him though. "Do you?" I squeak. "Want kids?"

His narrowed eyes result in an abdominal double loop, but then he says, "I thought all women want kids."

"I'm sorry, what?" My brain struggles with what to do with that zinger. "Did you just say that?"

My disapproval finally chips away a chunk of his morning mood, revealing a glimmer of humor. "Soph, are you telling me there's a possibility I'm going to dodge a very big bullet on this one?"

Is he joking? "Alejandro," I say, exasperated now. "Just tell me. Do you want kids or not?"

"Not," he says emphatically. "Definitely not."

Like someone's hit a release valve, I deflate, leaning back against the island. "Thank fuck."

"You dropping f-bombs now?" he laughs, putting his arms around me.

"God, you scared me. How did we not know this about each other?"

He nuzzles my hair. "Honestly, I assumed it was part of the deal."

"What?" I lift my head off his shoulder. "What deal?"

"The deal of keeping the only woman I've ever loved. I'd do anything for you. You should know that."

A hundred different emotions fight for dominance inside of me as I pull back to see him. "You'd have done that for me? That's . . . that's horrifying and romantic all at once."

Before he can respond, there's another knock on the door. He makes to go answer it, but I pull him back. "I really love you, you know that?"

"I do. I love you too." He kisses me square on the lips and it's a good thing whoever's at the door gets impatient or else we'd end up in the bedroom, noisily going at it with a fifteen-year-old kid in the house.

"¿Quién?" Alejandro growls loudly, making me jump.

"I don't care if *Fresita's* naked," Niner yells from the hall, his keys jangling. "I'm coming in."

"We still haven't talked about that," I whisper with mock outrage. "Niner can't have a key to our house."

He buries his nose in my neck to hide his smile as Niner, Ben, and Laney file through the door. "What's going on?" I ask.

"Jefe, sent us out for breakfast," Niner announces, holding up bags of takeout and heading for the dining table. "Where's the Padawan? You haven't lost him already, have you?"

Padawan? I don't know if it's the image of a young Niner watching Star Wars movies or Alejandro as a Jedi that does it, but once I start, I can't stop laughing.

"No," Laney groans, brushing past us to check the cupboards for plates. "If he thinks you find him funny, he'll never shut up."

"Fuck that. I am funny. Right, kid?"

A showered and dressed Tyler appears from the hall.

"Come on," Niner says, patting the chair beside him. "Come sit. I'll take care of you."

I think my heart melts a little when Tyler checks with Alejandro.

"Just don't do anything he tells you to," Alejandro says. "Or believe anything he says, and you'll be fine."

Niner gasps in mock horror. "You wound me, Jefe."

It's Ben who laughs. "Sure, babe. Sure." He approaches Tyler with his hand extended. "I'm Ben. And you can come to me if my true love gets out of hand."

Tyler follows Ben to the table and does indeed sit next to Niner. "You guys are together?"

I don't hear the answer because there's another knock on the door. It's like Grand Central Station around here. Alejandro answers it and Luis comes in, carrying another bag. "I got the *pan dulce* you wanted."

"Actually," Alejandro says, brows arched, "I asked Laney to get it. You weren't at her place when I called, were you?"

Grumbling something, he pushes the bag into Alejandro's hand and heads for Laney, who's making more coffee. He wraps his arms around her from behind and I feel my mouth gape open.

"No!" Niner shouts, standing to point at the new lovebirds. "Dammit, Laney. Are you guys officially doing it? Because if you are, I just lost a ton of money. Couldn't you have held out until Wednesday? The pool was really getting up there."

Laney plants a kiss on Luis's lips before she gives Niner the finger, then says, "I bet that new guy, Felix, won the pool, didn't he?"

Suspicion blaring, Niner asks, "How do you know that?"

"You ever meet the guy?"

"No, JJ made the bet for him."

"Yeah, and JJ and I are going to split the pot."

"Son of a bitch."

"Nope, no son involved, just a bad-ass bitch."

Breakfast turns out to be a raucous affair. JJ and Tony arrive and more razzing ensues and of course when Bruce is returned to a full house, he quivers with excitement, insisting on a greeting from each individual person. I can't help but feel a bit of a hole in our group with Rolando and Skippy missing, but I push it away for now. This isn't the time or the place to mourn them.

$$\bullet \bullet \bullet \bullet \bullet$$

The first week with his son sees a few bumps along the way; Alejandro is used to receiving obedience in all things, and teenagers, by their very nature, don't often give it. But they muddle through. Plus I think it's pretty sweet that Alejandro ditches work to play tour guide, taking Tyler to the places he asks to see.

One of Tyler's requests is a trip to Alcatraz, and when so many of us show interest in going, Laney organizes a private tour for the following Monday. Seems gangsters have a morbid fascination with prison and even I ask for the day off so I can go with them.

It works out well, because it's also the day the new house in Sea Cliff is scheduled to be ready. The security upgrades are finally complete and I'm pretty excited. I've only been back a few times since our initial visit, but from what I've seen, the designer has done an incredible job.

With the Alcatraz tour scheduled for later in the afternoon, Alejandro gets some work done in the morning, leaving me to supervise the movers. Since he has no plans to sell the penthouse, it's a simple move of our personal items, or so I thought. When the movers arrive there are five women and three men. I think it's overkill but I guess it'll go quicker this way. Jeremy stands beside me in the bedroom while I give some instructions. Aaron hovers at the door. They complete the task in under ninety minutes.

Alcatraz turns out to be incredibly creepy. Tyler loves it though, especially the towering cell block and 'the hole' used for solitary confinement. I don't let go of Alejandro's hand the whole time we're there and I promise myself I'll broach the subject of his slowly stepping away from his role again soon. The thought of him, or any of our family, ending up in prison is physically painful.

On the return ferry trip, Laney approaches Alejandro and Niner, wanting to talk. The ferry is docking when Alejandro returns to us. "I've got shi... stuff to handle."

Alejandro's attempts to curb his language around Tyler have been funny if not successful. I try to hide my smile, but Tyler laughs outright.

"Yeah, yeah," Alejandro gripes. "Just do as I say, not as I do. I'll see you guys back at the penthouse in a few hours, all right?"

"Are you taking Jeremy with you?" I ask. Since the loss of Rolando and Skippy, there's a shortage of men who Alejandro feels wholly comfortable with.

"No, he stays with you guys." He kisses me quickly and ruffles Tyler's hair.

As we disembark the ferry, he gets into an SUV with Niner that pulls up right to the exit. Jeremy, Aaron, Tyler and I have to walk the few blocks to the parking lot.

On the way, Tyler and I debate prison reform. I'm paying more attention to our back-and-forth discussion than to my surroundings, so when Aaron stops abruptly, I almost run into his back.

"What the hell?" he grouses.

Peeking around him, I get a look at a man sprawled out on the pavement by the front passenger door. "Oh my god. Is he okay?" I make to move forward but Aaron holds out an arm.

"Hey, buddy," he says, toeing the guy's foot. No response.

On the other side of the SUV, Jeremy gets in and starts the engine.

"Jer!" Aaron calls. "Hang on. Get over here."

Jeremy comes around the front of the truck, sees the situation and jerks his chin at the back door, barking, "Get in."

Aaron leans down to roll the guy over as I reach for the door handle. Muffled pops fill the air. Turning back, I have less than a second to absorb the shock of Aaron's body impacting the ground next to the man who's no longer playing dead, before I feel a sharp prick in my neck.

The world goes hazy, then dark.

• • • • •

I'm trapped . . . somewhere between waking and dreaming, urgency and apathy, terror and oblivion.

"Sophie."

The hissing sound of my name is stuck on repeat in my muddled mind.

"Sophie."

Tyler? I swallow, trying to quench the painful dryness in my throat, but my mouth may as well be a desert. I flex my fingers and jolt when I touch something lukewarm and fleshy and . . . dead. Panic rises as I try to yank my hand away. It won't move.

"Sophie!"

My eyes snap open and I struggle to make sense of my situation. I'm face down on carpet and my arms are secured behind my back . . . and one of them is completely numb because I'm lying on it. I flop around a bit until I'm able to get my knees under myself and sit up. The head rush almost topples me back over, but I manage to stay upright.

"Are you okay?" comes from somewhere in front of me. The light filtering in through a window illuminates Tyler in the dark. *Tyler!*

"Are you okay?" I wheeze.

His weak grin wobbles. "I asked you first."

"I think so," I say, grimacing when my fingers brush the hand that's asleep again. "You?"

"Yeah, just fuzzy from whatever they gave us. I was worried. You weren't waking up."

"How long . . ?" I close my eyes and take a deep breath in an attempt to clear my head. Thinking is like wading through a swamp.

"There's a clock," Tyler says, nodding his head at the wall behind me. "It's 8:15. So a couple of hours." His voice breaks when he goes on. "Sophie, what's going to happen to us?"

"Nothing," I tell him with more confidence than I feel, doing my best to ignore the pins and needles that are now creeping down my arm as the blood starts to circulate again. "Alejandro will find us." My eyes dart around what appears to be a generic bedroom. We're sitting on the floor at the foot of a double bed that's done up in a black and white pattern. *Why is it familiar?* "Do you know where we are?"

"No," he says, balancing a mountain of emotion on that single word.

I scan the room again. The wall clock, the bedding, the artwork . . . that I picked out last month. Adrenaline floods my system. "We're in the new house," I whisper harshly.

"What?" Tyler asks, confused. That makes two of us.

I struggle to my feet. "Have you seen the people who took us? Do you know where Jeremy and Aaron are?"

"No, I haven't seen anyone. And I don't understand. Why would we be in the new house?"

My legs are like jelly so I sink down on the edge of the mattress. "I have no idea. Do they have my purse?" Alejandro is always tracking my phone.

"I don't—"

I gasp. *My bracelet!* Frantically, I force my half-numb hand to search my opposite wrist. *Did they take it?* No, it's still there. I check the clock again. Alejandro left us at the pier at about six o'clock. *Does he know we're missing yet?* The panic that hadn't quite pierced my psyche starts to mix in with the adrenaline, and I yank at my bonds. They're metal. Jesus, I'm in handcuffs. Not having the use of my arms is more than a little disturbing. Lying back on the bed, I try to get my wrists low enough to go under my butt. After a bit of painful wrenching and twisting, I'm able to thread my legs through one at a time and bring my arms in front of me. What a relief.

Tyler stumbles to his feet and sits next to me. "Let me try." But it seems his arms aren't as long as mine.

"Don't worry," I tell him. "Alejandro will figure out we're not where we're supposed to be. He'll come." But as I look down at my handcuffed wrists, a horrible sense of foreboding comes over me. He might think we're just here checking out the house. *What if he doesn't come for hours?*

Needing to do something, I get up and move to the window. This bedroom is on the main floor with the kitchen and the living room, but at this end of the house, there's no yard below, only a sheer cliff face that leads down to a thin sliver of beach.

"Have you heard anything? Any voices? Or movement?"

"No."

The door beckons me. *It can't be that easy, can it?*

Desperately thirsty, I go into the en suite bathroom and drink from the tap. The cool water steadies me a bit and I quickly search the vanity in the faint light for anything that could be used as a weapon. There's not so much as a bobby pin and I have to fight back another flare of panic. Tyler needs me, so falling apart is not an option.

"I'm scared, Sophie."

"I know. Me too." I head for the door.

"Why would someone take us like this?" Tyler asks, the stress in his voice buffeting my back.

I have a few guesses, but I'm not going to share them with the poor kid. Tentatively I reach for the handle, but then recoil. It's not there. The door handle has been replaced by a flat plate so the door can't be opened from the inside. *What the hell?!* Our reality comes into razor-sharp focus, cutting into my attempts to keep a calm head.

Backing away, I sink down next to Tyler on the bed, trying to think. But all I can do is stare at the place where the door handle should be.

"What are we going to do?" Tyler whispers.

Then as if in answer to his question, the ominous sound of a key being inserted into a lock echoes in the room. My heart starts to thunder in my ears as I jump to my feet. Like something out of a horror movie, the door slowly pushes inward, the bright light from the hall spilling in and blinding me for a second.

Then more shock. "Skippy?"

CHAPTER 24

Alejandro

Mother fucker.

Another dead end. I am so tired of Harvey Sharkane slipping through my fingers. I want this piece of shit caught and I want him dead. Enough is enough.

After someone called in a tip, we headed out to Oakland. Harvey was spotted in a dive bar and though it took forever to make it over the Bay Bridge in rush hour traffic, I had a guy watching him. Harvey wasn't getting away this time. Except we got there and discovered it wasn't him. I. Was. Pissed.

Now with my rage wrapped around me like barbed wire, all I want to do is call Sophie and let her voice calm me on our way back into San Francisco. I hold off though. Putting my mood on her isn't fair. I launch the tracking app instead. She's still at the new house. I almost called Jeremy earlier to find out why they made the trip without me, but Sophie hates it when I do an end run around her. This whole mutual respect thing gets on my nerves more on some days than on others.

"Clay, head for the new house."

"Uh, sure, Jefe," my new driver stammers. "Where's that?"

Biting back the urge to lose it on him, I take a deep breath. "Just head for Sea Cliff." I never thought I'd see the day that I'd miss Skippy Arraya.

Next to me, Niner glances up from his phone to shoot me a commiserating look. We've taken to calling Clay and the guy beside him in the front seat, Carlos, Tweedle Dee and Tweedle Dumb. In reality, there's nothing wrong with either of them except they're new to the job. It's possible Niner and I are becoming intolerant old men.

By the time we pull up at the house, it's past eight thirty. We park on the street and Niner and I go through the gate, which isn't locked. Someone's going to get a piece of my mind. I look down the drive that runs parallel to the front of the house to the guard's booth, but it's dark inside and I can't see who's on duty.

As I open the front door, a hint of worry steals into my blood. It isn't locked either. "Soph!" I call as Niner grabs my arm, holding up his cell, letting me know he's going to take the call out here. The door clanks shut behind me in the dark entryway. "Soph!"

The single syllable dies on my lips as every muscle in my body locks up and I go down. I must black out for a second because the next thing I know someone's knee is between my shoulder blades and the metal snick of cuffs fills the air. In the back of my mind, I realize I've been tased but my body is still playing catch up. I've been dragged halfway down the marble stairs by a guy on either side of me before I even get a decent breath into my lungs.

I'm dropped like a bag of trash in the middle of my front room, my left arm taking the brunt of the fall. Good thing Sophie wanted carpet. I lie there for a moment, doing my best to get my thoughts compartmentalized. Not an easy feat when I know Sophie is somewhere in this house and I've been incapacitated.

"Well, well, well."

The slimy sound of Harvey Sharkane's voice crawls up my spine as I slowly right myself, first getting to my knees, and then my feet. I stretch out my neck from side to side before I deign to look at him.

"You are a *very* hard man to kill, Jefe."

There's no sign of Sophie, Tyler, or her team, but there are three men with Harvey. In my goddam house. Fury throbs in my veins. I'm only slightly mollified by the knowledge that even if I die tonight, they won't be far behind me. Whether Laney or JJ arranges their deaths, or Niner or Luis does it himself, this won't end how these bastards think it will. Which brings me to my next thought . . .

"What *the fuck* is this about, Harvey?"

A year ago, Harvey was a polished, high-powered attorney. Today, he's lost weight and the wispy thin hair of his comb-over has grown too long. Throw in dirty, ill-fitting jeans and the affronted look on his face, and he's now the poster child for a jaded, old-man's bachelor convention.

"This is about you underestimating my love for an incredible woman."

My blank expression clearly annoys the hell out of him.

"Leilani meant the world to me!"

"You're going to have to be more specific, Harvey." I know perfectly well who she is, or was, since he's talking about her in the past tense.

"You bastard! She was the love of my life."

"You mean your side piece?" I say, still sounding confused. And honestly, it's not much of a stretch. I have no clue what this has to do with me.

"You shut your mouth. The —"

"Harvey!" I yell. "Why would I care who you fuck? I could not give less of a shit about *Leilani.*"

He goes off on a tirade about what a murdering bastard I am. The man is obviously not playing with a full deck, which explains why none of the events of the last months have had any rhyme or reason to them.

Ignoring him, I take another look around. Harvey's men are spread out around the room, and as I assess them, I catch sight of something that has my insides tightening. A Marauders tattoo. So this isn't only Harvey's petty personal vendetta. The Marauders are an organization out of Texas who have a reputation equal to *Los Santos del Diablo.* In other words, they're not to be fucked with and my chances of getting out of this alive just shrank substantially. Real, gut-wrenching dread for Sophie and Tyler begins to bleed past the walls I've erected in my mind. But I crush it with my rage. The only way out of this involves keeping my head.

I cut Harvey off mid rant. "You realize you're a dead man, right? Dean Russell's use for you is over now that I'm here." The mention of the Marauders' long-time leader shuts Harvey up and I fill the sudden quiet with a derisive laugh. "It was *you* dicking around by sending the pictures when he just wanted me dead. I'm surprised he's kept you around this long."

"He needs me!"

"For what?!"

Outrage turns Harvey red, making me regret the comment. Escalating this is not the way to go.

"I'll be taking over your territory."

When I all I give him is utter scepticism, his eyes bulge, injecting even more crazy into his manic air.

"I will!" he insists.

"All you'll get, Harvey, is exactly what's coming to you."

"You son of a bitch!" He explodes forward, drawing something from the pocket of his jeans. *Shit.* I hear the snick of a switch blade and only have a split second to decide on offense or defense. Stepping toward him, I plant the sole of my shoe in his gut, sending him back onto his ass. I'm thrown off balance but keep my feet under me despite my bound wrists. That doesn't stop the line of fire that paints itself along my calf where the knife caught me. *Fuck, I'm lucky he didn't castrate me.*

Wheezing, Harvey is helped off the floor by one of the guys. Once he's vertical and can talk, he orders, "Hold him."

Shit. Shit. Shit. I back away as the three men move in on me, but I eventually run out of room. Harvey follows in their wake, brandishing the red-tinged steel.

"What are you going to do, Harvey? Have them sit on me so you can slice me up?"

"That's what you did to my Leilani."

"I don't know where you got your intel, but I didn't even know the woman. Why the hell would I take a knife to her?"

They finally corner me. I get a few good kicks in and a head butt, but without the use of my arms, they soon overpower me against the wall. Harvey peruses me like a canvas, the knife flashing in his hand. Then without warning, he strikes. The blade plunges deep into my shoulder like a fiery poker. "Fuck!" I roar, and in the ensuing scuffle I get a leg free and I clip Harvey again. He goes flying, taking the knife with him.

"*What* is going on?"

Too caught up in the nasty bite of the knife wound and the mind fuck of not being able to defend myself, I don't see who enters the room. It's a man, though, and he keeps talking.

"I go outside for five minutes to enjoy the view and I come back to *this?*"

"We're getting Leilani's revenge party started," Harvey says, picking himself up off the floor this time.

Breathing through the pain, I slowly raise my head and meet Dean Russell's creepy, pale blue eyes across the room. "You wouldn't know anything about Leilani, would you, Dean?" I ask him, letting the heavy sarcasm disguise how much my shoulder hurts. "Harvey's under the mistaken impression I had something to do with her disappearance."

"Mistaken? Word on the street is you did it. Harvey, here, isn't too happy with you." He shrugs. "But I'm just here to watch *the great* El Jefe finally get his due. You've been on your pedestal for far too long."

"Better a pedestal than bowing and scraping at the feet of Enrique Sandoval."

All he gives me is a flare of his nostrils, because at sixty-five, the man is smart enough not to be baited. But it's obvious he hates hearing the truth spoken aloud; he and I both know the Sandoval Cartel has their knives to his throat. It has to be the reason he's here, handling this little gong show personally.

"Let go of me!"

My head snaps up to where Sophie is being dragged into the room, struggling against Skippy Arraya's hold on her bicep.

"You're hurting me!"

"Settle down," he tells her, giving her a hard yank that reverberates in my own bones.

"Skip," I warn, the single word carrying the promise of a thousand excruciating deaths. Letting him live was a calculated risk, one I took because I hated the idea of putting a bullet in him. I thought maybe he'd redeem himself by delivering Harvey, but he's obviously reneged on our deal. An error in judgment that I may have to pay for with Sophie's life.

"Fuck you," he retorts, gripping her more tightly.

Sophie's yelp drains my reserve of common sense and I try to wrench myself free of the men holding me. All I accomplish is bright spots dancing in my vision from the pain. I take a breath and approach it from a different angle. "Sophia!" I call and she stills. "Look at me."

Her features are filled with fear. "You're hurt," she says mournfully and tries to pull away from Skippy again.

"Sophia, I'm fine. Please, calm down. You remember the cabin, right? That's what you're going to do."

"That bitch isn't doing anything now that we've finally got her," Harvey proclaims. "She's been damn near impossible to grab. Even the movers failed."

The movers? *Holy hell.* But that's not relevant right now. All I can do is pray Sophie understands that I want her in the safe room that's off our bedroom. Then I see Tyler behind her and my already see-sawing heart almost pitches over. He looks about ready to faint, his gaze searching mine for the answers to this impossible situation. It comes to me that with everyone listening to Harvey's rambling, no one's watching Tyler. I mouth, *Go,* and tilt my head toward the hall behind him, and slowly, he slinks backwards until he's out of sight. If he can hide, even if it's not in the safe room, it will give Niner time. And if Niner fails, then Luis.

"Shut. Up," Dean Russell finally tells Harvey. "You're getting on my nerves. And put that knife away before you hurt yourself."

"You promised me my revenge!"

"Harvey, you can't be that stupid," I say, my tone blistering. "Russell's the one who killed your girlfriend."

He whirls on me. "No. I know what you did."

Blood is dripping down my ribs now, having saturated my dress shirt and suit jacket and I'm feeling a little woozy. I force my head to clear. "I get it. Grief makes us do crazy things, but come on, you're better than this."

"No! She's going to suffer." He starts toward Sophie, knife in hand.

"Stay away from me," she cries, jerking against Skippy's hold, more wildly now.

Russell throws me a sly smile as Harvey moves past him and my stomach plummets. I get yanked back by the men holding my arms and almost pass out from the wrench to my shoulder. Harvey doesn't get far, though, because Skippy lets Sophie go and intercepts him. "I told you I'm not on board with hurting women."

"Get out of my way, you idiot." Harvey slashes at him, but Skippy grabs his wrist and lands a solid punch to his face. I feel a flash of pride as Harvey goes down. Skip grew up scrapping it out on the streets and then Luis honed his fighting skills. How I wish I'd seen the kid's betrayal coming. Nipping it in the bud wouldn't have taken much and I could have saved us all from *this*. The sadness mingling with the pride vanishes, though, with the *BANG* of a shot. Everyone startles . . . except Russell who's got his glock out. Disbelief crashes through me as I watch Skippy fall to the floor in a heap, his head thumping on the floor, a crimson patch growing on his back.

"Sorry," Russell says like he's bored. "But we really don't have time for this."

My eyes fly to Sophie, but all I catch is a glimpse of her before she disappears down the hall. "That's my girl," I whisper, which has Russell turning the gun in my direction. I don't care as long as Sophie and Tyler are safe, and he must see that on my face because he swears and stomps down the hall in search of my woman. But she'll make it. She had plenty of time.

CHAPTER 25

Sophie

I almost stumble at the crack of the gunshot, but I manage to push off the door frame of our bedroom, keeping myself upright and moving.

There's not a lot of space in my terrified mind at the moment. I can barely hang on to *2010 05*. Javier's death. Alejandro told me that's what it represents. I pray the numbers don't disappear into the haze of fear I'm wading through. *2010 05*.

Coming around the far side of our new king-sized bed, I throw myself down onto my knees, and with my hands cuffed in front of me, I almost face plant into the night stand.

Shaking like a leaf, I yank the door open and bang it into my knees. The pain barely registers in the face of the triumph. Inside is a gun safe, just like at the penthouse, just like at the cabin. I stare at the pin pad, frozen for a moment before I hear him down the hall.

"Where've you gotten to, you little bitch?"

My already overburdened heart pounds in my chest as I reach out and push 2-0-1-0-5 with sweaty fingers. *Denied. Oh my god! Oh my god!* Breathe, Sophie. Breathe. I try again, being more careful this time. 2-0-1-0-0-5. *Open* appears on the screen and I wrench the handle down and pull. Wrapping my hands around the cold butt of a 9mm settles my nerves just enough.

"What are you doing?" the man demands from the door, not able to see over the edge of the bed.

Deliberately I unlatch the safety, lean back from the bed, and swing my arms around. I fire. The first shot goes wide and takes him completely by surprise. He reacts almost immediately though, lifting his own gun. I don't hesitate and my second shot hits him high on the chest. My third and fourth shots hit him as well before he slams down onto the carpet.

My ears ring in the deafening silence that follows. The trembling worsens and my mind sinks into a quagmire of shock and terror.

"Sophie!"

The muted sound of Alejandro's panic snaps me back to myself. "I'm okay," I want to yell, but it's only a whisper. "I'm okay. I'm okay."

Then more gunshots, many more. And yelling. And I'm on my feet, staggering for the door. I don't acknowledge the dead body or the blood. There's only Alejandro and the dread of what I'll find. Even as I throw myself out into the hall, I can't seem to care that I may be about to walk into a bullet.

But the sweetest of sights greets me. He's coming toward me, bloody, but alive. I stumble to meet him and the impact of our bodies almost knocks us over without the use of our arms. Ragged sobs tear from me as I bury my nose in his neck, nuzzling frantically.

Into my hair, he repeats, "You're okay. You're okay. You're okay," like he can't quite believe it.

"*Fresita*, baby," comes softly from beside me. "Let me have the gun."

The gun? Right. I've still got it in a death grip and Niner has to pry it from my fingers. Then I hear, "Jefe, this is going to hurt," and the metallic sound of handcuffs being removed.

Alejandro grunts with pain and I pull back, remembering that he's been stabbed. The amount of blood soaking the front of his suit jacket is horrifying and I'm suddenly dizzy.

"*Mi amor,*" he whispers. "I need you to find Tyler."

Jerkily, my head bobs in a nod as I watch Niner cut the clothes from Alejandro's torso with the knife he always carries.

"Mariposa."

I jump.

"Find Tyler."

"Yes, okay."

It takes a few minutes but I find him in the laundry room, lodged in the small space between the wall and the washing machine. "Is it over?" he asks, jittery and in shock.

"I think so," I whisper with a sniffle, crouching down in front of him, rubbing at his knee in an attempt to comfort him. "Niner's here."

"You're bleeding?" His voice pitches high.

Scanning myself, I take in the blood all down the front of my top with detached horror. "It's not mine."

Our wrists are still bound so we struggle to get him out of his hiding place. Holding on to his shirt sleeve as if he might disappear if I let go, I lead him back to the main room where Niner is tending to Alejandro. Sitting on our new couch, he doesn't look well at all, but he lifts his chin, summoning us.

"Just let me try to stop the bleeding and I'll get the cuffs off," Niner says, sounding jumpy and not at all like himself.

I sink down onto the couch on Alejandro's good side and take his hand in mine.

"You're sure they checked the whole house?" he rumbles to Niner.

I don't register the response because the sound of heavy boots sends a bolt of alarm through me. Niner immediately has his gun trained on the stairs only to let out a loud breath when Luis appears. I never thought I'd be happy to see the man's cold, assessing gaze, but now I know this ordeal is truly over.

As Niner frees my wrists, I notice a wide trail of smeared blood on the floor. I follow it to the kitchen where an Air Force 1 sneaker sticks out from behind the island.

Tears prickle painfully behind my eyes and a new sob breaks free from my chest. Skippy. Stupid, juvenile, self-absorbed Skippy. He got what he deserved, didn't he? But he tried to protect me in the end . . . and he died for it. That has to count for something. So I cry. I can't keep it in anymore, especially when Tyler cuddles into me and Alejandro pulls us both closer.

• • • • •

Thank goodness for Laney. She meets us at the private clinic and takes charge of everything. All I have to do, after she provides me with a change of clothes, is sit with Tyler in the waiting room while Alejandro is examined and stitched up.

"Niner?" I'm so thankful that he's sticking close. "Do you . . ." I swallow back my trepidation. "Do you know what happened to Jeremy and Aaron?"

"Yeah," he says sadly, and my gut clenches. "Uh, last I heard, Aaron was out of surgery and in serious, but stable condition. Looks like he's going to make it."

"Thank goodness." Tears well again. "And Jeremy?"

His shoulders lift in slight shrugging motion. "It's not looking good."

Sorrow presses down on me. "But he's still alive?"

He nods as the door to the waiting room opens and Luis jerks his head at Niner, beckoning him. "Tony's going to sit with you for a while, all right?" Niner says, getting up as Tony comes in. I don't have enough left in me to be annoyed that their 'war council' is taking precedence over me and Tyler. But as I mull it over, I realize it's for the best. Once I see Alejandro, I'm not leaving his side again, at least not tonight . . . or ever.

Fifteen minutes later, we follow Laney down a hall with armed guards posted at either end to Alejandro's room. He's half-reclined on the bed, his shoulder heavily bandaged, the arm immobilized against his body. His eyes are glassy, telling me he's on painkillers and in desperate need of sleep.

"Are you okay?" I whisper from the doorway.

His gaze bounces from me to Tyler and back again. "I'm fine. Come here."

Tyler shuffles on his feet. "I'll wait out there."

"No. You'll stay." Then to me, he repeats, "Come here."

Feeling like the chains holding me back have been broken, I scramble forward on uncoordinated feet and reach for him. He lifts the hand with the IV and I climb onto the bed, careful not to jostle him and lay myself down. As if the missing piece of my soul has been found, I revel in being whole in his arms. He's alive and he's mine and never have I been more grateful.

Tyler is forced farther into the room when two orderlies roll another bed into the room. "That's for you," he tells his son. "I need you here with me."

The poor kid doesn't argue, just kicks off his shoes and gets on the bed.

Alejandro starts to fuss over me, murmuring *'tápate'*, trying to cover me with the blanket, but I place a quelling arm on his chest and get myself situated.

We're all asleep within minutes.

●　●　●　●　●

In the morning, we go back to the penthouse after another check by the doctors. Alejandro's expected to make a full recovery with a bit of rehab.

Once Alejandro is tucked into bed after some cursory moaning and griping, his pain pills knock him out almost immediately and I head for the shower.

I'm not sure what it says about me that taking a life hasn't been plaguing my every waking moment. I'd worry if I didn't have so much else on my mental plate, including the image of a knife-wielding old man coming at me and the sound of Alejandro's agony as he'd been stabbed. Plus, Aaron and Jeremy are still in the hospital. Though Jeremy's condition has been upgraded from critical to serious.

I know yesterday's events will never fade from my memory, but so far I haven't sunk into myself like I did after the gas station attack. Not even close. Maybe because back then, I'd had nothing to hold on to and now I have an anchor holding me steady. Now I have more than myself to consider.

I go in search of Tyler and find Laney, Niner, Ben, and JJ in the main room. Laney is at the stove . . . making pancakes.

"What are you doing?" I ask. I don't mean to sound cynical, but there it is.

Niner laughs. "I'm convinced it's a plot to poison us all."

Laney points a spatula at him. "Only you, my love." Then she turns to me. "The kid wanted pancakes, so I'm making pancakes. I'm a woman of many talents." She curtsies.

Yes, curtsies.

I walk toward her and the closer I get, the warier she becomes. She seems to consider using the spatula as a weapon, but I don't let it deter me. I pull her in for a hug. "Thank you for taking care of us."

"Oh, uh, yeah, sure." She pushes me away. "But that's enough touchy-feely crap. You're freaking me out."

Giggling, I decide to push one more button. "So, you don't want to do a girl's night? We could share about our lives while we drink wine and braid each other's hair."

"Will you be naked?" JJ calls from behind his laptop at the dining table. "If so, I'd like to secure an invite to this little soiree."

"Eww." Niner pulls a face. "Boobs freak me out. They're all squishy."

"You're missing out then," comes from the hall. Tyler is standing there, grinning, freshly showered with Bruce Wayne at his side.

"High five, buddy," JJ says, holding up his palm.

I chew on my thumb nail to hide my smile even though I'm probably supposed to say something about not objectifying women.

"We'll let this one go," Laney says in a low voice, an unfamiliar quirk to her lips.

It seems my anchor is heavier than I thought. I love my new family.

· · · · ·

I've been waiting for the lecture for the last few days now. I know it's coming. The ache in Alejandro's healing shoulder isn't the only thing causing the tightness around his mouth.

When Niner and Ben take Tyler for the afternoon on Thursday, I decide to get the ball rolling. We're at the dining room table, where Alejandro has been pushing the last of his lunch around his plate for a while now.

"Are you planning to send me away again?" I know he's not.

A little thrill pulses in my stomach at the way his eyes narrow on me. "I should after that stunt you pulled."

"What stunt was that? The one where I saved myself from being carved up into little pieces?"

"Don't," he grits out. "You should have gotten your ass into that safe room like I told you to."

"So *you* could be carved up into little pieces?"

"Niner was outside."

"Well, I didn't know that, did I?"

"You should have listened to me!" He chucks his fork down and it clatters against the plate.

I don't even flinch. Pushing to my feet, I lean toward him, my hands braced on the table. "Are you done?"

"No, I'm not done! You came this close to getting killed." He holds up his thumb and forefinger.

"Yeah. So did you."

"It's not the same thing!"

My indignant gasp doesn't impress him in the least.

"I'm going to have nightmares for years," he gripes. "Being helpless to stop someone from hurting you? It was . . ." He swallows back his emotions.

"Fucking awful?" I supply.

"Yes!"

"Then we're even. I love you, you love me. Let's move on."

He works his jaw from side to side. "Maybe if you suck my dick."

The smile that spreads across my face clearly both irritates and pleases him. "I thought you'd never ask."

"I didn't ask."

"Oh, sorry. I thought you'd never *order* me to suck your dick."

I kneel in front of him as he pushes his chair back from the table. "I'd threaten to spank your ass, but you'd probably get off on it."

"Probably," I agree, running my hand along the hardening length of him through his gray sweats. "But I appreciate the sentiment. A girl likes to feel loved."

A bark of laughter has me looking up at him in surprise to find his eyes lit up with all the love he has for me.

I may be the devil's own, but he too, is mine.

• • • • •

Tyler's last days with us are much more subdued than the first for obvious reasons, but he seems to bounce back: laughing, joking with us, and making conversation. Father and son went out somewhere yesterday and they had a good talk, Alejandro told me. He also mentioned how much he wished he could cancel today's planned trip to his sister's house. Then this morning, when the location was changed to his mother's place, he'd started pacing.

"My mother must have gotten wind of Tyler," he says with a very uncharacteristic note of insecurity in his voice.

"We don't have to go," I assure him.

"No. I . . . I don't know. It's been twenty years since I stepped foot in that house."

But Alejandro has never backed away from anything in his life, and *that house* turns out to be a very ordinary, small white rancher in East Palo Alto that's not four blocks from Scott's grandmother's house.

Tyler, picking up on Alejandro's reticence, says, "I don't mind if we skip it." He really is a nice kid. I know he's intrigued to meet a whole gaggle of cousins, aunts and uncles that he never knew existed.

"Nah, let's do it." Alejandro squeezes my hand before he knocks.

The door is answered by a girl about Daniela's age. "Tío Alejo," she says happily. "Mom said you wouldn't show, but I bet Matias five bucks you would. Thanks!"

He chuckles. "Glad I could help."

"Who is it, Mariana?" comes from inside the house.

"Tío Alejo," she yells over her shoulder and Nora, Alejandro's sister, who I met at Scott and Ellie's wedding, comes to the door.

"Alejo!" She pushes up on her toes to kiss his cheek and a stream of Spanish starts. I glean she's asking about his arm that's still in a sling and he's brushing it off. *And Alejo?* It makes me grin.

"Come in, come in," Nora then says in English. "Sophie, how are you? I heard rumors you were hanging out with this one," she nods in Alejandro's direction, "but I'm not sure I believed it until now."

"Guilty," I say as we kiss each other's cheeks. She freezes as she pulls away, getting a better look at Tyler.

"Good lord, Alejandro. He's the spitting image of you when you were that age."

And from there, everyone is very welcoming. It's slightly awkward at times, probably because no one is quite sure what to say to Alejandro, and it's difficult for me to smooth things over when a good third of the exchanges are in Spanish. One thing is certain though, after every handshake, Alejandro's hand makes its way back into mine.

It seems everyone was in the back yard when we arrived and as they head back that way, an older lady comes from the kitchen, wiping her hands on her apron. She's small and her dark, liberally streaked gray hair is styled in a short perm. *"Mamá,"* Alejandro says softly. *"¿Cómo estás?"*

She takes him in from head-to-toe, pausing on the sling briefly before moving her attention to me and then Tyler, where it stays for a long moment. "Bien, mijo," she finally says, tilting her cheek as if inviting him to kiss it. He does.

Alejandro introduces me and Tyler, and we nod and smile and shake her hand. And then they start speaking, back and forth. Even though I'm unsure of the content, it sounds formal and stilted, but surely some communication is better than none. I know he misses her terribly. My eyes wander the simple, rectangular front room and catch on a framed photograph on the wall. *Oh, wow, is that . . ? It is.* The image is the same one that Alejandro has tattooed on his back; the two cranes standing in water, one with its head raised and the other staring off in the opposite direction.

His mother follows my gaze over her shoulder. She's about to say something when the front door opens and Jorgie, Nora's oldest son and Scott's best friend, walks in.

"No shit!" he says loudly, then looks chagrinned. *"Perdón, Abuela.* I mean, no way! You guys came."

He kisses his grandmother first, who affectionately pats his arm. He moves on to me, but Alejandro stops him with a hand to the middle of his chest. I giggle. "Jorge Alberto," I say like I always do when we see each other. It's how he introduced himself the very first time we met in a brief attempt to seduce me.

"Sophie, what's up, babe? This is still going on, huh?" His finger waggles between us. "I don't see why Scott threatened *me* with bodily harm," he says to Alejandro, "and *you* get a pass. Hey, is this the new cousin?"

"Yup," Tyler says, a bit self-conscious.

Jorgie pulls him in for a hug. "Come on, man. You don't need to be standing around with the old people. No offense, *Abuela.*"

"Oh, Jorgie," she says dryly, and I almost laugh that she calls him by his English nickname of *Georgie* as she goes on in perfect English. "Why would I be offended by that?"

"I knew you'd understand." He grabs Tyler's arm to pull him away.

"You good?" Alejandro asks Tyler.

He shrugs. "Sure."

"Jorgie," his grandmother calls. "Bring him back later so I can talk to him."

"Sure thing, *Abuela.*"

The three of us are left standing there and she turns her attention to me. "You like the picture?" she says, drifting toward the photo of the cranes. We follow her.

"I do. It's beautiful."

"My husband took that shot when we first arrived here in California. I had it framed for his birthday many years ago. He always joked the two herons were us." She points to the one looking off into the distance. "That's me, the short one who's not paying attention to him. And he's the tall one, always trying to impress me."

I smile brightly. "That's so sweet." I turn to Alejandro. "I always thought they were cranes, not herons."

He clears his throat nervously in response and I frown at him.

"You've seen it before?" his mother asks, calling me back to her.

"Oh, of course, it's tattooed on Alejandro's back."

The woman blinks up at me in surprise. And it suddenly occurs to me that Alejandro may not want his mother to know that.

"Is this true, *mijo?*"

Another throat clear and I feel a flush of embarrassment creep up my neck.

He says something to her in Spanish and she responds. They go back and forth a few times before he reluctantly turns his back to us and murmurs, "Show her."

Show her? Right. The tattoo. I lift the thin cotton sweater he's wearing and expose the lower left side of his back, being careful not to jostle his injured shoulder.

"Oh." She seems shaken as she unfolds the glasses that are hanging on a chain around her neck and she puts them on. She studies it for quite a while before she says, "And with a Monarch butterfly in the sky." She meets my curious gaze and pats my hand to tell me I can lower the shirt. "When Alejo was about six or seven years old, we visited the Monarch butterfly sanctuary in Michoacán. He was fascinated with how they covered the trees and the forest floor like a living carpet. And when I told him they flew all the way from Canada, he was obsessed. He was always such a sensitive boy."

I fit myself under his good arm. "He still is."

It's then that his mother notices the scar on my neck. I guess with her glasses on, it became more obvious.

"Mijo," she says in a hushed tone and my stomach drops. *"¿Tiene puesta tu medalla de San Cristóbal?"*

I'm suddenly so worried that she's judging me as defective or damaged that I almost miss the only Spanish I recognize in that sentence. *San Cristóbal.* She's looking at the St. Christopher pendant, not my scar.

Taking the Catholic medal in my hand, I look down at it, then at Alejandro as he responds to her. The emotion on his face is not to be outdone by the tears that start to well in her eyes as they go back and forth.

When they finally stop, I hesitantly ask, "Is everything okay?"

"Your wear his medal?" she asks me, a few of the tears rolling down her cheeks now.

"Yes."

"I gave it to him the day we came to America, but he always refused to wear it."

Alejandro brushes a kiss to my temple under her watchful eye, and she graces him with a surprised, but pleased smile. *"¿Mijo, estás enamorado?"*

"*Sí, Mamá.*" He laughs softly. "*Estoy enamorado.*"

"What? What did you say?"

"That I love you, mariposa. More than anything."

EPILOGUE

Alejandro

5 years later

My mariposa is in the front row. From my vantage point up here at the altar, I have a stellar view of her in all her gorgeous glory; blonde hair framing her face, long legs folded demurely to the side, wearing a dress that defies logic. She's always been a master at making classy look sexy as fuck and today is no exception.

"Do you have the rings?" the minister asks, his voice echoing slightly in the cavernous great room of the house in Reno.

Right. I should pay attention. I'd never hear the end of it if I screwed up Niner's wedding.

Fishing the ring box out of my suit jacket pocket, I hand it over, not missing my best friend's wry look. He's obviously dying to let loose with some kind of inappropriate comment about my daydreaming, but he promised Ben he'd behave himself. I very much doubt he can hold off until the end of the ceremony.

Ben and Niner decided to finally tie the knot after eight years together, something I've had the pleasure of harassing

Niner about for months now. I don't know how I got so lucky with Sophie. Though we've talked about it and she wears an engagement ring at my insistence – mostly as a *fuck off* to other men – we have no plans to take the plunge. We're both perfectly happy living together in eternal sin.

I can't believe I ever thought I could live without her. When I think back on those days of trying to convince myself we weren't right for each other, I shake my head. Life hasn't proven me a fool often . . . but I've never been one to do things by half measures.

Honestly, it hasn't been easy. Relationships take *work*. And she can be just as stubborn as I am. We've butted heads too many times to count over the years, but they've been the happiest of my life. Sometimes I wonder at how her light hasn't dimmed at all under my influence. She's still the most compassionate and caring woman I've ever met.

It only took her a couple of years to get her nursing degree since she already had a biology degree from Stanford. Just how smart my girl is boggles my mind on a good day. When she started the program, I didn't like how much of her time it ate up. She called me out – like she always does – on my bullshit jealousy, telling me to stop being a little bitch. Okay, those are my words, but they're an accurate description. At least she didn't pull out a creepy doll reference. She saves those for my more intense episodes of misogyny, which have been fewer and further in between lately. Who says you can't teach an old dog new tricks?

As if my thoughts have conjured him, Bruce Wayne comes sauntering down the main aisle like he owns the place. When he reaches the front, he turns a couple of circles at my feet and lays himself out on the floor with a very loud groan as if to complain about how long this is taking.

A low titter of laughter ripples through the guests and Niner shoots me a look. After thirty years of friendship, it's not hard to realize he's going to die if he doesn't say something.

"Yeah, come on *Padre*," he says like it's a huge relief to finally be talking after ten minutes of silence. "The dog's right. Let's move this along and get to the good parts."

"I told you," the minister says in a low voice. "I have no affiliation with the Catholic Church."

Niner's mouth opens again, but Ben clears his throat, effectively silencing him.

In my periphery, I catch sight of Sophie narrowing her eyes at me. *Oh shit.* Her disapproval perks my dick up like it always does. *Not good.* I scan for something else to focus on. And there's Scotty, sitting taller than everyone else, glowering down the row at Daniela and my kid, who've got their heads together. Yeah, I'm going to have to have *another* talk about that with Tyler.

Moving Tyler to a different high school turned out to be exactly what he needed. He got his shit together and is now in the cinematic arts program at USC. He just finished his first year. Meaning he's looking at jail time – or the grave Scotty's probably planning to dig – if he doesn't pull his eyes off of fifteen year old Daniela. Once a punk, always a punk, I suppose.

Samson nudges his brother's shoulder, probably thinking the same thing I am.

Sophie and I went to Samson's Harvard graduation ceremony last year, and we took my mother with us. She and I have spent some time together over the last couple of years. Though we'll never be close, our relationship is a lot less frigid than it was. I'm happy with that. It feels good to have a firmer connection to my roots . . . and I can't help but think my father, wherever he is, is just as proud of Samson as I am. It's probably the height of self-indulgence to think of Samson's and Tyler's success as my redemption, but Sophie has convinced me that allowing myself this small forgiveness won't lead to my ruin.

As the minister seems to be wrapping things up, an obnoxious sigh comes from the audience. "When do we get to the part where I object?" Laney calls out, setting off open laughter now.

From beside Laney, Sophie sends me an accusing look as if this is my fault. *What?* I ask with my eyes. *Like I can control Laney.*

"Luis," Niner drawls. "I told you to keep her out of the tequila until after this was done."

Now it's me who laughs out loud – in front of all these people. *Like Luis can control Laney.*

From his spot on Laney's other side, Luis pulls a flask from his suit jacket and passes it to her.

God, Laney and Luis. What a train wreck. When they're getting along – like now – it's all good. When they're not? It brings new meaning to the word *toxicity*. It's a good thing Luis has a military background, because I'm convinced one day Laney will attempt to put a knife through his heart while he's sleeping. But that's only if Luis doesn't lock her up in one of his many dungeons first. If either of them goes missing, I'll know who to talk to.

"All right," Ben intones with weariness. "That's it." Stepping over Bruce Wayne, he crosses the short distance to the front row and wrenches the flask from Laney's hand. And tilts it to his mouth. More laughter erupts, Niner's the loudest of all.

Handing it back, he bounds back to the altar. "He's right, *Padre*. Let's finish this."

Looking exasperated, the minister huffs. "Yes, let's. By the state of Nevada, yada, yada, yada. You may now kiss the groom."

Cheers and applause break out as they kiss. When they come up for air, Niner turns to the crowd and yells, "Let's do some day drinking!"

There's a lot of backslapping and hugs and kisses to go with the congratulations, including mine. *"Felicidades, güey.* I still can't believe you fucking got married."

"Me either."

We pull apart and Sophie is there, beaming at Niner.

"Fresita!" He wraps her in a bear hug. Niner has always been in Sophie's corner, helping her, guiding her through this dark world we inhabit. We'll always be grateful to him. Plus, he did save our lives.

I ended up selling the house in Sea Cliff. Sophie didn't want to go back and I couldn't blame her. Besides, we're happy in the penthouse. From a security standpoint, it's the best place for us, and even from a social standpoint. Sophie likes having everyone around and she never did revoke Niner's key.

I didn't even mind the enormous bills she racked up with her redecorating. It feels more like a home now than it ever did . . . even if I could do with a few less of her *pops of color* in the form of throw pillows.

For both of our sakes, I've slowly been stepping back from *Los Santos del Diablo*. Nowadays, Niner and I let Laney and Luis handle most things. I figure at almost forty-six, if I don't get out now, I never will and reducing my exposure on the street makes our lives a lot safer. Admittedly, I miss it. I never knew how much I got off on intimidating people until the opportunity was gone. It's a hard pill to swallow after all these years as *El Jefe*. But I do it for my girl. There's nothing I wouldn't do for her.

Slipping my arm around her, I tune back into her conversation with Niner.

"I did good, right?" Niner is asking. "I didn't drop a single F-bomb."

"Yeah, you're a real hero," Sophie retorts. "Bordering on classy even."

His face screws up with distaste. "Take that back."

She giggles and he leans in to kiss her cheek. "Come on, let's get this party started. We've got some doves to pick off."

I laugh, but Sophie whacks him on the arm. "I told you, that's not funny." He's been needling her with his plans to shoot down the doves ever since she jokingly suggested they release some after the ceremony.

"You're such a softie, *Fresita*," he says affectionately as he turns to the next person waiting to congratulate him.

I pull her close. "It's moments like this that you must be so glad you took up with me."

Blue eyes sparkling, she smiles up at me. "I'll never regret it."

ACKNOWLEDGMENTS

Dear reader,

Thank you so much for your support! I sincerely hope you enjoyed getting to know Alejandro and Sophie as much as I have. That you've taken time out of your busy life to jump into their universe means the world to me.

Please consider leaving a review!

I'd also like to take this opportunity to thank my wonderful beta readers: Leila, Lana, Monika, Ursa, Whitney, Stephanie, and Christine. I can't thank you enough for all the time and effort you invested in this project.

An extra special shout-out to Leila for her daily encouragement, superior proof-reading skills, and being an all-round wonderful person. Without her, this duet wouldn't even be close to what it is. I love her so much!

Also, a huge thank you to my husband, Rodolfo, and my daughter, Mariana, for listening to me moan on and on and on about the plot and the characters. Their input was invaluable. You guys are the best!

And to my Instagram family of fellow authors and fans – Wow! You guys have changed this solitary pursuit of writing into an even more incredible process for me. Thank you for all your encouragement, kind words, and support. Also, to all the bloggers, bookstagrammers and ARC readers who took a chance on me and this story, I'm sending a huge hug and much love!

Contact the author:
Email: lisalynn_meyer@outlook.com
Instagram: www.instagram.com/author_ll_meyer
Facebook: www.facebook.com/lisalynn.meyer/
Goodreads: LL Meyer
Amazon Author Central: LL Meyer

Books by LL Meyer

The Worlds Collide duets:
Not So Far Away (Scott and Ellie, #1)
The Here and Now (Scott and Ellie, #2)

Fall from Grace (Alejandro and Sophie, #3)
The Devil's Own (Alejandro and Sophie, #4)

TBD (Shane and Desiree, #5)
TBD (Shane and Desiree, #6)

The Penny Books
His Lucky Penny, #1
Pennies for Wishes, #2
Find a Penny, #3
Pennies from Heaven, #4

Written as Lisa Lynn Meyer
A Touch of Silence

.